TAKING THE GOLD

On a Tall Ship in the
St. Lawrence 1000 Islands

TAKING THE GOLD

On a Tall Ship in the
St. Lawrence 1000 Islands

by M.A. Noble

M. Hockett, Canton, NY

Taking the Gold is a work of fiction;
any resemblance to actual persons is coincidental.

Copyright © 2014 M.A. Noble

ISBN: 978-0-9858345-3-1

. . .

V 03.1 2015

THANKS...

to Elizabeth Braunstein

for expertise and advice on depicting
tall ship activities.

Thanks to Tom Weldon & Staff at Singer Castle

for hosting personal tours and allowing exploration
of the magnificent estate.

And thanks to all the readers who have
offered their insights and suggestions.

TABLE of CONTENTS

Taking the Gold continues the adventures and mysteries of Corey "Worder" who lives in the Thousand Islands of the St. Lawrence River in Harts Landing, NY.

Cory solved the mystery of his mother's disappearance and exposed a 200-year-old lie to clear his family in *Taking Hart*. Now he must sail away on a tall ship to face his father and beat him to the British treasure. Only then can he win Samantha and claim his own last name.

1 ROUGH LANDING

VENTURE IVth & BACK

Corey gripped his binoculars with calloused fingers as he balanced on the footropes. *Will she be at the pier?* Too far away to tell. He felt his hair lift in the light breeze, which was also the only power inching the tall ship past another river village. All along the St. Lawrence, people admired the towering masts and billowing sails of the passing *Venture IVth*, probably dreaming of adventure and romance. Corey no longer grinned and waved back. He was proud of the traditional sail training ship, but now he yearned to feel the rumble of its twenty-first century engines. Corey had to reach Harts Landing by seventeen hundred hours—five o'clock to Samantha. Otherwise... He tried not to think about that.

He adjusted his weight and raised the glasses, and when he felt his biceps bulge, he allowed himself a smile. Sailing was hard work, but it paid off. He had trained less than three weeks, but late growth hormones had kicked in and, finally, he looked his sixteen years. Wait until Sam checked him out! Her brown eyes would get big, and those raspberry flavored lips would spill outward, like jam over toast. He wanted to sample them, and he wouldn't chicken out this time.

Midsummer. The smell of her hair, the warmth of her leg against his... They had distracted him from the flash cards, but she was a tough tutor, and she got him caught up to eleventh grade. Plus she took his mind off what had happened in June.

He pressed the binoculars to his face; he scanned and squinted. There it was! Wasn't it? But the pier was still just a speck among jutting rocks of the Thousand Islands. If Corey was late, Sam would leave with Auger Hart. The town hunk. Corey's muscles tensed at the thought, and his breath burst through tight lips as he willed the ship forward. But the topsail only flapped in the slackening breeze. He couldn't help yelling, *"Wait for me!"* before jamming a fist to his mouth.

Corey wasn't ready to talk about Sam. Not even with Woody, the third mate. He didn't want to hear Woody say, "Sure she'll be there—in the arms of some other guy!"

But his friend was only a few yards away, and he had big ears. "Don't worry, Worder—or *Redrow*—whatever name you're going by." Woody edged closer to the mast. "The home girls will still be there, lined up for your autograph."

Corey smiled. Woody could tease him about being a local hero for exposing a killer, or even about his name being a sham—*Redrow* had been reversed in 1812 to hide an identity. But Sam was off limits.

The ship had become like home to Corey, and now he couldn't get off fast enough. He put a hand to his chest and felt the metal hanging from a lanyard around his neck. As he patted the brass buckle that had once shielded him from a bullet, he noticed a shift in the wind and a gain in the ship's momentum.

Corey had gone off watch earlier in the day, and he had quit paying attention to the watch bells. Now he checked his own timepiece. It would be close, but he could make it. Sam's morning interview meant they would leave this evening and stay at her cousin's in Vermont—separate rooms, of course. Her dad had sold his car and needed the van at home, but Auger Hart had told Sam he was "going her way anyway." The guy just wanted to get with Sam. *Over my dead body.* Corey planned to drive Sam himself, but his license was only good for daylight hours. They would have to leave town right away.

"Hey, take it easy—you'll dump the newbie!" Woody yelled. Corey had been bouncing on the footropes as one of the recent recruits clung to the rigging. But Woody was being dramatic. The massive rigging towered through four levels of sails, and Corey couldn't have shaken the guy if he tried.

"By the way," Woody said, narrowing his eyes. "You got some girl at the pier waiting for you?"

Corey felt his face flush as he mumbled, "Just a friend." But he hoped he and Samantha were so much more. Sure she had been his tutor, but she had also explored the islands with him and found him this sailing ship. Corey gazed downriver and leaned into the memory of Sam's soft lips curling into that teasing smile as she tested his vocabulary. Now he swayed with the mast, his grip slackening and his eyes closing. That look in her eye...hadn't that promised more than "friends"?

A wave from the passing freighter pitched the *Venture IVth* and shook Corey half off the rigging. He swung like a broken door in a breeze; he flailed before catching a line and securing himself.

"Watch yourself," Woody hollered, "or you'll never make it home to see your 'friend'!"

Corey's breathing evened. He grinned at Woody, who extended a hand to his girlfriend, now on the upper ratlines.

"Sure you don't want to stay on?" Woody asked Corey.

"It vood be lufly to haf you vith us." Olga's sing-song drifted to Corey; it was the last day he would hear her voice.

"I've got, uh, plans." He carefully shuffled sideways along the foot ropes.

"You do have a girlfriend out there, don'tcha!" Woody grinned and lifted an eyebrow. But Corey noticed something new in his eye. An understanding. Woody knew what it was like to be head over heels for someone.

Corey sighed. Why should he care who knew it? He threw back his head and hollered into the wind. "Yes, I'm in love! With *S—*"

"Hands aloft to furl sail!" The captain's order cut the air and put a broad grin on Corey's face.

Finally. They would be under engine power. Crew members scrambled up the ratlines to take in sail. Corey joined his shipmates in rolling the sail and fastening gaskets to secure the canvas, but his hands trembled and his thoughts were on the future.

He and Sam would go treasure hunting after her trip. "We'll take the *Rover*, maps, lunch..." she'd said with a come-on smile. But it wasn't the lost gold of 1813 that excited Corey; after all, finding the "Estar Island" from his ancestor's journal would be a long shot. No, it was the idea of collecting her kiss that filled *his* sails.

He raised his binoculars once again. There! Where Patrice's Point jutted from the coast, he could make out the forms of humans crowding the pier. Corey scanned for a petite female. Bodies seemed to grow larger as the ship cut the distance, but he still couldn't see her. He pocketed the binoculars. He frowned and scrambled down to the deck; he patted the piece of brass again. He didn't really believe in luck, but his ancestor's buckle had saved his life.

Corey checked his watch: it would be seventeen hundred hours in three minutes! He went below and collected his sea bag from the fo'c'sle—which he'd learned to say instead of *forecastle*—and was heading for the ladder to the main deck when his eye caught the blur in the mirror. He had no time to admire his tanned and rugged image, but he grinned. When Sam got a glimpse of *this*, he'd have no worries. He hurried up the companionway to the deck, stroking the buckle. *If I was a girl, I'd stand in line to go out with me!*

His face fell as he glanced desperately around the pier. *But then maybe Sam's more particular than I am.*

A SIGHT FOR SAM'S EYES

Many of the locals treated Corey like a hero. People he didn't even know shouted "Ahoy, mate!" and crowded up to pump his hand. His popularity was a big change from last year, when he was just a "Worder Deserter." People who used to put him down now smiled up at him.

Last spring, Corey's mother was presumed dead, and his family were seen as deserters. Then Corey found the old journal, learned that Warren Hart was his ancestor, and found his mother alive. Together, they found the brass buckle that proved their ancestry, and Corey took a bullet from a false "Hart" who wanted to hide the truth.

But the name *Hart* didn't feel like Corey's own. And *Redrow,* from his other ancestor, didn't sound right. Maybe when Corey got with Sam, everything would settle into place.

Corey was scanning the walkway from the pier when a woman came up from the other direction and grabbed him by the shoulders. "I swear you've grown even taller!" His eyes snapped back to focus on a woman with eyes of sapphire.

"Mom!" Corey wrapped his arms around her. Her nose seemed even straighter, her forehead broader, than when he'd left. Last year's fall into the river had done a job on her, but the facial reconstruction hadn't changed those clear blue eyes.

Charlie, his stepdad, gave a wink and shook Corey's hand as he tried to control a hulking mastiff.

"Howler!" Corey dropped to hug his dog and roll on the grass with him. Busy as he'd been on the ship, Corey had thought of his dog every day at feeding and walk times—even though he knew Charlie would take good care of him. Now he hung on tight, even after Charlie tried to call Howler away for a vet appointment.

"Am I going to have to separate you two?" Charlie laughed. Finally, with leash in hand and Howler beside him, Charlie waved and headed for his truck. But not before scanning the crowd with a scowl and muttering, "Derrick will have to get himself to the *Stowe Aweigh.*"

"Derrick is Charlie's nephew," Mom said. "He's been helping Charlie with the fishing business...supposed to meet him here." She scanned the crowd. "Oh, there's Fred." She turned back to Corey. "I gotta run too. We're going to the office to look over publicity options." She tossed Corey the car keys, saying, "I packed you some sandwiches, sweetie!"

Corey had been glad to see Mom and Charlie, but he was even more glad to see them leave. He paced the walkway; he threaded the crowed desperately. He glanced at his wrist. Five-forty. He slumped. *Way too late.*

Had Auger persuaded Sam to leave early? Corey imagined Sam jumping into a red convertible, Auger grinning and throwing her bag into his trunk. The thought made Corey want to throw up. He was sweating; he pulled his shirt over his head and threw it down as he collapsed onto a bench. He hung his head. He no longer cared how much time passed.

If he could only turn the clock back and make things go differently! His gaze fell on his watch. He knew he had set it to Eastern Time, plus he'd synchronized it in Clayton before Woody borrowed it to show Olga about time zones.

"Hey, Redrow!" Woody himself was jogging by. "What time you got? I'm meeting Olga here later." He stopped and leaned over to check Corey's watch. "Hey, it's still on Atlantic Time. Didn't I tell you I changed it? Anyway, I still have time to rent a car before dinner at the resort. Later, Dude!"

Corey just stared as Woody ran toward Main Street.

Atlantic was an hour later than Eastern Time. Corey's eyes widened. Was it really only four-fifty-five? He felt a surge of adrenaline. Sam should just be getting here!

Corey jumped up and turned his head this way and that. He glanced toward the ship. Behind a line of tourists holding tens and fives as they shuffled toward the *Venture IVth,* he spotted the sun-streaked hair of a familiar brunette.

It was Sam. He breathed a huge sigh of relief. Then he took a trembling step forward. Wait until she saw him. Wait until she felt his powerful arms lift her off her feet!

Then Sam spotted Corey. He could tell she wasn't sure it was him—then a smile lit up her face and her step quickened. She was making her way through the crowd, and he was about to spring forward to meet her when it happened.

He froze. His joints had locked up, and he was stuck, immobile, like a ship run aground. His legs were like cement ballast, his arms rigid as the yards on a mast. And a voice echoed in his head with the words *You're dead!*

His mind was split. One half urged him desperately to run to Sam. Too bad the other part was stronger. That part had him in a death grip. What was it all about?

Sam approached, shouting his name, but he couldn't reply or even smile. Sam's own smile disappeared as she halted. Her gaze moved down his bare torso to the crossbones inked beneath his ribs. It was a temporary tattoo Olga had tried out on him.

Out of the corner of his eye, Corey noticed Olga herself approaching. She draped an arm around him and patted his tattoo, gushing, "Corey, my darling!" She kissed his cheek and said, "My favorite pirate." Corey knew it was just her fond farewell.

He could see Sam's jaw drop. He struggled inwardly to force air through his silent lips as his wooden arms refused to reach out. All Sam would see was a sailor with a beautiful girl, staring back coldly.

"So," Sam's voice broke as she backed away. "I guess things have changed."

No! Don't go! The shouts were only in his head, and he watched the back side of Sam's petite form as she ran away.

Olga and Woody took Corey to the ER and made sure he was okay before heading to the resort for a late dinner.

His mom took him home and helped him shuffle to his bed, where he fell to an exhausted sleep interrupted by disconnected images.

Rock walls surround him. A camera is aimed at Mom. He must get in the picture! The brass buckle flashes and pierces Corey's armor; it sears a hole in his chest. His chest opens to reveal a small cage inside, where something small is whimpering.

Corey jerked fitfully. He awoke enough to recognize the dream as some weird version of last June's shooting. But what about that armor, and the cage inside his chest? He fell back to sleep.

A baby cries in the cage. It reaches outward. From within the chest, it knock-knock-knocks on armor...

CLAMMING UP

Someone was tapping on Corey's bedroom door. He was barely awake as Mom hustled in.

"Oh sweetie, I was so worried."

Corey heard the swish of window curtains and opened his eyes to the sails of the fleet on his wallpaper. He tried to roll over, but his body was stiff and sore. Then he remembered. He'd turned to stone. Or was it brass? Things had gotten mixed up in his dream—the cave and buckle from June, and the weird freezing thing he'd just been through.

He bent his joints. *Whew.* He could feel his limbs.

"Thank goodness I was able to get you an appointment for tomorrow."

Appointment?

His mom sat on the bed and stroked his hair. "You must've had a real shock, locking up like that. Did it ever happen on your ship? They've ruled out any muscular disorders. But don't worry, Dr. Mason will see you. He'll help you sort things out."

Dr. Mason? Corey racked his brain. Was he a joint specialist? No. He was the guy that helped Mom remember who she was. But he was a...

"I'm not crazy," Corey mumbled.

"Of course not dear, I'm not saying—"

"I just had some kind of cramp." Corey still wasn't quite awake. How much had been a dream?

"I guess you didn't even get to see Sam."

Sam. Corey didn't hear the rest of what his mother said as his eyes locked on the wallpaper. The boats were now heaving, careening dangerously near the rocks. The scene at the pier came back clearly, and he remembered the hurt look on Sam's face.

He sat up with a stab of pain. Had Sam gone with Auger last night?

"Better get dressed, hon. After all, it's Wednesday."

"*What?*" What happened to Tuesday?

Sam should be back already! He tumbled out of bed in his briefs and pulled on his jeans.

Corey smelled freshly cut grass as he ran up the front lawn of the Mainsail. The tractor mower's engine sputtered off and a raspy voice called, "Hey, sailor man!" Corey slowed his pace as he turned to see Sam's father swinging his legs over the side of the mower. Corey wanted only to run inside and find Sam, but he waited to shake hands with Randy. There were dark circles under the man's eyes. It couldn't be easy running the Mainsail now that his partner was in jail for attempted murder. Ex-partner. Randy was innocent, but he was paying a big price for Johnny's crimes.

Corey dropped his hand. "I need to talk to Sam."

"Yeah, about that—" Randy blew strands of black hair from his eyes. "I thought you were going to drive her. She came by to grab some food, kept checking her phone while Auger waited. Finally had to leave, but wasn't very happy."

Corey clenched his jaw as he edged toward the front steps. "So is she back?"

"No, she decided to stay a few days, check out the area."

A few days! Corey slumped. *With Auger Hart.*

He stalked away as Randy yelled, "She waited as long as she could."

Corey heard the lawn mower start again as he kicked a tree stump and cursed his luck. He felt for the brass buckle, but it was not at his chest. It was not in his pocket. He hadn't seen it since before...the thing he didn't want to think about.

"It was just some freaky glitch," Corey said as he watched Mom pack Charlie's lunch.

"Dr. Mason can help you. He has a lot of experience, you know, and he helps *me* a great deal."

"I'm fine. It's just one of those things when you grow too fast. I read it somewhere." Corey almost believed it.

But it happened again after he took Charlie his lunch.

Charlie was cleaning the live well on his fishing boat and complaining about Derrick being late again. "He went to the Wedgewood for lunch, the prima donna. If he weren't my nephew..." Charlie shook his head and grabbed a sandwich from Corey.

On his way home, Corey was passing the Wedgewood when he froze up again. A busboy who was taking a break in the back alley noticed the kid on the sidewalk turn into a statue.

"You've just had our clams, haven't you?" he said, putting out a cigarette. "They'll kill ya faster'n these things, kid!" He dragged Corey to his truck and drove him home.

Corey was only out for a day this time. He still didn't like the idea of seeing a shrink, but he had to face it: something was wrong. Could Dr. Mason possibly have answers?

"He'll just talk to you, dear," Mom promised. "You won't have to do anything that makes you uncomfortable."

Well, he'd go to make *her* happy.

2 FIND THE DEMON!

DR. MASON

Dr. Gregory Mason was an okay guy. But when he suggested hypnosis, Corey remembered seeing a show where volunteers squawked like chickens. They were weak minded, and that stuff wouldn't work on him. He wasn't crazy and he wasn't a fool. He was here to make Mom feel better. Corey was relieved to find that Dr. Mason was cool with that; in fact, he was pretty laid back.

Before he knew it, Corey was chatting about his ancestry and how he'd nearly gotten killed last June. Dr. Mason was really interested, saying, "Wow, what an experience," and "How did you deal with that?" Corey barely noticed the time go by as he heard Dr. Mason's voice drone on, and he recalled things further and further back.

He was in a strange bedroom. His small feet had found the crosspieces of a wooden chair as he grasped the seat cover and climbed. His eyes were level with the dresser top when his gaze fell on the small piles of white powder. He pulled himself higher.

He stretched his arm. He could just reach the end of the first white row. He waved his hand back and forth, scattering grains with his fingertips. *Pretty white sand!* Standing at the edge of the chair, he stretched as far as he could. He dragged his fingers through three lines of powder. He was about to send them all into the air when a large hand clamped his wrist. He gasped in pain as another hand tightened on his neck.

"Freeze right there!" The gruff voice filled his ear.

Cigarette smoke filled Corey's nostrils, whiskers scraped his cheek, and a black skull cap filled his vision. He tried to yell, but the hand covered his mouth. His wrists were pinned behind him, and blue eyes blazed into Corey's. The voice warned: "Move or make a sound...and *you're dead!*"

It took time to unfreeze, but Corey's limbs relaxed as Dr. Mason coaxed him into the present. Corey could feel tracks of sweat from his face down his neck to his chest. But he had gained so much confidence since June—how could a memory wipe that out?

"Your mind is protecting you," Dr. Mason explained. "When you were distressed, your mind associated it with your surroundings. And you were convinced that if you moved, you would die."

"So anything that reminds me of that guy..."

"Could be triggers that prompt you to protect yourself," Dr. Mason said. "Psychological distress is expressed physically in a conversion disorder. Your subconscious mind was trying to save you from death."

Corey shook his head. "But I've smelled cigarette smoke—it never paralyzed me before."

"That's just one trigger. You may have experienced a combination."

"Somebody had a beard *and* cigarette *and*...?"

Dr. Mason took a deep breath. "Corey, your subconscious mind can block out the things you can't handle." He sat back in his armchair and crossed his legs. "By facing a killer last June, perhaps you removed a mental block to the triggers."

Corey blinked. "By doing something brave, I got worse?"

"Sometimes it feels worse because you're handling a bigger challenge."

Corey stared in disbelief. "Doctor Mason, something turned me into a stone. You call that handling things?"

Great. He'd moved to the next challenge, like in his video games. Corey had never gotten beyond level four. Outcome: annihilation.

The real question was *who* was the guy? He had become an inner ghost that could haunt Corey at any moment.

Dr. Mason wanted to desensitize Corey to his triggers. But he didn't know how long it would take or how many triggers there were. So even if Corey came for months, some new smell might make him freeze up when he was with Sam. How could she ever depend on him?

The more Corey thought, the more he was sure: it was the guy himself he had to deal with, not a bunch of triggers.

Corey spent a fitful night chasing a blue-eyed demon. But whenever he thought he had crushed it in his grip, it would vanish and pop up somewhere else.

In the morning, Corey pulled on his jeans and then grabbed a shirt from the chair. It was the one he'd left near the bench by the pier. Something clanged to the floor as a piece of paper floated down to join it. It was a note from Mom saying someone had found his shirt and buckle. Corey must have pulled the pendant over his head when he removed his shirt.

He grabbed the buckle and got a clean shirt before dragging himself downstairs. He was about to push open the kitchen door when voices leaked around its frame.

"It was so many years ago." That was Charlie's voice.

"I feel so bad..." Mom sounded like she was stifling a sob.

"Corey must've got into his stash."

They were talking about the guy with the white powder! Mom must have consulted with Dr. Mason after Corey's session. She never said anything on the way home.

Corey stood still, his ear against the door. Voices faded in and out, but Corey heard a few of his mother's words as her voice cracked: "...should never have left Corey with him."

He had to know who! But he couldn't upset Mom by questioning her. He pressed his ear harder to the door. Chairs scuffed against the kitchen floor and the voices turned away. He could only pick out a word here and there among the murmurs and the rattle of dishes.

PEG'S REMORSE

Peg picked up her plate and turned to the sink. She couldn't finish her eggs. It was sweet of Charlie to cook them for her, but she had no appetite. What little sleep she'd had was riddled with disturbing images.

She'd wanted to hold her son close and spill her grief, but Dr. Mason had asked her not to discuss the issue with Corey in her current emotional state. Corey had no idea the extent of her post-traumatic stress disorder. Being pushed to the river, robbed of her memory, and forced to see her son shot had done a number on her that couldn't be fixed with plastic surgery. The culprits were in jail, but they haunted Peg's dreams.

Now, no matter how hard she mopped, scoured, or scrubbed, her worries tainted everything. Charlie's hand stilled her own on the plate she was washing.

"You'll wear the pattern off, babe." He stood beside her and gazed out the window. The sun lit up his rugged face, reminding her of his quiet strength.

The garbage truck pulled up near their driveway, where several neighborhood trash bins were lined up, and Charlie's voice was almost lost in the din.

"I should let Derrick go."

Peg wiped an eye with her free hand—which was wet, so she grabbed a paper towel to finish the job.

"No, Charlie. We can't punish your nephew. He was only a teenager, and he's paid for his involvement with drugs. He's different now." She picked up Charlie's plate and took her time scraping it. "His mother was kind to take us in."

"My sister should never have let Derrick near Corey." Charlie started rinsing the forks.

"But Tanya had no idea what he was into—"

"Until he got arrested," Charlie grunted. "But I thought Tanya babysat while you were studying."

"She did, but he must've wandered into Derrick's room."

"I wish I had been there." Charlie scowled into the sink. "I would've kept closer watch."

"You had no control over things, Charlie, you were in the service. You didn't even know me then." She leaned against him as they gazed out at another trash can being emptied into the truck.

"When he showed up last month, I had no problem giving him a job," Charlie said. "Far as I know, he kept his nose clean." Charlie kissed his wife's neck. "I know the guy had it rough. But it'll be hard to look at him the same now."

"Promise me you'll treat him the same."

"Only if you'll promise to stop worrying and let Dr. Mason take care of Corey."

He was right. Peg would make it worse if she tried to explain things to her son.

"You can't blame yourself, either. You couldn't have known the guy was dealing." Charlie ran the dish towel over a clean plate. "Though he always did want to make a fast buck." He looked at the wall map of the St. Lawrence as he tossed the towel over his shoulder. "Remember how obsessed he was with that buried treasure—" The word was out before he caught his breath and said, "Sorry."

But Peg knew she should be more worried about Corey than herself. She shouldn't let herself get upset about her ancestors' hidden treasure, even though it had made her a target of online bloggers.

"Whoever emailed that link to the blog site hasn't sent any new posts lately." She tried to sound casual. "Maybe it'll die down." It had been several weeks since she had discovered the anonymous group questioning the events that spurred a local history revision. Some claimed the Worders were making a pathetic attempt to cast their ancestor in a favorable light.

"It's ludicrous. These people are crazy to challenge your ancestor's journal," Charlie said.

Peg had to face reality: "The experts only proved it was *written* in 1813." She took a big breath. "Some people deny that Fred Hart's ancestor Dirk Poole was a fraud. They say my ancestor Pat Worder made up the whole 'Estar Island' treasure story." A tremor ran up her spine. "Look, I've already gone through hell—I survived rocks and bullets. How could I let some web site..."

"Peg, Dr. Mason doubled your sessions for a reason." Charlie's voice was gruff, but his touch was tender on her neck as she leaned over the sink for support. "Being pushed into the river is one thing. Remembering who you are only to have your son shot—" He was shaking his head.

Charlie's voice came to her as if through a tunnel as she gripped his hand and fought a wave of panic.

"Give yourself a break. Don't go to that online site any more." Charlie's voice was pleading. "Post-traumatic stress disorder is nothing to mess around with. Even battle hardened soldiers can't deal with PTSD on their own." He paused. "You've suffered things I can't even imagine. Give yourself time to work through them."

He was right. But every time she got one step ahead, she'd get a link to another remark.

Now she was more concerned with what Corey had been through, not just yesterday, but in taking a bullet and saving her life. She couldn't let him know about the bloggers.

She fought tears again as she turned away from the window; she could not keep torturing Charlie by giving in to sobs. She assured him she was fine.

He poured two cups from the coffee maker at his elbow. "Since I brought up the treasure, maybe now's the best time to ask. How are you going to respond to that letter from the treasure hunter?" He joined her at the table, where they sat with their backs to the window.

She didn't like this subject any better than the other. Corey's biological father, Rob, never even knew Peg was pregnant. She'd been so in love... She had been about to inform Rob when she learned he had a fiancée. Devastated, she'd left to stay with Tanya, Charlie's sister. She never heard more about Rob until he was featured years later in a magazine about sunken treasure. And more recently, he had contacted Peg, having read about her ordeal. But she was still determined not to disrupt Rob's life or to complicate things for Corey. Even if Rob was an expert, Peg was not desperate enough to ask his help proving there was British treasure.

She still had another load of trash from her midnight cleaning rampage, stuff that wouldn't fit in today's garbage. Now the bin would have room for the rest of the junk. Including Rob's letter.

"My answer to Rob..." The roar of the departing truck faded, leaving her final words to stand alone: "is *no.*"

NO ESCAPING BAD GENES

Mom's and Charlie's voices had become too low to hear. Corey stood outside the kitchen door, his mind still stuck on the last thing he'd heard: "Shouldn't have left Corey alone with him."

Who was *him?* And why had his mother left Corey with someone who threatened him? He was debating whether to enter the kitchen when the voices became audible again.

"And you still won't tell Corey about his father?"

"No!" Mom was firm. "The less Corey knows the better."

My father. Corey was so stunned he almost felt paralyzed again. He'd thought Mom didn't know who his father was! She'd rather let him think she slept around than admit who he was?

Corey hadn't blamed his mom for her actions as a teenager. Her own father had been a drunk who messed up her life—until she had her son. And from then on, she'd just wanted to protect Corey.

What a fool he had been. Corey had thought everything was great now because his mother's ancestors had turned out to be heroes. Had he thought he was some kind of immaculate conception? It was his *father* who had contaminated him, his father who made him freeze. The man was a demon that still affected Corey by remote control! The only way to exorcise the demon was to confront him. Corey had to find out where he was.

Corey scowled and took a breath. He raised his fist, ready to explode through the kitchen door and get some answers.

Then a stifled sob leaked through the wood panel. Corey lowered his arm. *She feels even worse than I do.* He dropped his head. Then he turned around, dashed out the front door, and tore off toward the village to run off his adrenaline.

Quiet prevailed at the dinner table. Corey kept his eyes on his plate as he chopped strands of spaghetti into pellets. Out of the corner of his eye, he saw Mom's fork twirl pasta then pause, half loaded. She cleared her throat.

"About Dr. Mason."

Corey looked up, startled.

"He wants you to come two times a week; I think you should start Tuesday."

Corey didn't want to sit around being "desensitized," but he had come up with no other alternatives.

Taking his silence for agreement, his mom smiled and attacked her spaghetti. "I'll set it up."

The plan Dr. Mason described sounded like trying to stop the rain by collecting drops.

"What if we don't find all the triggers?" Corey said. "And if the source is out there somewhere—I could still be under his control?"

"Eliminating triggers should diminish the effects—"

"What if I went directly to the source? Wouldn't that take care of all the triggers?" *And be quicker.*

"It's much safer in a controlled environment. Otherwise, you could make things worse." Dr. Mason smiled encouragingly. "Many people do get better with desensitization." But even he admitted that it could take an extended period of time. He didn't say "years," but Corey was no fool.

Forget that! His relationship with Sam was at stake. He would not sit around while the culprit was running free. His father had messed up Corey's younger life, and now the man was ruining things with Samantha.

Until Corey had a name and hunted the guy down, it was foolish to think he could get out of his father's grip by "desensitizing." He'd have to see the man and banish him in person. But how to find him? He couldn't ask Mom, and Charlie sure wouldn't go against her wishes.

GAMES OF SAIL

Corey helped his mom do dishes and fold clothes. Twice he almost asked her.

He'd brace his knees against the bed and stretch a bath towel by the corners and say, "Mom..."

And she'd pause with a tee shirt or socks in her hands and say, "What is it, dear?" and her sapphire eyes would betray the shadows of her tortured life.

Then he'd sigh and say something like, "Those don't match."

Not even games could distract him completely, but Captain Video's *Scourge of the Sea* was the next best thing. Corey was engaged in a vengeful sword fight against his "father" when Woody walked in.

Corey looked up briefly. "Thought you left on the *Venture IVth.*"

"I decided to switch to the *Golden Aye,*" Woody said in a flat voice, "and sail as an Able Bodied Seaman."

Corey wondered why the guy would take a demotion, but he was distracted by the thrust of a digital pirate. Corey was only partly aware of the former mate sinking into oversized cushions near the gaming station.

"Sticking around on the *Venture IVth* would only remind me..." Woody's voice trailed off to a silence.

"She dumped me," he finally said.

"Huh?" Corey had picked off a swarm of pirates one by one. Then his avatar was obliterated by a surprise attack from starboard and Corey threw up his hands. He swiveled to face Woody.

"You mean Olga?"

"Said she needed something more stimulating." Woody picked at the hole in his jeans. "She was bored. After four weeks with *me?*" He plucked a mint from the ceramic frog on the end table and popped it into his mouth. "Anyway, she won't be meeting me in Halifax." He paused. "She took off with some editor from Manhattan." He bit hard, popping the candy. "Can you believe it?"

He could. Olga was out of Woody's league. "Sorry," Corey said as he swiveled to aim a carronade through his gun port.

Woody sat up suddenly and leaned forward, exhaling mint over Corey's shoulder. "Come with me on the *Golden Aye*—it sails Thursday."

Olga must've done a job on him if he was willing to give up being the youngest mate in the fleet.

"Look," Woody said. "You know how you froze up? Well, girls can do that to you." He tapped his fingers on the back of Corey's chair. "You could use a change of scene to help you move on."

Corey's eyes were on two escapees on the screen, but his thoughts went to Sam. He couldn't move on—he had to get her back. He stuttered his thumb on the control to move up the rigging, picking off snipers before he could get to the red-bearded rogue. *To get to the prize you have to remove the obstacles.* To get Sam, he had to remove his demon by facing his real father.

"You loved sailing, right?" Woody's voice overcame the electronic grunts and shouts. "Look at you pretending. Why not do it for real?"

Corey stared at the screen.

Woody persisted. "The Fielding Fleet is the best of the tall ship groups. The founder, Grayson Fielding? He used to hunt treasure, now he 'hunts solutions' for teens. He's doing a conference in New Orleans." Woody scrambled off the cushion. "Come on, we can go to that, and see the world! Florida, the Caribbean—" he slapped Corey's shoulder and lowered his voice. "I hear the island girls are friendly. They swim right out to the ship!"

Corey remained silent. Only one girl interested him.

Woody sighed. "Well, think about it. I'm staying right at the Hart Resort." When Corey raised an eyebrow, he explained: "Got a little extra this month from Aunt Adele." Woody's aunt was a successful romance author who had no kids of her own.

"Anyway, I'll leave you this, just in case." He waved a brochure in front of Corey's game screen then slipped it into Corey's back pocket. He stomped out, muttering, "Zombie."

DREAM CAPTAIN

Corey strained at the helm all night, but however he wrenched his pillow, he kept heading for the rocks. Then Captain Video told him to "think outside the game."

In the morning, Corey made his bed as he stared at the sailboats on the wallpaper. Was there a clue in the dream about how to find his father? How could he "get outside the game"? As he stared, something on the wall bothered him. Against the regular waves in the pattern, Mom and Charlie's wedding picture rocked crookedly. A fraction of an inch off. He leveled Mom and Charlie, and it made him think of something. Anyone who had known of Corey's biological father would have had a connection. Mom had nobody else, but Charlie had a nephew. Corey had not actually met Derrick, but he was right here in town. How hard could it be to find Derrick and pick his brain?

Corey pulled on clean clothes and grabbed the buckle before running downstairs. He wolfed down a piece of toast, grabbed a treat for Howler, and left by the back door.

There was no Howler in the yard. *Duh, he's out walking with Charlie.*

Corey tried to stuff the dog treat in his back pocket, but it wouldn't go. He pulled something out of his jeans and stared at it. That useless brochure from Woody. Corey slipped the dog treat in his pocket as he crumpled the brochure. He headed for the trash can to get rid of it as he thought about Charlie's nephew. There was only a slim chance Derrick would know anything, but he looked like the only possible way to Corey's father.

Until Corey found a way to his father in the garbage can.

TRASH OR TREASURE

"Hey, get your hands out of there!"

Charlie's voice made Corey jump away from the trash can; he backed up against a dog nose and felt the treat slide out of his pocket. Howler and Charlie were back from their walk. But Corey was too curious about the thing in his hand to pay attention to Howler, who now lay happily on the lawn, crunching his treat.

"What is this?" Corey held up the ripped envelope he'd somehow snagged from the garbage.

Charlie grabbed it. "None of your business." He mashed the paper into the trash bin, slammed the lid, and turned back to Corey, arms folded on his chest.

The two stared at each other. Three months ago, Corey would have been intimidated. Now Corey feinted and ducked around Charlie and dove for the can. Charlie tried to stop him, but Corey threw him off and retrieved the envelope.

"Fine," Charlie panted. "I guess it's no use hiding it." He caught his breath and rubbed his back. "Can't think of a lie any faster'n I can move the old bones." He looked left and right before dropping onto to the tree stump next to Howler.

"It has to do with my father, doesn't it?" Corey's throat was tight.

Charlie only sighed and shot a glance at the house.

Corey squinted at the name on the return address. "This Rob—" An appropriate name, since he'd stolen Corey's life. "He's my *father?*"

"Do not tell your mom I let you see that." Charlie's eyes were pleading. "She'd fillet me and fry me for supper."

Corey's hand shook as he read the physical address. Was it a dream? He pulled the envelope apart to see if there was a letter hiding in the crease, and he couldn't help shouting, "What did he want?"

Charlie shushed him.

"What, I mean is—" Corey lowered his tone and tried to control his excitement. "Where does he live?"

Charlie's nose flared. He spread his knobby hands flat, knuckle-up. "He just wanted some information, doesn't concern you." Charlie snatched the envelope and poked his finger at Corey. "Forget about him." He got up and walked stiffly to the garbage can and stuck the envelope in it. Then he threw a warning glance and huffed over to the car as Mom came out of the house.

Corey trembled. He knew his father's name! Okay, only the first name, but he didn't care about the last name anyway. Corey already had three to choose from, all better than taking his father's. The point was that he had Rob's address.

Corey acted cool and waved goodbye to Mom as she pulled out of the driveway, with Charlie glaring from the passenger seat. Then, when they were out of sight, Corey turned around, dove into the can, and pulled out every torn bit of paper that might assemble a letter from that envelope.

In his room, he pieced together a few phrases:
saw "History Revised" in the Times
cognized the name Worder at Harts Landin
glad to lend my experien
need the location of Estar Island to start looki

The writing was sketchy, but Corey wasn't stupid. It said enough to make him see red. What a pirate! The guy popped up when he thought there was money. He only wanted the location of the treasure. Plus there was some blarney about how he had "changed" and how Corey's mom had been "so important" to him. The guy had nerve. But no heart. He never even mentioned his son. Obviously, Corey was not important.

Corey found two more scraps that fit together. They were part of a letterhead that showed a ten-digit number. Now he had a first name, an address, and a phone number.

It was an hour before Corey worked up the nerve to call. He heard the other end ring as his mouth went dry. He racked his brain for the words he'd practiced. Then a message interrupted his panic.

"Catch me home October to early November then I'll be in and out again." Pause. Then, "Friends, call my cell phone any time." The voice box was full, so Corey put the phone down. He would have liked to leave a message: "Don't come near Mom, scumbag!" But it didn't feel right. He decided his first words to his father should be in person. Corey tightened his fists. Preferably delivered with the threat of bodily harm.

He sat on his bed. He and Sam had exhausted their leads to Estar Island, the treasure site named in the journal. Finding it would take a miracle. *And I don't believe in miracles.* Charlie didn't need him. Howler didn't need him. Sam wouldn't even answer his calls, which was his father's fault for making him freeze up. The only lead he had was his father's address, and the only one who needed him at all was Woody.

But the *FL* on the return address was a problem. How was he supposed to get himself to Florida by November? Mom would never let him leave during school, especially if she knew the reason. He could leave a note and hitchhike. No, he couldn't do that to her.

He frowned at the address. Twelve Coastal Drive in Key West, Florida, might as well be on Mars.

Wait. *Key West?* Where had he just seen that?

"Why are you digging in the garbage can, hon?" Mom's voice surprised him, and he whacked his head on the lid that angled over the can. Corey had been so excited he'd ignored the car in the driveway with occupants still in it. Mom and Charlie must've been having a conference in there.

He waved the brochure. "It's just something I threw out by accident." He could feel their eyes on his back as they followed him inside.

Sitting on his bed again, Corey smoothed Woody's brochure and turned it over. He read the section about earning high school credits on the sailing ship.

There. The next section listed port cities. Just above New Orleans was the entry *Key West.* The ship would arrive there early November.

Maybe there was such a thing as luck. He touched his brass buckle.

LETTING GO

"But this is so sudden!" Mom paced between Corey's bed and his door. She scowled at the foot of his bed, where the latest issue of *Tall Shipmate* lay open to a centerfold spread of a three-masted square rigger.

His mom had read about tall ships before Corey enlisted on the *Venture IVth*—how they had become popular for teaching the old ways of sailing, how teens learned skills and built confidence. She had no problem letting him sail to the Great Lakes—that was only a couple weeks during summer vacation. Signing on to the *Golden Aye* for months was a whole other thing. Before she'd even consider letting him go, he had to show her the educational program and the agenda. He explained that, though he would learn the old ways of sailing, the ship had modern safety features. And that they would do good deeds like deliver aid to Haitian quake victims.

"But you only just started with Dr. Mason..."

Corey stuffed a sea bag with clean underwear. "Dr. Mason says this could be good for me." Which was not a complete lie. He zipped a side pocket. "He gave me self-therapy assignments." Which Corey intended to toss when he sailed out of sight.

"I know he's available by phone. But what if you have...one of those *spells?*"

"Don't worry, Mom. The triggers are here up north." He refused to meet her eyes when he added, "I'm going south." He couldn't tell her he was heading directly for the biggest trigger, the mother lode—or *father* lode—of his trauma.

She sighed. "What about your friends?"

Corey jerked another zipper shut and pressed his lips tight. "Sam's busy with her own things."

His mom was quiet for a moment. "Corey, about your freezing up," she said softly. "I can't tell you how sorry..."

"Mom, it's not your fault." He glanced at her liquid eyes and felt guilty.

Then her gaze hardened as she pursed her lips. She gripped a pen and clamped her teeth over it as she studied the permission form.

"How would I get hold of you?"

"You can call whenever I'm in port." He tossed an old sailing novel in his bag. "You can always track our position with GPS."

She twirled her pen. "I hope Charlie can manage. You know he's expanding, adding ice fishing and survival treks."

Corey adjusted his bag strap. Charlie's business was booming, and he couldn't do it all by himself. But he didn't need Corey any more. "He has Derrick now."

"Oh." His mom dropped her gaze for a moment. "What about Howler?"

Corey opened his mouth and then shut it while he held a navy sock in suspense before joining it to its mate. How could he leave his best friend for so long? He fondled soft wool between calloused fingers. Corey was the one who had cared for Howler, fed him, whispered secrets in Howler's drooping ear. But since Mom had returned from the dead, Corey's stepdad had found joy in everything, including Howler...who now always ran to meet *him*.

Corey swallowed hard as he mashed and stowed the socks. "Howler is Charlie's dog now."

Corey was still brooding about Howler as he checked his phone. Sam hadn't answered any of his three text messages. He couldn't stand to think he might not see her before leaving. After they'd spent so much time together over the summer, Corey had expectations. He and Sam would talk on the phone, study together, explore the river on weekends.

If she only understood his problem and his plan, if he could just explain it to her. He'd even called the B&B, but Randy said Sam was still away. Visiting a 'girlfriend.' Right. He hadn't noticed Auger Hart around town either, but he couldn't let himself think about that.

Corey clenched his teeth. He had to face his father. If he could do that, he knew he could overcome the trauma. Otherwise, Corey would have to live with the fact that any unexpected sight or sound could control him. Even if he never met another trigger, he would be controlled by the fear of it. And he could never have a relationship with Sam.

Corey didn't need a therapist to tell him to quit messing around with triggers and confront the source—the man who was ruining his life!

3   EMBARKING MAD

BOARDING FAUX PAS

The *Golden Aye* towered over the pier, miles of crisscrossed rigging supporting its masts and neatly furled sails. Corey walked ahead of Mom and Charlie while Howler, seeming to sense Corey's departure, trotted loyally at his side. Corey felt like he was swallowing a boulder as he stroked Howler's head. He reached to his back pocket for a treat but felt only the folded paper, the one where he'd copied Rob's address and phone number.

Corey checked his text messages one more time before Mom hugged him tightly, saying, "Love you dear, remember to call." Charlie shook his hand and squeezed his shoulder. Corey choked up, realizing he would miss them too. But as he waved goodbye, he caught himself glancing at passing cars.

"Wait, isn't that...?" He'd thought he'd seen a van like Randy's. No, it wasn't. Was he a total nut case? Did he think Sam would come chasing after him, like in the movies? He shook his head as he walked up the ship's gangway, alongside several tourists, but he still couldn't keep his eyes from straying to shore.

Which was why he got off on the wrong foot as soon as he stepped on board.

"Are you with us, Maverick? Or still out in the field?" At the sound of a woman's husky voice, Corey caught his breath and jerked his head forward. Whose feet had he trampled?

His eyes worked their way up from canvas deck shoes and rolled trousers to an untucked linen shirt and bronzed face with gray and sandy tufts fringing a burgundy cap. Corey's stomach clenched as his eyes locked with the blue-eyed glare of the captain. Did he already have a strike against him?

Corey's cheeks heated; he'd told Captain Harper he was a seasoned deckhand. What he was showing her instead was a clumsy landlubber. A few days ago, he still had his sea legs; now he staggered with the ship's sway.

The woman looked him up and down, and with a powerful grip on his shoulder said, "Steady there, Mr. Redrow." Her gaze met Corey's as she added, "We'd better get you squared away before you do me in." Then one blue eye crinkled into a wink, and her mouth drew back over square jaws to show large teeth. "At ease, sailor. Stow your bag in the fo'c'sle." She pointed forward and turned to consult with the mate.

Corey was about to pass her on the way toward the bow when he heard as much as felt a slap on his back.

"What the—!" he choked out as he lurched forward, jerking his hand out and nearly slapping the captain, this time from behind. He swung around to face his assailant when he heard the familiar voice.

"Knew you couldn't stay away," Woody laughed as Corey let out his breath. "It was the Caribbean girls that changed your mind, right?" He put his arm around Corey's shoulder and steered him amidships past a pin rail terminating a web of rigging lines. "C'mon, I'll show you around." He tipped his head aft. "I see you've already met Cannonball Harper."

Relieved to be out of the captain's range, Corey took in the scene on deck. The ship swarmed with crew, trainees, and tourists. Some bustled about with purpose; some were new sailors who worked carefully with partners; some held brochures as they smiled and pointed here and there.

The trainees included teens enrolled in the education program plus a couple of middle-aged recruits. The crew included the captain, three mates, the bos'n in charge of rigging, an engineer, a teacher, a carpenter/medic, a galley cook, and three able bodied seamen, or ABs.

Corey learned more about his new captain.

"Rosalind Scotty Harper," Woody said, "is from a horse farm in Kentucky. Come to think of it," he whispered, "she kind of looks like a horse!" Corey couldn't help staring at her profile and imagining a whinny as she lifted her lip at a new recruit. When she glanced his way, Corey's laugh became a cough, and he turned to follow Woody.

"Why 'Cannonball'?"

"She was a gunner's mate in the Navy," Woody said. "Then she got into battle reenactments. Some landlubber gave her the name and it stuck." Corey's eyes strayed to a hinged flap in the hull and wondered if the gun port was still used.

"Only weapons I know of are the water guns we hid in a deck box."

As Corey surveyed the visible storage boxes on deck, he noticed the pungent odor that permeated the air. Woody didn't seem bothered by it, but Corey had to ask.

Woody sniffed. "You get used to it after a while. But if you know what's good for you," he lowered his voice, "you won't go near the galley. The cook's trying a new recipe—"

"Trying is right." It was a new voice. A raspy one.

Corey pivoted one-eighty and nearly smashed into a graying man in ragged cutoffs and T-shirt. Was that a smile, or were his lips curled to balance the cigarette?

The man coughed as he moved away, "That girl could destroy a TV dinner. Rather eat my cigarette."

Corey thought the guy must be an old hand, but Woody set him straight.

"Morris? Only been sailing a few weeks. He just walked away from a career on Wall Street." Woody smirked and added, "He traded his suits for jeans, and his wife for his freedom."

"Happy to see my behind, she was." The man had reappeared out of nowhere. "Long as I left the money behind!"

Woody's face reddened as Morris adjusted the coil of rope that hung over his shoulder, saying, "I don't care who knows it." Woody seemed relieved to be called away by the second mate.

Corey found himself staring at the roll that bobbed in the man's lips as Morris said, "Don't worry, it's herbal. Coltsfoot's good for my cough."

In the fo'c'sle, each bunk had its own privacy curtain. Corey dumped out his duffle bag and placed his clothes in the drawer beneath his bunk. Then he followed the sound of old rock and roll—and the strange smell—up to the galley. Corey stared past two ovens and an industrial cooking range to see the blur of a woman shaped like a dumpling.

Marty French's platinum hair was fastened in a lopsided bun that threatened to abandon ship as she bobbed to the music. The dotted scarf draping her shoulders skimmed its surroundings, and Corey stared as flying fringe threatened to join unidentifiable lumps sizzling in the fryer.

"I specialize in French-fried everything!" Marty called out in rhythm with the radio. "Don't you love Fleetwood?" She gave a wink. Corey said his mom played them all the time.

Marty passed him a crispy chunk from the cooling rack and watched him nibble. He tried to smile as he stowed the rubbery mass in his cheek.

Corey made it up the ladder and was a few feet from the rail. Close enough. He was so focused on expelling the putrid wad, it didn't register when someone at the rail turned to ask if his day had improved and would there be "further assaults?" Not until she swung around fully to face him.

That's when the lump hit Captain Harper in the eye. Her smile disappeared as Corey's saliva oozed down her cheek.

Near Harts Landing... MACK BACK & ON TRACK

Mackenzie "Hart" Poole meekly took the pills and tossed them down her throat with water from a paper cup. At least that was what the meds administrator thought.

Mackenzie stored the pills in her cheek until she got to the restroom and flushed them. She splashed cold water on her face. She had quit taking the medication several days ago and now felt as though she were waking up from a dream.

When she had arrived at the correctional facility, she had been somewhat dazed. *This was not the plan!* She was supposed to be enjoying her role as first lady of Harts Landing—without those pesky Worders in the way. And training her grandson in the art of influence. Not wasting time in jail.

But she had snapped out of her disappointment. Time here did not have to be a waste. Influencing Oscar, the corrections officer, was easy. He had proved a valuable ally in her new plan—until he went and eloped with the medications lady. *How could he abandon me for weeks?* The new meds guy always made sure she swallowed, and the drugs had fogged her thinking.

Now Oscar was back, along with the pill lady.

As Mackenzie's mind cleared, the memories returned: pushing Peg Worder Stowe off the cliff, using the woman's amnesia against her when she survived, stealing the journal

Peg's son had found; and then Mackenzie's arrest for attempted murder. And the fact that her own grandson had blown the whistle on her!

Mackenzie had assumed Auger would help her guard the Hart secret and capitalize on the name. Now the journal was exposed, and many people believed her ancestor had stolen the name.

Most people in Mackenzie's position would have given in to circumstances. But she knew psychology better than anyone; minds could always be molded.

"Don't worry, Mack," Oscar murmured through unmoving lips as he escorted her. "I didn't forget you while I was gone. I stirred things up online."

Mackenzie flashed on a new memory: the map on a page she'd hidden before the journal had been confiscated. Experts had verified the journal's age, and people had believed its author. But people were like sheep, and since the treasure had not been found, all they needed were a few doubts planted here and there to turn into a pack of wolves.

By now, Oscar should be ready to carry out the next step. "I'll need you to do some research," she began.

He listened obediently as he returned her to her cell.

LEARNING THE ROPES

Corey sank to the deck below the rail as the captain stepped away, still wiping her face. He was shocked and relieved to find that she had a sense of humor! She had even apologized for coming between Corey and the rail.

"It isn't the first time I've seen that look on a sailor," she'd said. She explained that Marty used to work in a greasy spoon restaurant that failed—*big surprise*—and the crew should "be patient as she adjusts."

Corey's breathing slowed and he felt relieved, even self-satisfied, until Woody came along. "The new recruits are as ignorant as you," he snorted. Then he added, "*Used* to be."

Corey followed Woody's gaze to a couple of his new *Golden Aye* shipmates. One was being teased by a sailor from another ship because he thought a sheet was a sail instead of a line. When the other forgot the term for a sail's lower corner, the sailor called her "Clew-less."

"Don't let it bother you, dear," a jolly looking woman told the girl. "I used to think a shroud was a head covering!"

Corey glanced at the shrouds that fanned from the mast to either side of the ship. He knew what it was like to climb the ratlines as the deck below appeared smaller and smaller. The new crew members would face enough challenges.

After the visitors disembarked and Woody was called away, Corey found himself explaining terms to one of the new trainees. Soon he was surrounded by several more.

He pointed up toward the mast. "Those crosspieces are *yards.*" He waved at the moveable lines and blocks. "You use running rigging to move the sails and yards." He pointed out each of the sails stacked on the mainmast. "Starting at bottom, it's the course, or *mains'l*. Then topsail, t'gallant, and royal."

"What about that sail?" a boy pointed aft, toward the mizzenmast. "It's not square-rigged like the others."

"That's a spanker—the boom at its foot can be trimmed to the wind."

Woody passed by again. "Don't get too comfortable standing around!" He loved to harass the newbies.

Corey ignored him and continued. "You'll learn to tie knots, secure lines on belaying pins, hoist sails using halyards, brace the yards to catch wind in the sails, furl sail by securing it. You'll even stand watch and take the helm."

Woody returned. "But you'll spend lots more time..." He tapped each of his fingers. "With deck washing, sanding, oiling, and painting, helping the cook, and cleaning the head— that's the bathroom, in case you didn't know." He grinned. "It won't *all* be glamorous, though." The others laughed uncertainly. "At first, you'll spend time hanging your head over the rails—"

"And not just because of Marty's cooking," Corey added.

"You make a good teacher." The jolly older woman, Chazy, sat on a bench as she rubbed her feet.

And you make a good talker, Corey soon concluded. Chazy was a widow whose kids had grown and left her "nest."

"Biggest adventure last month was watching a movie! It was time to have me some fun." As the woman talked, a gold locket bobbed up and down at her throat. When Corey admired it, she stroked it, and her voice softened.

"That was from my Alfred on our last anniversary." She opened it to show a tiny photograph. "That's him...and there's Betty and Junior." She closed it. "Solid gold," she said with a proud smile. "I always put it below when I'm on watch."

When she left for the companionway to the lower deck, Chazy called out to a boy and girl gawking up at the mast, "Now I know that rigging looks scary." Her upper arms jiggled as she shook a finger. "But you kids will be climbing circles around me in no time!"

The "kids" were eighteen-year-old twins from Rochester, Brian and Darian. Darian pushed her glasses up closer to her dark brown eyes and smiled wordlessly. Brian smiled broadly and chatted as he ran a hand over his neat cornrows. Then he slapped Woody on the back and suggested they partner up. He had mistaken him for a trainee.

Woody froze. "I don't need help 'learning the ropes,'" he said stiffly. "And furthermore..."

Corey noticed the captain approaching from starboard as Woody poked a finger at Brian's chest. But before Brian could find out what was 'further,' Woody's brows shot up as a firm hand pulled him sideways.

"He's a little sensitive," Corey explained to Brian and his sister. But Corey couldn't help overhearing the captain tell Woody, "Rein it in, Mustang—no one's going to steal your oats."

Woody's red face was doused by the end of the fire drill. Two other safety drills included man overboard and abandon ship. The trainees practiced throwing life rings. Darian was a natural, and she partnered with a freckled, slightly plump girl who took a little longer to catch on. It was Hannah, the girl some guy had called "clewless."

They all learned how to pull on buoyant suits in case the ship ever capsized. They checked "ditch" kits, which held emergency supplies. They learned how to 'cast off the falls' to release the lifeboat.

They reviewed watch rotations and learned that each day would be divided into four periods, six hours each.

"Don't be surprised if we switch watches now and then," the first mate added. "Fielding says people learn best under changing conditions, with different people." His face darkened as a shaven-headed boy strutted by.

"And there *are* different people around," Woody whispered. "I hear that kid is only here as a condition."

"Condition?" Corey furrowed his brows as his gaze followed the teenager with bones tatooed on his scalp.

"Of probation."

CRACK THE WHIP

The student trainees gathered about the chart house. On its wall was a large chart of the St. Lawrence River and the whole eastern seaboard. Several pushpins marked ports at which the *Golden Aye* had stopped since its journey began in Duluth, Minnesota. The only river towns to be so festooned were Cape Vincent, Clayton, and Alexandria Bay. Mr. Crakov inserted a marker for Harts Landing as the crew clapped. Then he encouraged the teens to get comfortable near the hatchway. The crew would take care of setting sail while the students got oriented.

"Call me Cracker." The teacher spread a river chart on a makeshift table and secured the corners with weights.

"As in Cracker of Whips!" shouted the first mate.

"Watch out, kids...he's a tricky one." The bos'n winked from the starboard pin rail amidships. Cracker ignored them.

"Even though this ship has modern equipment for backup, we'll learn traditional sailing methods to develop responsibility and teamwork." He paused. "Now, you might have heard how things are on other tall ships. But the Fielding Fleet is not other ships. We sail by stars, climb aloft for lookout..."

The bald boy suppressed a snort. The idea of the portly man climbing the rigging *was* entertaining.

"But that's not what *I'm* here to teach," Cracker said. "I'll be responsible for your class work." He glanced at the boy. "And grading you."

The boy's grin disappeared.

"Lesson one: always know where you are." Cracker ignored the whispers and giggles. He traced a path with his finger on the large chart.

"First, let's get oriented. Here's North America. What river are we sailing, Steve?" He gestured to a stocky boy with sun-streaked blond hair over dark eyebrows.

Steve wrinkled his nose. "*Duh*. It's the St. Lawrence!"

"Right." Cracker zeroed in on the local border area between the U.S. and Canada, his finger sweeping upward along the illustrated river. "And are we sailing upriver or downriver?"

"Up." Steve rolled his eyes with a grin at an older girl, a tall brunette whose violet eyes flashed him a look before darting back to the sailing manual in her hands.

"No," Brian said, "*That's* upriver." He pointed a large, dark finger aft, to the southwest.

"Right. We're headed downriver." Cracker swiveled to face Steve. "Downriver doesn't have to be south." When Steve's smile disappeared, Cracker added, "Don't feel bad. It's a common misunderstanding."

He turned back to the group. "And how do you know you're going downriver?"

"It's when you *go*...with the *flow*." The words came out in a slow rap. It was the bald boy.

Cracker consulted his list. "Orville Dickory." He looked up. "You are correct."

"Aw, don't gimme that formal crap," Orville tossed his head. "We're family now, right? I'm the *Dice*." He looked around coolly, with intense gray eyes that appeared half closed.

Cracker stared at him. "Dice it is."

He continued. "The river goes from its source in the Great Lakes to its mouth near Quebec. Then it flows from the Gulf of St. Lawrence into the Atlantic." He pointed along the river's flow. "We'll sail downriver..."

"Which is northeast!" Steve said triumphantly.

Cracker gave him a thumbs-up and pulled out another chart. Steve stole another glance at the brunette, who was trying to suppress a twitch of the lip. Instead, a dimple appeared and she told him her name was Sherrie. Steve sat back with a broad smile.

"We'll be passing a number of islands." Cracker unrolled a portion of chart showing the nearby river area. "The bigger islands are upstream." He pointed aft. "But around here," he swept his hand toward the bow, "we find some smaller ones, like Rocky Island and Ironsides—"

"Ironsides is made of iron and Rocky is rocks, right?" Dice gave a half grin.

Some of the crew laughed, but Cracker said, "Good question. Anybody know what type of rock?"

While the others were speculating, Darian and Hannah started their own conversation near Corey.

"Wasn't it Rocky Island I saw on the news a couple of months ago?"

"That cave, the shooting... Someone found an old journal." Darian's eyes widened. "Claimed there's British gold."

"Buried treasure?" Dice muttered nearby. "Yeah, right."

"It's for real." The new voice came with authority.

Dice narrowed his gray eyes at Corey. Others turned to look at him, too. It was the first time Corey had spoken since settling on a deck box, shades over his eyes, filtering everyone here out of his memories of Sam. Until the comments seeped through.

When he had first seen the blog challenging his ancestor's journal, Corey was outraged. Sam had calmed him: the bloggers were zeroes with nothing better to do. But Corey was sure the journal was true. It was solid as...

"Granite," he said. *Better change the subject.* "That's what these islands are." He pointed beyond the port rail, where Chazy stood.

Cracker gestured for Corey to continue.

He sat up. "Glaciers scooped out the land between granite columns, and then water filled in." He pulled off his shades. "The islands are the pillars of granite sticking up, with added dirt and greenery." Corey smiled at what he had learned from Sam. Everything reminded him of her.

Hannah was in awe. "Are there really a *thousand* islands?"

"Hah!" Dice snorted. "Not likely."

Everyone looked aft toward Wellesley, nearly out of sight, and other large islands upriver. Many smaller ones were scattered here and there.

"There can't be more than a hundred or so," Steve said.

"The 'Hundred Islands' just doesn't sound right." Chazy said.

"You're right, Dice," Corey said. "There's not a *thousand* islands."

"I knew that." He looked bored.

Corey turned to the others. "It's nearly *two* thousand."

Dice glared as the others snorted. Then he seemed to shrink into the crowd, popping up here and there around the group as Cracker and Corey discussed island history.

Corey was describing a nearby sunken battleship when Dice finally passed behind him to settle on a deck box.

"The *Spitflame* was from the War of 1812." Corey gestured aft toward the Landing from which they had just departed.

"Why, I never thought I would sail right over another ship!" Chazy grinned at Corey and reached for her locket. As she patted all around her throat, her bright face turned the color of ash.

"It's the first time I've ever seen that woman un-cheerful," Woody said as everyone searched the deck for the locket.

Chazy's eyes looked like two pieces of coal stuck into a big marshmallow. She choked, "I just had it, not two minutes before I leaned over that rail." She looked into the water. But by now they had motored farther downriver. Chazy's voice was a hollow drone. "I must not have clasped it after showing it to Corey."

She had dropped to the hatch cover, her shoulders heaving, when the captain called, "Stand by to set sail!" and the crew scurried to take positions.

A singsong voice pierced the air from behind Corey. "Hey, is that gold? It's a nice piece—the one in your back pocket..." Marty, the cook, had emerged from the galley. She snapped her fingers. "What was your name again?"

Corey was shocked to think that anyone here would have the locket. *What kind of creep?*

When he looked around to find the culprit, everyone else was staring at...

"Corey!" Marty shouted with a grin. "So where'd you get the gold piece?"

Horrified, Corey craned his neck to see the chain that dangled from the back waist band of his own pants. He felt his stomach drop. He turned back to face unfriendly stares.

Gravity seemed to increase in the silence; the locket pulled on Corey like a lead anchor that would bury him in the islands and kill any chance to find his father.

In Harts Landing... THE WHOLE TEXT

The northwesterly breeze lifted Sam's bangs. The way the early September sun shone on the river took her back to the island days of July and August. She had pulled the van over to take in the scene along the cliff...and figure out what to say to Corey. As she looked beyond Rocky Island, she saw a tall ship heading downriver, its white sails luffing. Or was she imagining it? After all, she'd been stuck on the image of Corey's ship coming in, wishing things had gone differently that time at the pier. The last time she saw him.

How excited she had been! She could hardly wait to run up and plant a big kiss on his lips. The sight of him had taken her breath. How muscular he was! And how natural he looked... *With a tall Scandinavian beauty draped over him.*

Her stomach seized up, and Sam closed her eyes against the memory, but the unwanted scene only popped more clearly in her head. It had been like a punch in the stomach when Corey had stared at Sam and said nothing. It seemed that he didn't want to acknowledge her in the presence of his new girlfriend.

Samantha had planned to return home on the bus after her interview—the day after Auger dropped her off on his way to visit his own future college. But she'd changed her plans after seeing Corey's reaction at the pier. And she would *not* answer those lame texts. Some story about a "trauma."

The passage of a few days had softened her. Maybe she had judged him too quickly. Corey had been through a lot. Anyway, by now that girl had probably sailed on. Maybe now Sam could face Corey and give him a chance to explain. His last text said he would be at the pier today.

She smiled and started the engine.

"You missed him," the guy said without looking up. The guy—Darren or maybe Derrick she'd heard his name was—scowled at a spot on the hull of the fishing boat he was pretending to wipe down. As if the spot would disappear by his staring at it. When he looked up, the scowl vanished. The wide blue eyes were framed by sandy waves that escaped the black rag around his head, and reluctant lips fought the curl of a smile. His skin was free of sweat, though the hot sun beat onto his face and shoulders.

Sam's face fell. "When's he coming back?" She glanced at her wrist watch. "I could just wait..."

"Hah, right," he said as he eyed the bare skin between her sun top and hip huggers, his lips giving in to an appreciative grin. "Better bring your cold-weather gear." He stared at Samantha and continued his circular hand motion even after he ran out of boat.

"What are you talking about?"

"You have a long wait." He corrected his aim and gave a swipe at the bow section. "Months, from what I hear."

She stared, blank-faced.

"He's on that sailing ship." He nodded downriver. "Heading to the Caribbean for winter."

"No...no," Sam shook her head. "That's not right." She checked her phone messages. "He just says he's going sailing today." She noticed there was a line of text she hadn't seen earlier. She scrolled it up and widened her eyes. "And 'will be gone...the rest of the year'?"

Her hands went cold. Her breath came in gulps. "No! He did *not* sail away from me!"

She stood as still as Corey had the last time she saw him.

ISLAND OF DARKNESS

Corey could hardly breathe as cold eyes glared at him. He felt like a convict awaiting sentence.

As the captain approached, none of the crew even acknowledged Marty's new shout: "Look, we have a stowaway!" referring to the canine form limping along behind the captain.

"Marty, Mr. Gray is with me." The captain's eyes never wavered as she headed toward Corey. "Now, please go check the galley bins."

Behind the old dog came Morris, also looking stern, without his cigarette.

This was it. Captain Harper would tell Corey he was through. She didn't need Morris to back her up. Corey would go peacefully. The ship would be turning back to shore any minute. Corey glanced at the others; they looked at him with anger and confusion. Only Dice gave him the hint of a smile.

"Stealing is bad enough," the captain said as she took her prisoner toward the chart room, "but letting a fellow shipmate take the fall?"

Corey was shocked to see the captain lead Dice away as Morris whispered the magic words: "Corey was framed—saw it with m' own eyes."

After assuring Corey they "knew all along" that he was innocent, everyone was buzzing about Dice, who was now with the captain in a conference call with the probation officer—and Grayson Fielding.

A fresh breeze had come up, and the mate had relayed the order to loose the topsail. As Corey edged sideways on the footrope toward the yardarm, he asked Woody about Mr. Gray.

"He's old and can't see good." Woody undid the gasket that secured the rolled sail. "But he's been with Captain Harper for years."

"Wish I'd brought my dog," Corey mumbled as he loosened sail.

"Your monster?" Woody said. "The ship would capsize every time that dog saw a fish."

Corey had to admit, Howler would be a risk.

Woody climbed back down the ratlines behind Corey. "Besides, you're not the captain."

They stood on deck and watched the sail fill with wind. Then the ship rolled with the wave of a passing freighter. Mr. Gray, who had come out of the captain's cabin, nearly lost his balance before the captain shooed him back inside. *Conference must be over.* Would Dice be dumped on the nearest island?

Corey watched an overhead cloud pushed along by the same wind that filled the sails. Then a much smaller puff drifted past his nose. Smoke. It was from Morris.

If it hadn't been for him, Corey might be an outcast right now. If Morris hadn't caught a glimpse of Dice slipping something in Corey's pocket and later realized what it was...

Corey gave Morris a smile of gratitude as the *Golden Aye* sailed near Grenadier, the long Canadian island.

Some of the trainees were at the port rail, watching the scenery.

"What's that house with the glass thingy on top?" Hannah asked, pointing at the structure on a small island.

"Reminds me of the top of my wedding cake." Chazy fondled the locket that had reappeared under her throat.

Everyone stared at the gray stone building topped by a glass dome.

"It's a lighthouse," Morris slurred past the roll between his teeth. "Sisters Island."

"The lantern in that dome hasn't been used since '59," Cracker added. "Now the place is privately owned."

Steve's eyes were wide. "Somebody *owns* a lighthouse?"

Corey had taken the helm, under Woody's supervision, as they headed downriver past familiar islands. In his mind, he was sailing in the wake of his ancestor, Warren Hart, who had defended the United States two hundred years ago. As they glided northward, they approached a small island just inside the US border, one that would have been all granite and trees in Warren's time. But now Dark Island supported a grand estate that rose from a rock foundation to red-tiled roofs.

Corey's thoughts were interrupted by a shout.

"I thought the castle was in Alexandria Bay!" Steve stared over the port rail. "Did we get turned around?"

"That was Boldt Castle," Sherrie said with a grin.

"This one is Singer." Cracker rubbed his hands together, warming to another lecture. "It was built about the same time as Boldt Castle, early nineteen-hundreds. But unlike Boldt, Frederick Bourne actually lived in his castle, at least in the summers."

As the crew ogled the island kingdom, Corey looked sadly at the west side. He and Sam had come ashore there and shared a secret picnic under the trees. He could almost feel the warm touch of her hand.

"Looks like something out of a storybook," Darian said, tightening her glasses strap.

Woody grinned. "Supposed to be full of secret passages."

"And I've heard it's haunted," Chazy said, her voice low.

Corey felt the hairs stand up on his arm as he recalled Sam talking about the early 20th-century man, dark-haired and white-shirted, who had been seen walking the island every full moon. But Corey's goose bumps were not caused by any ghost. It was the memory of the real girl brushing her arm against his. Corey had felt the thrill of Sam's touch as they sat in the shadows joking about the ghost. Was the island haunted by Frederick Bourne, the castle's first owner? Or maybe a servant? Corey hadn't cared who it was as long as it kept Sam whispering in his ear.

Fairy tales and ghost stories had been fun back then. Now Corey was all too aware that he was getting farther and farther from Sam. "I don't believe in ghosts," he grunted as he yanked the helm hard to starboard.

Mr. Gray, who had been wobbling his way onto a bench, happened to lose his balance and fall to the deck. "Easy, partner," Woody said to Corey as he glanced at the captain, who stood with Morris near the chartroom. Woody's lips were stiff as he warned, "You don't want to join Dice on the captain's SHIP list."

"Huh?"

"Screw-ups, Hacks, Idiots, and Pirates."

LOCKS TO THE KEYS

They had passed another lighthouse, the one at Crossover Island, and moved into Canadian waters by the Brockville narrows when Corey heard murmurs around him. Dice had appeared, wordlessly, and was sanding a deck box. From the look on his face, nothing in the world could be more important than stripping that box down to raw wood.

"Man how'd he get out of that one?" Brian said, and someone else said, "Worked out some kind of arrangement."

Woody nodded. "If anybody could turn him around, it's Fielding."

The owner of the fleet was either a fool or a genius. Corey watched as Chazy approached Dice and spoke in serious tones. Then she smiled and actually hugged him.

They were edging past sunlit cottages and elaborate estates when Steve called out, "Hey, we're in Canada. Don't we have to, like, show our passports?"

"Not unless we anchor," Morris said.

"Which we're not...yet," Woody said, his eyes gleaming. What was he so excited about?

"Stand by to furl sail!" The order came long before Montreal and would not be the last time the crew would take in sail and resort to engine power before reaching the ocean.

The captain had already radioed the intention to navigate the narrow passage ahead of them.

Corey scrambled up the rigging along with several experienced crew members while newcomers watched.

"Hey, I can help with that!" Brian offered, but Woody waved him off, saying something about his "inexperience."

It didn't take long to furl the sails.

The *Golden Aye* approached a queue of private craft to wait its turn. New crew members gathered near the pin rails, at one side of the ship then the other, and learned to check belaying pins that held the movable rigging lines. Each had to be secured in a way that allowed quick removal.

It was soon time to motor forward. Hannah's eyes were big. "What are they going to do to us in that box?" She had seen each ship sink lower and lower upon entering the enclosure ahead of them.

"They're going to dunk us," one of the AB's said with a straight face, "then check for leaks."

Hannah's eyes grew even larger until Morris whispered, "He's a moron," and gave her arm a squeeze.

"Don't worry, boys and girls," Cracker announced. "We're just climbing downstairs!"

Woody glanced at Corey and rolled his eyes.

"It's no joke," Cracker said. "This 'lock' is literally a step in the stairway that all outgoing ships use to get to the ocean." He explained that as water flows down from the Great Lakes to the Atlantic, there are a number of drops.

"And in these gated enclosures, the water level is raised or lowered so boats can move between sections." He looked all around the area. "We're lucky today, won't have to wait for cargo ships." He added, "Commercial ships get priority."

Morris muttered to Sawtooth, the carpenter, "Remember in July they made us wait for hours, now that was a pain in the—"

"Yep," Sawtooth said. "Fell asleep on deck and burnt the top o' my head!"

"Well if you'da kept your cap on..." said a salty crew member, "or growed some hair..."

"By the time we got through, I *had* growed some hair!"

The banter of the old-timers receded to the background as the teens became distracted by the lock procedure. They watched as the ship was guided into the enclosure and the gate closed behind them. The *Golden Aye's* channels and hull were protected by wooden boards and inflated rubber fenders, and soon the ship's two-dimensional world expanded to three. Corey' head tilted back, and he had the sensation that the world was rising above the ship.

"Send all lines as able!"

"Ease handsomely!"

Raising or lowering within the locks required eyes on all sides, as fenders were in danger of shifting and allowing contact between hull and cement walls. Lines had to be kept taut to keep the ship in place but let out gradually so the ship could lower with the level of the water as it drained to match the river level ahead.

"Eyes to portside—shove that fender board!"

Corey felt disoriented as the walls closed in. He flashed back to last June and visions of the cave where he'd been trapped underwater. He shut his eyes, knowing that in a few moments, the far wall would open and release them to sail out of the lock and downriver.

For now, his eyes opened on a darkened cement wall.

"Eww!" someone said.

Corey's gaze followed Hannah's to the slimy green fringe waving from the wall. He forgot his claustrophobia at the thought of the slime he needed to remove from his own life. He couldn't let anything stop him from getting to his father!

Released from the lock, the *Golden Aye* proceeded through clusters of small islands and stepped down through several additional locks, passing Massena, Cornwall, Coteau-du-Lac, and Lachine before descending to Montreal.

Be patient. Corey reminded himself that Florida was a long way from home, and there would be a lot of delays before getting there. For now he had to be fully present on board.

"You're in for a treat!" Woody said as they waited for passport checks at Canadian customs. "You'll get to meet Jay-Boy the playboy!"

4 EVERYTHING GOES SOUTH

They had neatened the *Golden Aye* with proper harbor furls in Montreal. Now Corey and his mates had a few hours of shore leave for some sightseeing.

At the Notre Dame Sailor's Church, old ships hung in the cavernous space, and stained glass windows pulsed with reds and yellows enlivened by the sun's rays. *Like shining gold pieces.*

Afterwards, they took in the sights along the old Port before reporting back to the ship. There they met Morris and several crew members leaving in search of a cheap restaurant.

"I thought Marty was serving dinner on board," Hannah said.

"Exactly," the carpenter called over his shoulder.

After one bite of batter-fried meatball, Corey ate two bowls of salad. Then he filled up on cheese and crackers as he joined in the easy chatter among his new shipmates.

The *Aye* was berthed for the night. Corey's bunk was a little harder than his bed at home, but least he wasn't forced into a sling like on the *Venture IVth*. He had never quite gotten used to his own weight curved into a hammock.

It had been a busy day and, for the first time, Corey was left alone with his thoughts. He checked his phone. Samantha had not returned his text. Didn't she even care that he had just sailed away for months? He almost called her but stopped himself. He would only make things worse if he kept trying to contact her. *No.* He made a pact with himself: He would not contact Samantha until he faced his father for once and for all, and vanquished his demon. Until then, he would focus on sailing.

Only exhaustion allowed Corey to relax as the soft sounds of a guitar lulled him to sleep. Or had that been a dream?

In the morning, they welcomed two new crew members: the dark and quiet William and the wise-cracking Jay.

James "Jay" Town was the blue-eyed twenty-six-year-old Woody greeted with a side-body hug. When introduced to the new sailors, Jay lingered just a little longer with the girls, who blushed and flirted. Corey didn't get it. He shook Jay's hand and gave him a half smile. "Jay-Boy" was okay, but how was he a treat?

How became obvious when the guy leaped onto the hatch cover and launched into a rap about his new acquaintances, timed to hip hop moves. Crew members either laughed or turned red as they heard Jay's interpretation. Corey felt his ears go pink when Jay hinted at Corey's 'Secret Desire'—until the punchline: 'For Marty's Meatballs.'

The mood on board made watch go faster, and Corey hadn't realized how hard he had been working until he collapsed on the foredeck with a cold bottle. The captain was right, water was the best thirst quencher.

He gazed out past the stays and the headsails, and when he caught his breath, he stood up to lean over the rail. He turned his head this way and that, enjoying the breeze. A familiar profile caught his eye. There, at the end of the bow was a perfect image of Sam! It was the first time he had looked at the ship's figurehead, a wooden sculpture like an angel leading them onward. He wanted it. He stared at the deck, wondering. Could he create a replica?

Corey sank to the deck and imagined carving a piece of wood into the form of Samantha. As he gazed back toward the foremast, he noticed Dice working with a crew member. Corey had almost forgotten the guy was still on board. He looked down and shook his head as he remembered how the boy had framed him.

When Corey looked back up, Dice was headed his way. *Great.* Did he make nice with the captain just to get another chance at Corey?

The boy stopped in front of Corey and stared at his own feet. "They said I had to apologize."

Corey didn't say anything.

"But not 'til I could mean it." He eyed Corey and sighed. "You made me look stupid."

Not much of an apology. And he'd made himself look stupid.

Dice turned and leaned over the rail. "They said you didn't mean nothin' by it. He rubbed his ear, turned and walked away as Corey stared after him.

The whole crew bubbled with energy as they departed Montreal. With a new pushpin on the chart house wall, the *Golden Aye* headed toward Quebec. Woody and Jay had a chance to catch up on old times as they worked.

"So what woman you running away from this time?" Woody was showing the quieter newcomer, William, how to "fake a line," looping it onto the deck so it would run freely.

"Hey, that hurts," Jay said as he finished belaying. He pressed a hand to his chest. "The only woman I ever ran from was my sister when I was eight—don't roll your eyes at me!"

"What about the redhead, chased you off the end of a pier in Nantucket?" Morris asked in his monotone.

Chazy piped up from amidships: "And even I've heard of the little gal whose father chased you away in Jacksonville." Her flesh jiggled as she chuckled. "With a shotgun!"

Jay held his hands palm-out. "All right, I admit I've had a colorful history." He pressed a hand to his chest. "But I've turned a new leaf. I am happily engaged." He pulled up his sleeve to reveal blue inking in the shape of an anchor, the name *LouAnn* woven through it.

Stix, the engineer, was passing by. She took a swipe at the tat and checked her finger.

"Hey! Yes, it's permanent," Jay said, mock anger flashing in his blue eyes.

Woody stopped working the knot he was demonstrating. "And she doesn't mind you going off for weeks?"

"Mind? McGill is a tough school, it takes all her concentration." Jay shrugged his shoulders. "Thought I'd do her a favor and get out of her hair."

As he corrected William's latest attempt at a knot, Woody said, "You just want to grab a chance to visit your old ports while she looks the other way!" He punched Jay in the arm.

Corey was giving Brian pointers on climbing, saying, "Just take one step at a time." But he knew he'd better listen to his own advice if he wanted to climb his way back to Sam. What would it be like, being engaged? He knew one thing: If Sam ever said yes, Corey would never leave *her*.

It took four days to get to the Gulf, including overnights, a Quebec festival day, and allowing ship tours. By now, Corey's head pulsed with new sights and fresh memories. But his real purpose was never far from his mind. He created an image of his father to keep him focused: a dark, horned silhouette. Whether occupied with hauling sheet or doing a deck wash, Corey held the image. And when Quebec receded in the wake of the *Golden Aye* and he had jabbed a fresh pin in the chart, the image seemed to stare down from the clouds, luring him seaward. As the river widened into the Gulf of St. Lawrence, Corey could hardly wait to get to the Atlantic.

They had cleared Prince Edward Island and passed through the Canso Strait, and when they entered the open waters of the Atlantic it was like emerging from a cocoon. From Corey's perch on the yard, he could see for miles. But the best part of entering the ocean would be turning southwest toward Florida. That was where Corey would slash his bonds and claim freedom from the man who came between him and Sam.

In Harts Landing... B&B GOING SOUTH

Sam ran up the front steps of the B&B, through the open door—was something different?—and barely grunted at her dad, who was taping a large flat carton. She grabbed the stair rail but stumbled when she realized what was missing.

"Randy, what are you doing!" She forgot her promise to call him "Dad" like normal kids did. She ran back to him. "You can't sell Corey's window. Mr. Murphy left it for him." The colorful stained glass ship had meant a lot to Corey when the previous owner had left it to him. But who was she kidding? Now that Corey was on a real ship, he'd probably forgotten that too. It seemed he had no interest in Sam. He hadn't contacted her since sailing away.

"The kid said we could keep it." Randy wiped dust off his face. "Besides, now that he's a Hart he'll have plenty of money." He frowned and scribbled on the package, shaking his head. "I thought we could handle the renovation costs, but..."

"I know, too many debts to count." Sam was glad to change the subject, though this was painful enough. Randy's former partner had ruined Randy's credit.

"Look, Samantha."

Oh oh. He usually called her Sam.

He let out a breath. "Just keeping the Mainsail open will be hard. And you can kiss college goodbye."

"Hey, not necessarily."

"Well, don't get your hopes up about that prize."

"It's a scholarship, and if I don't win it," she nodded at the carton, "*that* isn't going to make a difference." Then she stared up at the hooks that dangled, useless, without the framed glass sailing ship. She couldn't help remembering the summer days, exploring islands with Corey in a real boat, gliding over sunlit waves.

"Listen, I'm telling you something here." Her dad's face was serious. "I've really been trying to keep this place going." His voice faltered. "I know you like living here, but..."

"What! You don't mean—"

"My folks know a guy down south."

"In Georgia?" Was he considering moving? She'd never see Corey!

"This pecan producer needs a manager by late summer." Randy raised his voice. "Hey! Where you going?"

She could hear him call her name as she stumbled down the front steps. But there was nothing he could say. If she had only seen the signs last June, maybe things would be different. "It's my fault!" she cried.

"I'm the one that trusted Johnny," Randy's voice was fading behind her. "Unless I win the lottery, what can I do?"

Sam ran past the van, its bumper boasting "Sailing Rules!" reminding her again of Corey leaving with that blonde. She put on a burst of speed to run it out of her mind.

FLAMES OF GOLD

The students had just finished their first formal science class as they headed southwest past Halifax and toward the New England coast. Cracker had reviewed the anatomy of several sea creatures and gave the assignment to find and illustrate one of each species during the next few days. They had to compare and contrast its parts with the parts of a sailing ship.

Now the *Golden Aye* skirted the southern coast of Maine and headed for Portsmouth, New Hampshire, to pick up a new trainee and offer "sailaway" tours.

The sunrise deck wash had been delayed because the variable winds had required frequent trimming of the sails. When things settled down, Woody sent Corey below for buckets.

As he descended into the bowels of the ship, Corey was seized by a pulsing sensation, and the closer he got to the engine room, the more distinct the throbbing became. It was...music. As he entered the jungle of metal and plastic, Corey saw the engineer with drum sticks blurring among pipes. *So that's how she got her name.* Then, beyond Stix, he noticed someone else's fingers picking strings to create a Spanish melody. Long legs stuck out over a work bench, and the guitar rested at the torso, but the face was hidden by pipes. Corey didn't have time to see who it was, but they sure had a sensitive touch. Must be Sherrie. She always made herself scarce when she was off watch.

Back on deck, Corey noticed the ship was giving wide berth to a field of buoys along the coast.

"What are those?" Corey wondered, setting the wash buckets on deck so William could fill them.

"Each one is attached to a rope—" Morris said.

"Which is attached to a trap." Woody finished.

"Hey, we're in Lobster Land, dude!" Jay shouted. "Those lobster pots are probably full of somebody's dinner. Too bad I can't afford it on sailor wages."

Corey wondered what lobster tasted like. More important, he wanted to see one up close, since it was one of the assigned creatures. "Hey, Woody, how could I get a look..."

But Woody was clapping someone's shoulder, saying, "Ready for your first sailaway, buddy?" It was Brian, who had just made his way down the shrouds. Like the other newbies, Brian had seemed nervous about hosting the people willing to slap down twenty-five bucks for a two-hour sail. Woody punched the guy's arm. "Don't worry, you'll be fine. Just remember: you already know more about sailing than ninety-five percent of the people."

"It's nice to see Woody taking Brian under his wing," Chazy whispered. "After their little run-in."

"Woody doesn't hold a grudge," Corey said.

Then he heard Woody holler. "Better hide, Jay! After all, this is Portsmouth!"

Jay took a position at starboard and mumbled, "I got no problem with Portsmouth."

"What's that about?" Corey asked as Woody came over to help check line placement.

"Ex-girlfriend claimed Jay was a daddy."

Jay had good ears; he swung around. "Told you, I never! She was just trying to frame me. Anyway, her kid has brown eyes."

"So?" Steve asked. He had moved closer as he scrubbed a patch of deck with a stiff bristled brush. Others, too, seemed to be paying less attention to their jobs than to Jay. Even Dice, who had appeared quietly and was arranging the contents of the newly varnished storage cabinet, glanced his way.

"Four blue eyes don't make two brown ones," Jay said. "It's genetics."

Steve paused his back-and-forth motion and wiped his face. "I don't think that's a hundred percent true, I heard there's a chance..."

"There's a chance you're a moron!" Jay dipped his hands in the water bucket and swished it at Steve. Corey laughed along with everyone else as Steve gave Jay a taste of his own. Corey hooted at Jay's look of surprise until he felt a cold shock himself—a powerful stream to the chest. He looked up to see Dice's familiar scowl, but this time the guy was holding a water cannon. The two boys locked eyes in a mutual glare. Then a smile spread over Dice's face. Corey grinned, grabbed the water gun and turned it on Dice.

Before long, the deck was the scene of a full-scale water fight with everyone drenched and shrieking.

"What's going on here?"

The deck became a gallery of dripping statues. The captain looked slowly from one to another before barking orders for harbor preparations. As the mate repeated the instructions to the crew at large, the captain turned away, but not before Corey noticed the hint of a smile.

Corey acted as lookout as they approached the coast. The ship had radar, but the trainees were learning the old "hands-on" methods and they had to take their responsibilities seriously. They kept a sharp eye out and had to report the location of anything that could threaten a close encounter.

As they approached the landing site, the most threatening thing Corey could see was standing on the pier under a splotch of orange. As the call for mooring lines spurred a burst of activity, a high voice drew the crew's attention.

Red hair exploded over a set of blushing pink shoulders. Flying elbows and palms were directed toward an unfortunate woman nearby. *Must be her mom.* The lady shook her head as she faced the girl and jabbed a finger at the trunk resting between them; the woman's body puffed and deflated as she blew disapprovals. But it looked like she was only fanning the flames.

Morris piped up. "We've got ourselves a lighted match."

"Is that our new shipmate?" Chazy chuckled. "Looks pretty hot under the collar. And over it too!"

"Surprised that ole pier don't go up in smoke," Sawtooth, the carpenter, muttered.

As the ship came alongside, Woody leaped overboard, stretched to his full height, and strode to the girl as crew members pretended to focus elsewhere.

A sharp voice could be heard clearly: "I can't go anywhere without my hair straightener."

"Only a small bag," Woody spoke stiffly. "And only essentials."

The mother gave an exasperated smirk and threw up her hands, as if to say "I told you so."

The girl ignored her mother and looked at Woody with a patronizing smile. "You don't understand, I need—"

"No, you don't understand," Woody countered.

The girl glared at him as her lips tightened around the words: "I want to speak to someone in charge."

Pink coloring crept over Woody's cheeks, and his body puffed up. Fireworks shot from his eyes, igniting an onboard bet.

"Five bucks says he blows." Sawtooth slapped a bill on the hatch.

"Nah." Morris stopped scratching Mr. Gray and pulled out a five. "The boy's got this."

Morris collected on the bet.

After Woody had hovered for several menacing moments, his color returned to normal. He spoke clearly, robotically, "I am in charge over you, and you will follow my orders." He did an about face and stalked onto the ship. The girl's mother made her open the trunk, make choices, and stuff the bag. Only the girl's hair burned in protest.

By the time the captain appeared at the gangway to welcome April P. Goldstein, the flames had died down to warm embers shining from behind emerald eyes.

"Just call me Goldy, Captain," she said with a handshake and a determined smile. Goldy turned and swung her sea bag over her shoulder so it rested next to her bared lower back, where navy blue inking proclaimed her the *SASSY I*. Below the tat, muscles rippled under white stretch pants as she followed Chazy to sleeping quarters. Corey stared, mesmerized, until Woody shoved a paint can at him. As Corey wiped new paint on a deck box, his brush slapped out a rhythm: *"Goldy is a hot-tie."*

When he finished his deck chores, Corey had no more time to reflect on the new crew member. He had to greet visitors and answer questions as the ship made three two-hour sailaways. Being the "expert" was new for Corey—and a little scary. But he liked the way the kids looked at him as he showed how to keep the wheel steady, and how they clapped as he showed off his climbing skills.

Finally, the last of the public adventurers were returned to shore, and the exhausted crew could look forward to a night's rest.

In the morning, Corey stuck a pin in the chart by the word *Portsmouth*. He was eager to get underway and see the town shrink into the coastline. He'd worked hard, he'd waited long, and it was time to let the northern coast slide out from under him.

"All hands on deck!" *Yes.*

The captain and mates were on the quarterdeck. The trainees stood in pairs, ready to coil and put away docklines.

Corey smiled as the engines came to life. The order was given to cast the lines. Corey practically danced on his toes waiting for the line to pile onto the deck so he could coil it. He could barely contain his excitement, and a shout escaped without his permission.

"Grab it!" he hollered at the top of his voice. Woody caught the end of the dockline but turned to see what the problem was.

Meanwhile, his line sagged to the water. Woody was unable to haul it out fast enough as it disappeared under the ship. Soon, the prop stopped turning.

They would not be leaving any time soon.

CUTTING BAIT

Corey adjusted his snorkeling gear and held his breath as he glided into the darkness under the hull. He willed himself not to panic. The last time he dove underwater, he had been trapped in a rock cage, and he ran out of air.

Now he felt like he was in shock. Was it the cold water seeping through the wetsuit? More likely, it was the humiliation of what he had done. He was glad there had been snorkeling gear on board because now he had a chance to redeem himself. Besides, he'd rather be down here than topside facing the shipmates he'd disappointed.

As he scanned for the prop, he simultaneously scanned his brain for that Fielding quote. What was it? *Fear is from ego; success is a push beyond fear.* Beyond his fear was success in Key West. Corey focused on a mental map of Florida as he turned under the stern. He had to free that line.

There. A tangled, knotted mess. He felt around his waist for the sheathed knife and fumbled for a few precious seconds. He worked the blade over the mooring line as quickly as he could. *Almost free.* His lungs were bursting. Would he have to make another trip? One more jerk of the knife...the line fell away and the prop was free.

He pushed hard against the prop and glided away. He could see the sunlit surface as he rose. He swallowed against the urge to suck, but then he could wait no longer. His lungs took a hard pull...just as he broke the surface. He wheezed and coughed as he heard his shipmates yelling, clapping, asking questions.

"Did you do it?"

"Is it free?"

"Are we good to go?"

His breathing evened out as he calmed himself, relieved to be in the open air. But something bothered him. Something he had glimpsed as he'd scrambled from the prop.

Corey took several gulps of air, dove, and went back under the ship.

There. With his light, he could see another line, smaller, made of nylon, hugging the propeller. Must have caught it coming to port from that last sailaway. Not yet tight enough to affect the prop's action, but it would. He tugged at the strands. No luck. He pulled out his knife and, holding the nylon line, worked until it was free of the prop. Then he followed it back to a mess of broken pieces of plastic and metal. Lobster pots?

He broke the surface with the bait that had lured him back to the propeller: the remains of a lobster pot and its contents. Woody was the first to recognize Corey's new haul.

"Hey, guys—looks like we get seafood tonight, compliments of Coriander!" Corey grinned, too caught up in the mood to be embarrassed by his real name. On deck, the girls hugged him and the guys slapped his back—even Dice.

"You're the dude!" Morris collected the haul before Marty could get her hands on them, muttering, "She's not going to ruin this dinner."

That's when Corey caught a glimpse of the captain approaching, and he remembered the reason he was wearing a wetsuit, the reason for their late departure. He had overstepped his bounds and distracted Woody.

"We should've been underway by now." No smile broke the captain's lips; her eyes were like marbles. "Your job is to follow orders, not give them."

Strike two? And they hadn't even left New England.

"Lucky for you," she turned with gleam in her eye, "I can't resist a lobster dinner."

In Harts Landing... BLOGGING DOWN

Peg held her fork tightly, the Landing Lunch special clinging to its tines as she glared at her husband. "How can you say that?"

"Because it's true." Charlie wiped chowder off his chin. "Nobody who matters gives a dam about those blobs."

"*Blogs*. And they're right there for everyone who googles Harts Landing." Peg attacked the meat loaf with her fork. "It could affect the business, just when Fred and I are turning things around." And what was worse, it could devastate Corey. But her son had never mentioned the online comments, and she assumed he knew nothing about them.

"Look, Peg," Charlie laid a hand on her arm. "People don't like change. They want to cling to the stories they grew up with."

"But to smear my family, claiming we're making things up? After all Corey and I went through." She gripped the water glass tightly, her fingers white. But she knew Charlie was right.

People identified with the Harts Landing legend. They were proud of Warren Hart and Dirk "Hart," the man they believed was Warren's son. They needed to believe that Dirk had saved the town, not that he had gunned down their forefathers. People didn't like being fooled.

"Corey took a *bullet,* for godsake, to bring out the truth!" Her gut still clenched at the memory of holding what she'd thought to be her son's dead body last June. "People are vicious."

Charlie stroked her arm. "It's going to be okay."

Peg breathed in and out, in and out. She hated the panics. But since smashing into the rocks and then being almost killed again... Like Dr. Mason said, it would be unusual not to have side effects.

By dessert, she could discuss things more calmly. "Actually, Fred thinks a mystery could be good for tourism."

"It wouldn't hurt to bring some money into the corporation after what his mother did."

Fred was a dream to work with, and Peg admired his tenacity. She didn't blame *him* for the fact that Mackenzie had tried to kill her; after all, Fred had been a victim of his mother too, at least financially. He and Peg, now partners, had managed to run the Hart Resort on a shoestring since mid-summer, and they were continuing with the expansion Fred had planned before Mackenzie had tampered with the accounts to launch an illegal operation.

"Fred claims his mother is devastated about the damage she's done," Peg said thoughtfully.

"Well, she finally got medicated."

"He says she had a mental illness and when she 'came to' she was mortified to learn what she had done."

"That must've been hard for her to swallow." Charlie waved at the waitress for the check. "The woman probably *is* sorry and wants to make amends."

Peg put down her fork and stared at him. *Mackenzie Hart, sorry?* That's what was hard to swallow.

AN IMPRESSION

Corey dropped to a bench near the hatchway. The sun's warmth penetrated his wetsuit, meeting the heat of embarrassment that seared him from within. As the ship left Portsmouth, he was definitely not feeling elated. He had acted without thinking, and he'd better be more careful if he wanted to stay on the ship.

He peeled off the top of his suit.

"Where'd you get that scar?" Goldy blurted.

He gazed down at his jagged white splotch, glad to take his mind off his stupidity.

"I jumped in front of a bullet," he said. But that sounded just as dumb.

Goldy's eyes narrowed on his, and she crossed her arms. "Right, you stopped a bullet."

Woody scowled at her on his way to the bridge. "You don't cut anyone any slack, do you?"

She gave him a sour look and turned back to Corey. "But you wouldn't still be here if a bullet hit you...there?"

Corey twisted his body to remove his wetsuit. "I got shielded by a buckle."

Goldy nearly choked as she burst out laughing. "A buckle, at your chest? Were you wearing your pants up to your arm pits?"

"It's a military buckle from 1813. I had it in my shirt pocket."

Her mouth hung open briefly. "Okay, I'm listening." Her breath heated his shoulder blade as he turned and stowed the wetsuit. He pulled his shorts on over his trunks as the ship rolled, and he collided with her. They ended up entangled on the deck, and he was surprised to feel her bare skin pleasantly warm on his.

She got on the bench and patted the spot beside her. "Tell me more, oh stopper of bullets."

Corey sat next to her.

"So you got in front of a gun." Her green eyes were wide.

He looked down, visualizing the scene from last June as he had so many times before. He shook his head.

"Had no choice." His eyes darted to hers. *Am I really telling a stranger?* Her gaze was soft. He looked away and focused on a knot in the deck. It seemed like a portal, sucking him back in time.

He told how he'd discovered a 200-year-old secret that someone wanted to cover up by stealing the journal and getting rid of Corey and his mother. He told how he had charged at the shooter in an island cave. "I had to. My mom could've died."

The watch bell rang. Corey shivered. He got up, unsteady, as Goldy stared at him. But her flames shone through her emerald eyes, and they warmed him.

GETTING CLEAR

Corey wanted no more trouble with the captain; he kept his head down and his hands busy. When he wasn't on watch or educating tourists about sailing, he concentrated on school assignments. Cracker wove the lessons into real life so Corey actually looked forward to them. He was passing everything, and he'd even gotten a ninety-five on his lobster assignment. Dice, who had finally asked Corey for help, had begun passing his English tests.

Corey volunteered for dirty work no one else wanted, like cleaning the head. He helped train the new hands in basic knot tying, line hauling, and maintaining the deck.

"Hey, scrub that deck, no slacking!" Woody snarled as he passed Goldy, who glared back and growled under her breath, "You're not our watch leader."

"Why do we have to do a deck wash *every* day?" Hannah asked, her arms quivering as she pushed a brush next to Goldy.

"It's like pledging a fraternity," Dice said. He stopped waltzing with the long-handled brush and applied his "girlfriend's" head to the deck.

"It's called hazing." Goldy scowled in Woody's direction.

"It's not that." Corey grabbed a brush and dipped it in the bucket of saltwater before sloshing it over the planks. "It keeps the deck clear of any buildup you could slip on," he said. "Plus, if you don't keep the wood swollen, sea water might leak through." He didn't tell them that it would take many months for that to happen.

Hannah and Dice looked down, as if staring through the deck to their bunks below, and they doubled their efforts. Goldy had no complaints either, and Corey thought he saw her smile as she glanced his way.

The days went faster when he took them one at a time. Just like climbing the rigging.

In Boston, Corey learned about the ship *USS Constitution*. In Connecticut, he visited the Mystic Seaport and saw demonstrations of old navigation methods, like using a sextant to measure star altitudes. That was where he caught his first glimpse of Grayson Fielding—in a video. There was something about this guy. Corey could see why Woody wanted to meet him and why Dice had decided to become a real member of the crew. The man radiated energy as he shared his passion.

If Corey hadn't been planning to ditch the ship at Key West, he could meet the founder of the fleet in person. But even if he never met the man, Corey would always remember what Fielding said about navigating: "Find your own stars and follow them."

Corey's stars would lead him to Key West and freedom.

It was nearly evening, and a low fog had rolled in faster than expected as the ship sliced past the Delaware coastline at eight knots. At last visibility, the area had proven clear for several miles, except for a distant schooner, broad on the port bow, and a freighter heading into Delaware Bay. The captain ordered foghorn blasts, one long and two short, every two minutes.

Climbing to the topsail yard, Corey emerged from the fog. The sun barely peeped above the heavy blanket of mist, and its rays gave an eerie glow to the fog bank. Corey sighted the top of the freighter's stack and the mast of the schooner glistening in the last light, confirming their projected positions. No worries here.

Corey looked down toward his feet, partially hidden in mist. He felt isolated, cut off from the ship below, where visibility was spotty and mists gathered and rolled unpredictably. Up here, things were clear and peaceful. The sun was sinking below the fog and the stars were coming out like shy children from hiding, even while the remnants of sunlight cast a sheen over the blanket of cloud.

Here above the fog, echoes of orders and deck chatter slowed and settled around the edges of Corey's mind, leaving space for thoughts and desires he had put away. He gazed to the south.

He knew it would be impossible to see Florida from here, but he drew up his binoculars and fixed them on the southwest. Puffs of fog, twilight, a distant wisp. In his mind, he could pretend they were clouds over Jacksonville. He smiled. He took a deep breath. It was magical up here.

Shouts from the quarterdeck disturbed his reverie.

"Throttle back!" Then: "Sound the horn!"

Corey pulled the glasses down and jerked his head right as the mate echoed the captain's shout.

The top of a small mast approached from southwest off starboard amidships. Within minutes of collision!

Ordered back to the deck, Corey scrambled down the ratlines—*Don't hit!* His stomach was full of rocks. *Please don't hit.* He had taken his eye off the ball. Wasn't the ship's radar working? Had he endangered his crewmates, his captain, his ship?

He rushed to starboard, joining the crew witnessing the spectacle, a fishing boat that had lost control and could not respond to warnings. In the distance the Coast Guard was approaching to aid the vessel. The boat had shown up on radar, and there had been time enough to avoid a collision.

Still, Corey had shirked his responsibility. He sagged onto a deck box.

"Don't feel bad, Redrow," the captain said, all too understanding. "If your sharp eyes didn't catch it, none of my lookouts could have. Must've been invisible."

Corey caught his breath. He was going to get off free! As the captain turned toward her cabin to check on Mr. Gray, Corey started to walk away. He tightened his lips against a pull of conscience; then his smile fell and his shoulders drooped. He sighed.

"Wait," he said. She halted.

"The mast was visible." he choked out. "I just wasn't looking." He froze into a familiar stance as he dreaded the captain's reaction. Was *this* strike two?

She scowled. "What were you doing up there, stargazing?" She walked back over to Corey and looked him up and down. "You have a lot to offer, Mr. Redrow." Her eyes looked at his, back and forth. "And you do own up to your mistakes." She seemed to reach into his deepest parts, where even his inner demon squirmed. "But if you're going to stay on my ship," she said, her lips barely moving, "I need you one hundred per cent." Her voice was stone cold. "Decide what's important."

Corey stared at the mast and imagined that it rose up and up, to a place where today's problem was a dot on his map. He squeezed his brass buckle.

The resonance in his voice surprised him: "Protecting the ship is important."

The captain gave a slight nod and turned away.

Because Sam is important.

In Harts Landing... ROMANTIC FARCE

It was a warm fall evening in the Landing, and the theater looked busy.

"Hey, don't get any ideas," Sam said as Auger ran around his car to pull open the passenger door. "This is not a date."

Auger shrugged and locked the door after she got out. "Don't worry, just keeping up my image." He winked at some younger boys at the ticket window. "Besides, I'm doing you a favor—you need to get out more."

The movie, *In Ruins*, was about an archaeologist couple whose relationship hinged on a mission to find a lost village. The man had lost faith in the woman—until her discovery of the site triggered a breakthrough in their relationship.

Sam couldn't help seeing a parallel: Corey had wanted to prove the treasure was real, but he had abandoned the hunt. Those online comments must have gotten to him when he couldn't find any clues to Estar Island. Had he run away with that girl to escape the criticism? If Sam could find any evidence of Estar, would he come back?

She voiced her thoughts as they exited the theater. "Maybe it's a sign, that I need to look harder for that island."

Auger halted on the sidewalk. "That's what you got from the movie?" He snorted. "All the action, the adventure, the hot scenes?"

She tightened her lips.

"Don't waste your time on Worder." Auger turned toward the car. "Sounds like he's just not into you— Hey, where you going?"

His shout now came from behind as Sam right-angled down the street.

Auger had been good to her, even covered for her in history class when she was distracted. But when he asked her out, she made it clear she was accepting as a friend and would pay her own way. But as a friend, maybe she had confided too much, and she didn't like Auger's "friendly" advice.

He followed her. "Look, if you're so hooked on the guy, call him." He sighed. "For god's sake, text him, email him..." He caught up and spun her around. "If that's too scary, write an old fashioned letter."

"It's not that easy." She pulled away.

"Hey, aren't you the same girl that called me last June and demanded I meet you at the library?"

"I was only helping Corey with his ancestry—you know, the *real* Harts." That was hitting below the belt, but it did shut him up. For two seconds.

"Well, that's my point." He drew a breath. "You put yourself out there because you wanted to help him. You should be just as willing to help yourself—and the sooner you get back to being your usual bossy self, not the other *b* word, the sooner you'll be doing everyone a favor."

She dropped to the bench by a potted tree facing the Roma Restaurant, wearing a scowl and crossing her arms.

"Sorry." Auger sat next to her. "Look, even I wasn't always so smooth." He ran his fingers through his sun-bleached hair. "Even I had to learn how to get what I want." He framed her with a make-believe camera. "You're a hot girl, you can stand up to competition."

Sam nearly gagged. The memory of Corey with the tall blonde girl brought angry tears to her eyes, and she grabbed at her purse for a tissue. What she drew out instead was the crumpled copy of that journal page.

Estar Island. It taunted her. It should be near Harts Landing. Why was there no evidence of its existence?

Those comments online about Peg Stowe and Corey perpetrating a hoax were totally unfair. But Sam could understand why there were doubters. No one had heard of Estar Island, and there was no reference to it on the internet. The name must have been discontinued long ago. Still, she and Corey had vowed to keep looking—together. But Corey seemed to have given up.

"If I only had something, a clue—about Estar Island," Sam murmured. "Maybe he'd come back to his senses."

"His senses?" Auger said. "Luring him with treasure on an unheard-of island, yeah, that's sensible."

She couldn't help unfolding the photocopied page once again. She hoped to find something they hadn't noticed, some clue.

Auger leaned over the page. "Hey, what's that?" His voice held suspicion mixed with sarcasm. "It has something to do with that fairy tale, right?"

"How can you say that?" She yanked the paper behind her back. "You of all people have no reason to be snarky—"

"Okay." Auger held his palms up. "It's just that this is getting weird."

He leaned closer. "For your own good." He gazed into her eyes. "We need to throw that..." He reached around her. "Into the trash." She moved the page farther behind her.

Each stretched an arm farther and farther behind Sam, their eyes locked together. They were barely aware of the owner of the Roma changing his specials board and gesturing toward the bench, clueless, murmuring, *"Amore!"*

Auger's eyes shone with cool intensity as he demanded: "Give it to me."

Sam smiled sweetly. "Bite me."

She slid off the end, and Auger was left face down to ponder his social skills, along with the landscaping at the end of the bench.

SAILORS TAKE WARNING

It was early October, and the *Golden Aye* had been sailing south for two days straight. It was on the mid-Atlantic coast, approaching Chesapeake Bay, and there were meet-ups, festivals, and history reenactments to get through before Florida would even be in the scopes.

Corey latched onto the yard and glanced out at the skyline. It seemed only moments ago the rigging had cast shadows on the deck and the sun warmed his skin. But now, blue skies had given over to purple-tinted mists and darkening grays. A squall had materialized from an unusual weather pattern that gave short notice.

Up here in the rigging, the sway of the ship was multiplied; Corey planted his feet on the footropes and let the wind press his body around the yard as he shuffled sideways to secure the topsail. Corey and Brian had been the first to clip into harnesses and hustle up the shrouds when the captain gave the order to strike sail. Woody was moving slowly; he remained below to haul sheet.

Now, the puffs of wind threatened to grow into a gale that could wrench the ship apart. Corey gripped the rolled topsail, his fingers like claws. He reached to pull the line of gasket and tie it around the sail as Brian did the same alongside him.

Corey's hand was numb with cold; the wind howled around him and whipped a sail, which cracked and popped so he could no longer hear the shouts of the crew below. He barely heard the mate echo the order to strike the course.

That's when things really started happening.

As the crew hauled, Hannah lost her grip, and a burst of wind whipped the line from Woody as he was trying to get new purchase. As they yelled and grabbed in vain, the sail was one sheet to the wind, and the line whipped about as the sail snapped and crackled.

Ordered to the deck, Corey shinnied down the ratlines. The sea seemed to approach and recede from his position with increasing tempo. He used all his strength to keep from being blown "like a tin can off a fence," as the captain would say. As he clung to the shrouds, he saw the horizon go vertical. Before he could even think of vomiting, he got doused with downpour, upwell, and side splatter. He lost his footing and slid, ropes scouring his hands before he could catch another foothold.

When he swung over the side of the shrouds, the deck was awash; seawater had poured over the rail and through the scuppers. The trainees were in their harnesses, working hard to stay upright. Crewmates and bos'n had scrambled to secure the lines while the captain shouted orders.

Woody dove for the loose sheet and helped an AB secure the sail. He planted his feet, and together they gained control. Corey had reached the deck and was shifting position when another surge swept through the scuppers near his feet.

No one else saw Woody drop to the deck after his feet flew from beneath him when the ship pitched and dipped the port side rail into the sea. Corey made a grab for Woody's waistband just as he was about to slide overboard.

5 TASTE OF THINGS TO COME

The wind had died down, and they had come through the storm intact. Woody had thanked Corey profusely for saving him from going overboard. But as the ship settled into its course along the coast, Woody sank to the deck and leaned against the hull.

"You should've let me drown."

Corey's mouth hung open.

"It's Olga's fault." Woody held his head in his hands.

"What are you talking about?"

"I'd just heard—before the weather..."

Something about Olga. Was that why he had been so distracted lately?

Woody sighed heavily. "She's getting married."

"To that editor?" That was fast.

"No, moved up the ladder to some big shot *publisher.*" Woody said the word like it was the worst kind of vermin.

"Sorry."

"Olga was only hanging around me until something better came along." Woody frowned. "She's been writing a romance novel." Suddenly, his eyes widened. "Come to think of it, she only dated me after she found out about Aunt Adele."

Corey had forgotten about the author who sent her favorite nephew a nice contribution every month.

Woody looked miserable. "I wondered why Olga was emailing my aunt all the time, asking her stuff." He looked like he wanted to say more. Then he did.

"The worst part is *how* she used me."

"What do you mean?"

Woody grabbed the phone from his waterproof pack and punched it. He handed it to Corey. "There it is on Amazon, her story." He jabbed his finger at the screen three times. "Just read that." Corey read the book's sample text, flowery language about a girl sailing on a tall ship and the guy...

"Hey, that's you!" Corey recognized the description, and as he got into a romantic scene added, "Did you really do *that?*"

"Hey, working a squall really builds a thirst." Woody changed the subject as he reached for one of the bottles on the hatchway and took a gulp.

"PLAHHH!" He sprayed water out of his mouth, some of it landing on Corey.

"That's my water!" Corey said as Woody scowled at the bottle.

Woody slammed it down. "So I noticed. It's flat." He picked up the bottle next to it and took a couple chugs. "Ah, good ole cream soda."

"Why do you drink that—doesn't Captain Harper get on your case?" Corey quoted: "'Water's the best quencher,' you know."

"Well, that's why I don't use a clear bottle." Woody gave half a grin.

He took another pull on the bottle and put on a look of indifference. "I'm lucky I missed the Olga boat." He stretched his legs and forced a smile. "Time for a new direction anyway. By the way, I meant to ask. What's so important about the south?" He raised an eyebrow. "Yeah, I've noticed you perking up at every mention of Florida. What gives?"

Corey hesitated, but since Woody had confided in *him*... Corey looked around to be sure no one could hear before whispering, "I'm jumping ship."

Woody stared blankly and then laughed out loud.

"Shh!" Corey sat close to Woody as he glanced around at the crew, but no one was paying attention.

"What are you talking about?" Woody asked.

"The real reason I came—"

"Was girl problems." Woody gripped Corey's shoulder. "C'mon Coriander, what better way to fix the problem than to get some experience? You still don't know which type of girl is for you."

Was Woody trying to convince himself?

"Try all the ones you want, there's always more!" Woody had a wild look in his eye. "Imagine..." He swept his arm, palm outward. "Sunny skies, coconut trees, bikinis."

"I don't want more girls. I just need to get to Key West." Corey sighed and dropped his chin to his chest. "My father lives there." He stared at the gulls diving for fish. "The reason I freeze up is, I have a...defect. A black mark inside, from when I was, like two. The therapist said—"

"What?" Woody's eyes widened. "You saw a shrink?"

"It's not a big deal," Corey snapped. Then he lowered his voice. "He helped me remember something bad that happened. Now I have to fix it." Corey explained his plan. "I have to face my father to get rid of this mental block. It keeps me from having a relationship with...a girl I might be in love with."

A hooded figure appeared at the companionway. Fiery strands escaped the head covering. Where had she come from?

"I'll tell you what." Woody scowled as his gaze followed the figure. "Some girls might be worth getting away *from*."

Corey had seen Woody get irritated, but it didn't usually last long. Goldy was the only one that got under his skin and stayed there.

"She's always been nice to me." Corey stared at the spot where she'd just been. *Must've gone toward the bow.*

Woody was still going on about her. "Always making me look foolish." Woody tightened his voice up a few notches: "'Oh, these lines are on the wrong pins—don't worry, I'll fix them for you.' As if *I* screwed them up. And right in front of the captain."

Corey furrowed his brows. "I've never seen..."

"She's crafty, but I know what's going on behind those cat eyes." Woody shook his head and glared at Corey. "How can you even think of leaving me on this ship with her?"

He was quiet for a while as he sipped his soda. Then he faced Corey. "So...that's the only reason you signed on to the Golden Aye?"

"Well, yeah." But Corey had to admit, he had also gotten new skills, confidence, and friends.

"Look, dude, who do you think made this all possible? Grayson Fielding built the whole program."

"Sure, I guess." Corey did admire the man. He'd love to meet him some time.

"Buddy, you'll miss out if you get off in Florida. Fielding's the real deal. If it's a father figure you're looking for, you gotta come to New Orleans!"

Corey had a lot to thank Fielding for, but if he was going to have a shot with Sam, he needed to be where she was. Mom would send him a plane ticket any time he wanted to go home, which he planned to do as soon as he banished his father from his mind.

"I gotta get back to the Landing," he said.

"I can't believe you'd leave us for...a *dream*. If things don't turn out like you want once you get there, you've wasted everything. Like I said, there are plenty of girls in the south."

Woody's eyes lost focus as a new smile played at his lips. "Just think about that."

Corey's eyes were drawn by a movement on port side; Goldy flashed him a smile as she headed aft.

Woody groaned as Corey smiled back at her. "Hey, I said think about girls, not walking nuclear threats."

STARRY EYES

"By the mark, seven!" Corey called out from the starboard sounding station. He hauled in the lead line and again swung it two times around, releasing it forward, almost parallel with the water's surface. He plunged the line again. Then he leaned over to recheck the mark that appeared just above water level. He had just confirmed the first depth finding and made a notation on his homework sheet when he felt a squeeze on the shoulder that made him jump.

It was Goldy. He relaxed. He'd had his doubts about her that day at the pier, but first impressions could be wrong, and Goldy had proved herself. She had learned to make do with limited possessions and was on good terms with her shipmates—except Woody.

She looked girlier than the other females; she was wearing a skirt—most wore cutoffs even off duty. He squinted at her mouth. *Is that lipstick?*

"I heard you talking," she said.

His brows sprung up. Had she heard the secret he'd shared with Woody?

"You know, I wouldn't mind following..." She picked a piece of fuzz off his t-shirt and raised her eyes to his. "If you were giving the orders."

Maybe she'd only overheard what Woody said.

Corey noticed how the colors in her eyes mimicked those of the shimmering waves. "Like emeralds," he blurted. "Your eyes, I mean."

She smiled and said, "Topaz."

"What?"

"Your eyes." She smiled. "I have a pendant just that color." She lifted her gaze to the evening sky.

"I overheard the plan, the one you told—" She rolled her eyes. "You know who."

Corey stiffened. So Goldy did know his secret.

"Don't worry, I won't tell." She reached over and squeezed his arm.

They reviewed the depth-finding assignment and compared notes on the results using a lead line versus the modern methods.

"Sonar measures the time it takes for a ping," Goldy said as her finger lightly touched Corey's lips, "to bounce off an object and return." She touched her own lips. Then she laughed. Her sense of humor was a little weird.

It grew dark while they discussed how sound waves traveled through water. Then she pointed at the sky.

"Look up there." She offered the telescope she had taken from the folds of her skirt.

Corey took the glass and looked through it to where she pointed.

"It's Gemini," she said. "Those stars were named for Castor and Pollux, twins of mythology. Patron saints for sailors. They were fated to be together, as one."

Oh, yeah. He felt himself blush. She must've heard him talking about Samantha.

"It's their destiny." She moved toward Corey.

My destiny to be with Sam. Now Corey liked the way she was thinking.

She lowered the telescope. "Look, about your plan to leave." She put her hand on his arm. "I don't mean to pry, but I can be a very good...friend."

GETTING LOOSE

They sat on Goldy's bunk holding cups of cola. Corey didn't often drink soda and was ready to lift it and say "Cheers!" when Goldy looked side to side and from behind her pulled out a bottle. It was half full of amber liquid. Part of the label was visible: "Kentucky Bourbon."

"Some of the crew were drinking it last shore leave," Goldy said. "They left it behind."

Corey didn't have to ask why they left it. Rules were strict: no alcohol onboard—and never within eight hours of watch.

"Why waste it?" She grinned. Then she hid the bottle as Darian passed to retrieve something from her bunk. Goldy whispered, "Come on, we aren't on watch for almost eight hours!"

Corey saw his mom drink whiskey once. Though he hadn't known it then, she was about to face her dying father, a father she hadn't seen for years after escaping his abuse. Now Corey was dealing with his own father issues. He could use some courage. "But I won't even be seventeen until November first."

"That means you're already legal in Jamaica!" Goldy said.

Darian came back through. "Aren't you guys coming topside? They're going to winch up the old cannon—I mean *gun*—from the cargo hold." She glanced toward Goldy's elbow and then left.

After he was sure Darian had disappeared topside, Corey held out his cup of cola. Goldy smirked and covered her mouth with one hand as she pulled the bottle from behind her and splashed some of its contents into his soda.

She touched her cup to his and tipped her own to her lips, keeping her eyes on Corey.

He took a sip. *Not bad.* The only alcohol he'd tasted was a sip of beer, which he had drained from one of Charlie's bottles. Disgusting. But now he hardly tasted anything but the cola; this stuff was going down easy.

Corey began to loosen up. He noticed a tingling sensation in his arms and legs, and the tension seemed to be melting away. Goldy was singing a sailor's limerick that would never reach the captain's ears, and Corey guffawed as he caught the puns in the *Schooner from Altoona.*

"You're a nice guy," Goldy said suddenly. She topped off his glass and scowled at the bottle. "Not a know-it-all, like a certain other sailor." She looked at Corey and smiled again.

"Woody's all right," he blurted.

Her face soured again, and she rolled her eyes. "He treats me like a child, just like my mother." She turned away and mumbled, "She's been such a nag ever since..."

Corey remembered the woman at the pier the day Goldy joined the ship. "She was just watching out for you." He took another gulp. "At least she was there."

He barely heard her say, "Yeah, well Dad wasn't."

Corey was feeling a little loose. *One sheet to the wind.* He was warm and comfortable. He smelled the shampoo of Goldy's hair. Like Mom's. Even the roll of the ship made him feel cozy.

They were talking about parents, and before he knew it, Corey was saying, "My dad deserted too, but not before leaving his black mark—" He clapped his hand across his mouth.

"Black mark?" Goldy said. "Is that what makes you so shy?"

Corey stared into his cup. This stuff was dangerous.

"Tell me more."

"Nope." He burped and tightened his lips. Then he burst out, "I've already said too much."

"Okay." Goldy put her finger to her lips. "Here, have some more." She poured from the bottle into his cup.

Corey took a gulp. He stared at the floor. The grain of the planks resembled a man's head, with horns, and it seemed to be laughing. Corey blinked at the vision. He moved each limb and sighed, relieved that he hadn't frozen up.

"See," he shook his head, "as long as my father has control, I can never be with...with a girl I really like." He fiddled with his cup. How could he make Goldy understand that he couldn't even talk to Sam as long as he lived with this fear? "I have to be in control of myself."

"A girl you *like*, huh?" Goldy repeated, sliding closer. "What's so scary about a girl you like?" Goldy's voice softened, and she sounded almost shy. "Are you afraid she would judge you? I think a girl you like, if she cares, would take you as you are." She paused. "Look at me."

Corey looked. Two shining emerald eyes probed his, promising their support. He could trust those eyes.

He hesitated then shifted on the bunk to face her. "See, I have to confront my father so I can believe in *me*." But he wasn't even sure he deserved to believe in himself. Had he really left home to find a way back to Sam—or was he abandoning the relationship out of fear? Now he was planning to leave his shipmates, and he was confused. "Maybe I am just a Worder-Deserter." He explained his hated nickname.

"Corey, you have to believe in yourself," Goldy said. "You're a stand-up guy." She looked down and muttered, "*You'd* never duck out on a commitment." She looked up and grinned. "And you're cute. What else could a girl want?"

He smiled. She was probably right. He'd signed on to the *Golden Aye* to find his father, but he had become part of the ship. He had friends here, and there were probably other girls who'd like him. *Just that none of them is Sam.*

Goldy smiled. "You belong here. On board."

He took another swig. Could he really just 'be here now' and let tomorrow take care of itself? "The only way I could really be with a girl," he said slowly, "is to erase my defect—" She made a face, and he said, "Yes, I can admit it." He was slurring a little, and his tongue was disconnected from his self-consciousness. They both started laughing. The ship seemed to be rolling more than usual, and it shifted him closer to her.

"Everybody here is great." So many people had helped Corey learn and grow. "My friends, Cracker, the captain—the Cannonball is awesome! And..." Corey's mouth hung open for a moment. "You know who else is great? Grayson Fielding!"

"Well, then you should meet him."

After Corey banished his father, it would be good to meet a real man. A role model.

Corey felt lighter. Confiding in Goldy had lifted a weight. He gazed at the floor; the pattern of the grain had shifted. The image morphed into the face of Grayson Fielding. Fielding was no quitter. Corey smiled. It was a sign. Corey should see things through on the *Golden Aye* after finding his father—at least to New Orleans. That way, he could complete a semester of school.

He pointed at the bottle. "I sure don't want to get on the captain's list—but I'm glad we did this." He paused. "I was gonna jump ship." The vessel pitched, and he pressed against Goldy. "Maybe," he smiled at her and remained close, "I can stay a little longer."

Goldy's eyes widened. "Oh, Corey!" she breathed and opened her arms.

A loud call for "All hands!" erased her smile and wiped out their free time.

Near Harts Landing... SHAPE OF REALITY

"What's the matter, Gran?" Auger leaned closer and waved a hand. "Did you hear me?" He hadn't seen his grandmother in several weeks, but he wondered if this visit was a good idea. She seemed no more responsive than last time. Did she even recognize him? Did she remember the insane things she did that got her locked up? Maybe the drugs they gave her here made her a zombie. He should just leave now and get over to the county historical society, where he could do some research.

He gave it another try: "I said I found a map." When her eyes returned to his, he added, "It was in your suite. I guess it fell out of that journal before, you know." He lowered his eyes. He didn't want to mention what she had done. Auger still had mixed feelings about the scandal Corey Worder had unearthed: Auger's ancestor Dirk stealing the Hart name and heritage from the "Worders," who were the true descendants of Warren Hart, the 1813 hero. And Gran had imagined some grand destiny for both herself and Auger. He shook his head; it was still hard to believe she had stolen that journal and tried to kill Corey's mother to cover up the truth. *Delusional paranoia can claim anyone.* That's what Dad had said. Even a brilliant psychoanalyst like Auger's grandmother.

"I found it under a squeaky board—" he blurted. "When I went in your suite to do repairs. I hope you aren't mad."

Gran's eyes cleared, and her wrinkles readjusted into a grin.

"Of course not," she gushed. "How wonderful!"

He was relieved. Maybe she had hidden the page but forgot about it. After all, she'd been possessed by some mental thing.

"Did you bring it with you, this map?" Her eyes gleamed.

He pulled a paper out of his pocket, unfolded it, and held it up. "Don't worry. It's just one of the copies—the original is pretty delicate."

He let her scrutinize the page. Then he lowered it, saying, "Sam will want to show it to Corey—"

His grandmother's head snapped up, her eyes narrowing.

"Well, she wants to help him and his mom," he said. "They'll be able to check its shape against other islands." He doubted it would do any good, but it might shut Sam up.

Gran's eyes returned to the paper. "So no one else has seen this map?"

"I was going to show Samantha before coming, but I didn't have time."

She let out some air. "Good, Augie." She shifted in her seat. "You know, it would be wonderful to help those people." She tightened her lips before saying, "We just don't want to get their hopes up."

Those people? Gran never called Corey and his mom by their names. But then Corey's last name was not exactly clear.

Gran closed her eyes. "Oh, Augie," she sighed. "You know how sorry I am, don't you?" She shook her head as her eyes opened and probed his. Then she examined her fingernails and continued, "I can hardly believe the things they say I've done." She leaned forward. "But I wasn't myself, was I?" She sank back slowly. "Rare condition. Combination of genetics and—well, I won't bore you with details." Again, she sighed. "I can't believe I actually tried..." She looked aside, shaking her head. "Thank God they're all right."

Auger was relieved to see his grandmother rational and remorseful. It was a good thing Corey had exposed Gran's condition, but Auger was sorry to lose his heritage. It still seemed unreal that his family's history was a sham. And some freakish condition drove Gran to attempt *murder* to protect the 200-year-old lie! Luckily, Corey's mother had not sued for property, but went into partnership with Auger's dad. After all, it was Auger's family who had built the original properties into an empire. And now, Peg Stowe and Dad were both better off since Gran had stopped draining the corporation. Still, Auger wished he'd never learned the truth.

Gran was still talking. "I did wrong, and I'm right where I deserve to be—" She raised her hand as Auger opened his mouth. "No, don't try to deny it," she said. "I have to pay for my crime."

Auger changed the subject. "So, about the map. You don't want Corey and his mom to see it?"

"Well," she said with a wink. "You and I have a couple of good brains. Let's keep it to ourselves until we've had a chance to look it over." She shook her head sadly. "I'd hate to get their hopes up and then disappoint them after what they've been through."

"Sure, Gran." Auger said, glad his grandmother was now in the real world.

In the parking lot, Auger held his coat over his head and hopped over puddles. He'd thought the treasure was a fairy tale, but he had to humor Gran. If someone as brilliant as she believed in it, even when she was rational... Who knew?

Auger turned on the wipers and pulled out of the parking lot as rain spattered the windshield.

In Key West... CHANGE OF KEY

In his home office, Rob fondled artifacts from his last dive, thankful the storm hadn't done any inside damage. His gaze continued along the shelf to a letter he'd stuck between books. He unfolded it and read again: "Do not come. Even the best of hunters will fail without a map." He gently touched the signature, *Peg Stowe*, and lingered before tearing himself away. He had other things to deal with.

"Hey, thanks for helping out," Rob told his friend as they removed the last of the boards from his windows. Andrew was slender but muscular, like Rob, and the work went fast. Rob's travel schedule had changed, and his regular house sitter was out of town, so he was glad to let Andrew stay here in exchange for keeping an eye on things. Since he'd been attending Alcoholics Anonymous, Andrew had proven very dependable.

"I'm glad I could help." Andrew dusted off his sleeves and ambled over to the billiard table. "Small price to pay for getting another chance." He closed one eye and rolled the five ball into the corner pocket. "Once I get a job, I'll find a place of my own—but don't worry, I'll watch your house as long as you need me."

Rob recognized the rush of optimism, but he knew Andrew faced a long road. "Just promise me you'll keep up with your AA meetings." Alcoholics Anonymous would give Andrew the support he needed. "Sorry I'll have to leave you," he added, "but you can call me if...you know."

Andrew grinned and brushed off his slacks as he grabbed a cue stick; he twisted a chalk cube at the end. He ran the low balls one after another and started on the high balls. He aimed and slid the cue stick back and forth between his finger and thumb. He rammed the cue ball into the nine-ball, which jumped the bumper, bounced on carpeted cement, and rolled into the wine cellar. Andrew followed it, ducking to avoid hitting his head.

Rob was glad he had removed the bottles from the wine cellar. He had seen the best and worst of Andrew—the days he had cracked had been bad, but the days he was able to resist sometimes seemed even worse. Andrew had an active imagination, and his ghosts could visit days after the last drink. Then Andrew would repeat his own name to reinforce his identity, feel a sense of control. Andrew was desperate to beat his problem, and if he ever passed out, it would more likely be from fear than from alcohol.

Rob was just starting to wonder what was keeping him when Andrew came out holding the nine-ball. Must've rolled way under the wine rack.

Andrew proceeded to run the remaining balls.

SNIFFING OUT THE TRUTH

"Reporting for duty, Captain!" Corey shouted to be heard above the luffing sails after charging up the companionway, still grasping his cup. He could see several on- and off-watch crew and trainees around the open cargo hatch. There was no gun on the deck.

When he met the captain, he wiped his forehead with his left hand then shielded his cup. The wind had increased, and large droplets splattered his face and hand.

Goldy had clamored up behind Corey, yelling something incomprehensible until she froze at the sight of the captain. The captain frowned at Corey and glanced at his right hand. "I need a two-handed sailor, young man." She pointed at the cup. "What have you got there?"

Oh oh. Corey realized his mistake too late. "J-just some soda?" He tried to sound casual.

The captain might have gone for it, but just then a lull in the wind exposed some ongoing portside gossip.

"...a bottle of bourbon..." Darian's voice trailed off as she realized her disclosure had reached more ears than intended.

The statue that was Goldy came to life and blurted, "Oh, it's not bourbon, Captain." She forced a laugh as she looked around at the slack-jawed crew members. "It's not!" Her face was red as her hair as she glared at Darian.

Corey's palms were sweating. How could he be so stupid? He should have left the cup below.

The captain's eyes bored into him. "You know the rules, young man—I'm sure you would not put the crew at risk, not on my ship."

Core's shoulders sagged. Not only was his trip to Key West on the line; so was the respect he'd gained from his crewmates. And worst of all, what was left of the captain's respect for him.

"You know I'm from Kentucky," the captain continued. "And if that's bourbon, I'll know it quicker'n a cat on nip. Hand it over."

A drop of something more like sweat than rain streaked down Corey's cheek.

The captain lifted the cup to her nose.

Corey stood still. After all he had gone through, had he squandered his chance for Key West?

The captain scowled into the cup.

Corey hadn't felt so ashamed since he'd been mocked at the hockey game last March.

He hung his head—Strike three?—when the captain thrust the cup back at him.

"Just as I thought," she said. "Some people can't handle their soda pop." She turned and barked something about weather conditions and scrapping the plan to lift the gun.

Corey stared into the cup of liquid that had loosened his tongue. Then he remembered the stuff Woody had hidden. He suddenly envisioned Goldy pouring into an empty whiskey bottle... "Cream soda?"

She avoided his eyes and grabbed his cup. "Do you really think I'd let you get thrown off the ship?"

6 STORM-TOSSED

Captain Harper's old gun never made it topside. The crew battened down the hatch cover and anything else that could fly off in a hurricane.

The *Golden Aye* had already turned west toward Chesapeake Bay when they got the news. The capricious storm had changed directions.

Every year, tropical storms incubated in the Caribbean Sea; many died out before heading north, but under certain conditions, a storm would develop into a hurricane. Even then, the whirlwind might only wreak havoc in Florida before heading to sea and dying out.

This storm had moved north and was supposed to head for the open ocean. The prediction was wrong. It had reversed direction quicker than anyone could've guessed, sending ships racing for shore. The *Golden Aye* was on the edge of the storm.

Seawater washed over the deck, and the pitching of the ship swept Goldy off balance and set her sliding in the seawater on the main deck. Corey yelled, "Are you all right?" but all he could hear was the howl of wind and the spray of water. He pulled her up and steadied her as she attached her harness, as he had, to the lifeline of the ship. He glanced southeast, marveling at the sudden change of weather.

Corey climbed aloft to help strike sail. He was used to the ship's movement on waves, but this felt more like a washing machine. As he bundled sail in spattering rain, another roll of the ship sent his stomach to his chest. He had never worried about going down at sea. Modern communications gave storm warnings ahead of time, and though they learned ancient sailing methods, the *Golden Aye's* powerful engines gave them an advantage.

Descending to the deck, Corey clung to the shrouds as they swung to the rhythm of the waves like an upside-down pendulum. A blur of orange jackets showed through the misty spray. The helmsmen worked hard to head the ship into the waves—if it went parallel, it would likely go under.

Corey could barely hear voices over the train-like roar as he crept down, rung from rung, to the deck. As the mate now wrestled with the helm, the captain cupped her mouth to call impossible orders. The mast was forty degrees to the horizon; Corey felt a sudden drop and grabbed for a mass of ropes; another wave countered the force of gravity and righted the ship. Thanks to Stix, who kept the engines going as the *Golden Aye* ran with the wind, they were able to keep the ship steady and moving northwest. Meanwhile, crew members clung to lifelines to stay on their feet.

Corey was at the helm when he noticed a squeaking between roars of wind and splashes of wave. He checked the rudder housing. The torque of the rudder had opened a crack in the joint that transferred the power of the wheel. How could it be fixed in this storm and keep the ship from sinking?

One thing was sure: if the rudder stopped responding to the helm, they would be at nature's mercy.

Stix staggered to the wheel, dragging her welding gear. Corey and Woody held part of an old canvas sail over the housing to keep the rain from filling it as she worked. She got a torch lit and began, shaky at best. Then a splash of wave doused it and she had to begin again. After four tries, she was able to weld a bead that kept the socket firm...for now.

BANNER STILL WAVES

It was a ragged ship and crew that crept northward up Chesapeake Bay. Aside from a few scrapes and bruises, the crew had escaped injury, but the rudder joint would need some work.

They would lay in for the remainder of the storm. Plenty of repair work was needed on hull and sails, and general order needed to be restored. The battle reenactment in Baltimore was cancelled, but if Cannonball Harper was disappointed, she hid her feelings. There would be more than enough to do securing and restoring the ship.

After fastening anything that could come loose, and tripling up the mooring lines, the crew worked with other members of the Fielding Fleet to help local volunteers. Corey secured loose items, boarded windows, and stacked sandbags but, fast as he was, he couldn't keep up with his partner. When he found out Gary was a member of the *Workman Ship*, he didn't feel so bad. It was part of a specialized division of the Fleet that included vessels like the *Scholar Ship* and the *Steward Ship*. Another division emphasized interpersonal relations on vessels such as the *Friend Ship* and the *Court Ship*.

The rain and winds finally abated as the exhausted crews, in turn, were dispatched to hotels.

The city showed its appreciation to the volunteers with a large-screen viewing of a Battle of Baltimore re-enactment. The national anthem came over the speakers, and a huge flag was shown being raised at Fort McHenry.

"Did you know a lawyer wrote the Star Spangled Banner?" Woody said.

"Francis Scott Key? What was he doing on a British ship?"

"Negotiating for prisoners. The British didn't want him leaking their battle plans so they kept him on board."

All Corey remembered from history class was that Key had watched the battle and penned the famous lyrics. But seeing where history took place made it real. The people who risked everything so long ago, right *here*, made the US what it is. Corey shivered with goose bumps. Then he wiped off his stupid smile. *Lame.*

His gaze followed the massive flag on the screen, illuminated in the night's glow, and he lost himself in the music. *Does that star-spangled banner yet wave?* The stars and stripes seemed to weave themselves into a feminine face. Was his mind playing tricks on him? Lately, his thoughts of Sam had been overridden as he fought the elements. But now... *Yes*, that banner was yet waving! Sam was still his purpose and his colors.

DELAY

By Tuesday, Corey was itching to move on. The crew were assessing the ship for storm damage when he heard, "All hands muster on the quarterdeck!"

This is it. The captain would give the order to prepare to get underway. Corey had been patient. He had worked hard; he had kept his mind sharp and his nose clean. They had to leave soon to make the Key West stopover before the New Orleans conference. Besides, it would be nice to get Goldy back on board. Corey hadn't seen her since Woody suggested she help out on the short-handed *Hard Ship*. That vessel had lost a couple of crew members when their worried families managed to arrange their transport home. It wasn't clear whether they were more worried about the storm or the ship's tough regimen.

Finally the *Golden Aye* was about to put south.

All crew were gathered topside. Captain Harper's face was hard to read. Corey licked his lips waiting to hear the watch arrangements and orders to set sail. Any job was fine with him.

"We've had some damage."

Sure they'd had some minor stuff, most was taken care of, and some could be done underway.

"The crack was the tip of the iceberg. You all know how critical the rudder joint is. We can't leave until it is replaced."

Corey's face fell. So did everyone else's.

The part had been ordered and would be available in a couple of days. Ship parts were in demand, and a replacement would have to come from Jacksonville. Great. They couldn't ship out to Florida until they got a shipment *from* there.

Corey dove into preparations for departure. He volunteered for any task the captain requested. Every part of the ship had been scrubbed and painted, all lines checked and spliced or replaced where worn. Corey took advantage of down time to study for his science, math, and social studies exams. And he even practiced his desensitization drills from Dr. Mason.

He visualized the scene from that day at the Harts Landing pier when he'd returned on the *Venture IVth*. He worked his mind backward from "frozen" to memories of the surroundings to find a connection. A strobing image? Curls? Faces? One that passed behind several others? A dark cap? Corey must have experienced several of the triggers that day at the pier. Was there a smell of smoke? Maybe a barbecue at the Seaside Grill? And what about a voice? Had someone spoken with that same gruff voice Corey had heard as a small child?

In his bunk, with closed eyes, he recreated the images, the sounds, the smells that he remembered from Dr. Mason's regression. He got better at relaxing while imagining the scene. And he envisioned standing up for himself. At first, he just looked his father in the eye, breathing deeply. Eventually, he was able to say, "You have no power over me." He was getting eager to face the man for real.

After watch on the second day, Corey's growing excitement filled his exorcism regimen. His demon-bashing incantations cut through the fo'c'sle.

"You are not real! You have no control—"

A voice came back: "Well maybe I don't have control," the curtain slid open to reveal Woody's grin. "But the ship does! We sail in the morning."

Woody moved away as Corey sat up, but before he could slide off his mattress, Corey felt someone else drop to his bunk.

"I missed you, sweetie." Goldy leaned toward him, and Corey thought she was going to kiss his cheek, but she whispered in his ear, "We have some business to discuss." She jumped up. "In the salon!"

BY CANDLE LIGHT

"It'll be fun," Goldy said as she looked at the other faces. "We need a party!"

"I overheard the plans," Dice said. "We're joining the *Hard Ship* for the 'lifting of spirits.'" The off-watch shipmates were demolishing a bowl of chips with salsa, one of the few dishes Marty couldn't spoil, as they heard her "singing" near the companionway.

"It's party time!" Marty shrieked. Everyone laughed; they knew she would be whirling around with her scarves.

Then she hollered, "Hey—does this mean I have to make the food?"

Almost everyone shouted, "No!"

"A party's supposed to have *good* food," Morris grunted through his rolled herbs.

"Don't worry." Goldy nudged Corey. "I'm ordering your birthday cake from a bakery!"

"Cake?" He'd forgotten he had mentioned his birthday to Goldy. He hadn't had a party with anyone except Mom and Charlie for years.

"Yes, this calls for cake, birthday boy! Seventeen is worth celebrating."

Did he really want to share his birthday with the crews of two Fielding ships? The answer bubbled up with a warm feeling. *Yes!*

Corey had to work to get presentable for the rendezvous with the crew of the *Hard Ship*. They had a reputation as tough characters, but Corey would be their equal. He put on his one pair of black pants, with borrowed suspenders over his bare chest. Showing his scar couldn't hurt. And now it was emphasized by his six-pack abs.

As he passed the chart house a feminine voice claimed, "You've got a devilish look about you, Sir."

Corey spun around to face Goldy, who lived up to her tat in a red dress she'd found in a second-hand store. The form-fitting outfit challenged her ringlets for attention.

He felt bold, even dangerous, as he surveyed her look. "A sexy lass like you could make a devil of any man." Her face was made up like a magazine cover girl, and was set off by curls gathered with a tortoise shell hair pin.

"It was my grandmother's." Goldy gave a mock scowl. "And if you don't behave," she said, touching the end of the pin, "it will become the enforcer!" It came to an actual point, unlike the new plastic fasteners.

Corey grinned. He filled his chest and swaggered next to Goldy onto the *Hard Ship*. They climbed aboard to raucous greetings and upbeat music. Paper streamers hung from the stays on deck and from the galley's overhead.

"Hey, sailor," said a tall brunette with a single braid falling to one side of her neck. She wore purple eye shadow and bright red lipstick.

"C'mon Corey," Goldy insisted, pulling his arm.

"She's just being friendly," Corey whispered. He appreciated Goldy's attention, but what was she afraid of? That he'd forget Sam? He smiled at the girl and found out her name was Sylvia while Goldy huffed off to the refreshment tables.

The night was great. Corey was the center of attention for several girls and boys who admired his scar but didn't ask too many questions. Goldy kept an eye on him as she talked with a guy named Chester who appeared to be fascinated with her hair pin. Woody told tales of Jay and other crewmates he had encountered. Jay was too excited with recent news to care.

"She's due early June—I'm going to be a dad!" he'd exclaimed. He was doused with shaken bottles of soda. His eyes gleamed through soppy strands of hair. "I'm going to surprise her and come home early." It was a happy and noisy crowd that laughed and joked and jabbered as the music became more energizing.

Perry, one of the *Hard Ship* crew, had been quiet until he was persuaded to dance on the hatchway. Stix tapped a Latin rhythm on cooking pots, and everyone clapped along as Perry flipped and spun his body. Soon, someone was strumming a pop tune on guitar. It was the same style Corey had heard in the engine room of the *Golden Aye*, only with more energy.

"Way to go, Strings!" someone yelled. *Did Sherrie get a new nickname?* Corey turned to find the source of the music. On the far side of the crowd, the musician sat on a high stool but, once again, the face was obscured—this time by hanging balloons. Before Corey turned away, he heard three pops and caught a guilty grin on Chester's face. In his hand was the incriminating weapon: a tortoise shell pin. Where the balloons had floated, a head now appeared. A head with a new growth of brown hair; a head under which intense gray eyes gleamed with merriment.

The night was full of surprises. Dice—er, Strings?—was a sensitive musician!

Goldy watched over Corey most of the night, like a protective sister. She even introduced him to some nice girls she had gotten to know. Two were married to crew members and one had a fiancé in Georgia.

"Watch out," Woody said. "'Flames' is trying to get her hooks in you." Woody just didn't understand Goldy.

It was time for cake. Corey was glad Goldy hadn't made a big deal about his birthday up to now. He could see her watching him through the galley door as she lit the candles...until he got distracted by Sylvia, who insisted on a close inspection of his eye color—*"so golden"*—and a hands-on inspection of not only his brass buckle but his chest scar. That was the last thing he remembered before the blazes tore through the galley and shot up the stays like sparklers, and three fire extinguishers drenched all the food.

COREY'S DETOUR

"Sorry about your birthday disaster!" Goldy wailed the next morning as they prepared for sail.

"It's okay. I had a great time until—well, you know." Corey had to suppress a laugh as he remembered Goldy's head of ringlets turning into a frizzy ball.

"I should've noticed those streamers over the cake."

"At least they didn't have any structural damage." Corey gazed down the pier toward the *Hard Ship*, where the crew members were cleaning the deck and replacing stays. "And fortunately they aren't in a hurry to get moving like us." He waved at Sylvia until Goldy yanked on his arm.

The New Orleans conference itself had been delayed, but Corey still worried about the timing for Key West. Goldy persuaded him to punch his father's phone number again, and he heard a new message: "Due to the storm, my travels have been delayed..." Corey could still make it in time!

Finally, they were underway.

At the end of the second day, Corey was at the helm; Woody was next to him complaining about his stomach.

"I told you to stick with the vegetables last night," Corey said. "That other stuff smelled pretty spicy."

"But Marty said Mexican was her new specialty," Woody groaned.

Corey noticed Mr. Gray waddling along the deck. The captain must have left her cabin door unlatched when she went below.

Then his gaze fell on the chart. It showed a channel that would cut off several miles.

"Hey Woody, do you think—"

"Gotta go!" Woody's face was pale and he clutched his middle as he ran to the head, yelling something to Corey about not doing anything stupid while he was gone.

Corey knew the ship, and he had enough experience plotting a course. The depth was adequate. Goldy, who had appeared when Woody left, agreed that the channel would be quicker. Corey bore to starboard as Mr. Gray struggled to mount the hatch cover. But the chart didn't account for the buildup of sediment from the recent storm.

The captain reappeared on deck, laughing about something with Webber, the bos'n. The two went quiet as they noticed their surroundings.

They were halfway through the channel. Corey felt a drag and his stomach turned. The *Golden Aye* groaned as it caught bottom.

A flurry of activity ensued when the captain yelled orders to reverse the ship through the shallow muck and back to the planned route.

When the ship was back on course, the captain began to lash out at Woody, who was pale and confused. His illness was obvious, and the captain turned to Corey, her voice stiff.

"We have some things to talk about, Mr. Redrow."

This time it's the SHIP list for sure! Corey racked his brain for a way out of this one. His hand flew to his chest, but he'd left his buckle in the black pants. *Figures.* He might as well start packing. He braced himself as the journey flashed before his eyes. He couldn't blame his father for this. But before he could stutter *Aye*, Goldy spoke up.

"It was my fault, Captain."

Corey and the captain both stared at Goldy.

Her voice was solemn. "Mr. Gray nearly fell overboard, and Corey ran to save him; I grabbed the helm." She paused, lowering her eyes. "And I took the wrong route while Corey checked him for injuries."

The captain looked at her dog with alarm and seemed to realize for the first time that she had left her cabin unlatched. When she looked up, she opened her mouth and closed it again. It was the first time Corey had ever seen her at a loss.

Her lips gave a twitchy smile before she led Mr. Gray back to her cabin.

Corey stared at Goldy.

He wavered between telling the truth and saying nothing. This was just too good—Goldy's way must be fate.

She is a goddess. She had risked her own good standing to save Corey.

Wait until Woody heard.

Checking the ship for damage cost an extra afternoon. But that evening, Captain Harper had some good news: "No real damage...and we'll make the conference." The crew cheered.

"Bad news is," the captain continued, "we'll have to make a beeline to New Orleans."

No stopping in Key West.

GOLDY SUBSTITUTES

How could he be such a moron? After all Corey had been through, even with Goldie's heroic efforts, had he lost the only thing he'd signed on for?

He wanted to jump overboard and attack a shark. *Keep your cool.* Nothing ever happened according to plan.

After an eternity on watch, Corey fell into his bunk. His mind turned this way and that looking for a solution. Could he release the small boat by himself as they passed Key West? Could he jump overboard and swim there? He fell asleep with no answers.

He was the mains'l, Goldy's arms the yard, Sam the breeze that moved him...until a cold wind took over. It became a terrifying face, and the sight froze him into a sheet of ice. He crumpled into pieces that fell and shattered on the deck.

Corey's eyes sprang open, and he drew his curtain over to see Goldy in the dimming light gathering plastic hair pins that had scattered all over the sleeping quarters. *It must be evening.* He swung his legs over the side of his bunk and sat up. He was rubbing his eyes when he felt the weight of her body depressing the mattress and rolling him sideways. He remembered the last time she had sat there, and he regretted how quick he'd been to drink alcohol. Not that it really *was* alcohol, but he didn't know that at the time.

Goldy set down her bag of captured pins. She released the tortoise shell that anchored her curls, smoothed her hair, and refastened it.

"I'm sorry about Key West," she sighed. "I know you were looking forward to it." She put some cheer in her voice. "But New Orleans will help you forget."

"I doubt it." What he needed was a clear head. He almost wished he could be in the storm again. It had a way of focusing the mind.

He would find a way to get to Florida eventually.

Goldy leaned close. "I can help you forget." She kissed him on the cheek. "Look, I know what it is to live with disappointment." She looked down. "I may complain about

Mom, but it was my dad who betrayed us both." Her face darkened. "Leaving us for that *woman.*"

So Goldy had been abandoned too. She and Corey had that in common.

Goldy's face brightened as she leaned close and squeezed Corey's hand. Her scent of jasmine reminded him of the cologne Sam had worn last summer. He smiled at her.

"So what if you can't be with your father?" Goldy whispered in his ear. "You're with me. I'll be him." She sat back and put on a serious look and lowered her voice.

"Well, here I am, boy, what do you have to tell me?" She added, "Go ahead, spill it."

Corey almost laughed. But then, he thought, role playing couldn't hurt. He cleared his throat.

"I–I'd tell him...er, ask him..." he looked down, suddenly undecided.

"Keep going," Goldy adjusted herself to face him. "Here," she said, pulling his arm so he'd face her squarely. "He's–" She lowered her voice again. "I mean, *I'm* right here in front of you."

She had a way of lowering his defenses, but he surprised even himself by blurting, "Why didn't you love me?"

Silence.

He looked down, embarrassed. When he stole a glance at Goldy, her hair seemed to have taken the shape of horns, and the next words were plain and brutal.

"Because my drugs were more important."

Corey's brows shot upward; hot blood surged through his body. He was hardly aware of a feminine voice saying *"so sorry"* and *"didn't mean it."* His eyes narrowed and his temple throbbed as he projected the form of a whiskered man next to him. Something undefinable was bubbling up. Corey's knuckles tightened into fists as an unfamiliar voice spilled over his own tongue. "Stay away from my mother." It was a menacing growl. *"Or you're dead."*

The man morphed back into Goldy, who now stared back, white-faced. How threatening Corey must have seemed!

"I'm sorry—" he started gently, thinking she might back away from him. Instead, she shifted her weight forward and pulled him off-balance as her nose zoomed in toward his. Her lips, soft and moist, latched onto his, and he felt he was being drawn through them as she pressed herself to him.

When she finally released him, he stared at her, open mouthed. His head buzzed as she murmured, "I knew there was more to you," and her eyes made fireworks of the rays of sun streaming through the porthole.

Goldy had knocked him off balance. What was that *kiss* all about? But then Corey suddenly realized something had shifted inside him. His demon had loosened, had become unstuck. He felt like—just maybe—he *owned* some more of himself. He was a step closer to victory!

He cracked a smile, leaned in, and gave his friend a big hug.

"Goldy, you're awesome!" She had made him realize his power. She had also rekindled a powerful desire for Sam that put things back in focus. As long as he had the will, nobody could keep him away from Key West. He'd find a way!

Goldy had put herself out there, risked playing the fool. He sat back and relaxed as he studied her face, soft and pretty; her wild red-gold hair was framed into a halo with her grandmother's hair pin; her eyes were green gems. She was a magnet—she would never have trouble finding a boyfriend.

Goldy was still leaning into him, eyes shining like the moonlit sea, when she blew his mind again. Her hands slid under his shirt and her lips latched onto his with urgency.

What is she doing?

Didn't she know he was into Sam? Was she really *coming on* to him? But that soft skin, that scent... He forgot everything else as he felt *Sam's* lips on his, *Sam's* fingers stroking his chest. His gut insisted he just go with it. He tasted her velvety tongue. He slid his hand down her back. He pulled her around him and lowered them both to horizontal. They ignored the thump of his knee against the hull. His nose sucked in the sweet aroma of her neck as her heel found the hull with another thump. But Corey only heard the clunk of logs on the coals, on an island beach. He hungrily kissed the girl whose eyes flickered in the flames of his memory.

His words slipped out between kisses: "Brown eyed beauty..."

The other lips stopped moving.

Then a drawn out whisper escaped with his next breath: "Samantha."

Wild hair swept his face as the girl jerked away, her hair fastener springing loose.

Corey vaguely heard the thud of heels on the floor and felt the words scraping him back to the present: "...eyes are green... name is Goldy!" and then, "Just another traitor!"

The vision of Samantha vanished. Corey opened his eyes and sat up, hitting his head on the wood beam. He rubbed his scalp and looked around the sleeping quarters. He wasn't on an island; he wasn't with Sam.

He wasn't with anyone.

UNNAMED FEAR

"If exhaustion doesn't get you, the sharks will." Woody didn't react well to Corey's idea of jumping ship, literally, to swim to the island. Woody parceled a rope by winding it with cloth strips to prevent chafing. He gave every other twist an emphatic jerk. "Anyway, now I'll have to watch you like a hawk." He scowled up at Corey. "You know I have responsibilities." His hands ceased their work and spread wide to emphasize his point. "And once I call 'Man overboard,' don't you think it will delay the whole crew?"

Corey avoided Woody's eyes. "Never mind. I was only brainstorming."

"Well take your storm somewhere else." Woody said stiffly. Then he sighed. "Hey, I'm sorry how things worked out. I'm just a little tense since, you know." He glanced up at the topsail yard, where Goldy was edging over the footrope, checking gaskets Woody had already secured. "I don't know what made her ask for my watch. I think she did it to make my life miserable. But the captain okayed it."

Corey was still thinking about Key West. Even if he was willing to risk the elements and the sharks by jumping ship and swimming, could he really abandon the captain or the shipmates that had become like brothers and sisters?

Corey wanted to talk to Goldy and make things right between them. But he had hardly seen her since she'd gotten reassigned to this watch. Whenever he did see her, she was too busy to talk.

Would he have to depend on fate to get him to his father? Maybe the conference would inspire him with a solution. Or, maybe with Goldy's help, he had already passed some kind of test. Maybe he was already cured! How could he know?

The questions swirled in Corey's head as the ship rounded the Florida peninsula, heading west into the Gulf of Mexico. Whenever Corey had a solid plan, he knew who he was. Right now, he felt like a man without a name.

Could he find it in Louisiana?

In New Orleans... FIELDING MEMORIES

Robert G. Fielding had left his personal life at home. Now *R. Grayson* Fielding scanned his conference keynote speech in his hotel room. But something was bothering him. The hotel cocktail menu on the desk made him think of his wine cellar. When he'd removed the bottles, he'd forgotten that aged Scotch—Andrew's favorite—on the far side of the rack in a gap next to the stone wall. Had Andrew spotted it that day in the cellar? If so, he would probably take it out later, maybe set it on the coffee table, and gaze at the label. He would have no intention of drinking it, but the memories it would bring could be dangerous. His buddies were drinkers, and he'd be lonely. Without a job, it would be easy for him to slip into old habits. Grayson wished he could've been "Rob" for a few more days.

But, as he told his trainees, it did no good to worry. Fielding returned to his speech. He read the first paragraph three times. How could he think with that raucous street noise? He pushed his chair away from the desk and walked to the sliding door to the balcony. He wasn't much for air conditioning; he was used to the fresh breeze of sailing on a close reach. Before sliding the door shut, he paused to survey the scene. There was the city skyline and beyond it, he knew the Gulf stretched to the waters of the Atlantic. But beneath his deck, the streets burst with color. Cafes and lunch carts leaked Cajun aromas, and jazz musicians launched rhythms that entered the ears and exited the toes of tourists. Tourists who would gladly pay top dollar for this view.

He couldn't wait to get out of here.

As he turned back to the room and slid the door over, a new sound edged through the diminishing crack, a somber melody that snaked through his ear and down his arm, arresting his hand on the door. Jazz funeral players marched through the intersection a couple blocks over, headed for Green Street. He remembered seeing the cemetery from the taxicab. The funeral dirge was an old gospel tune—something about a "closer walk." It irritated him; it gladdened him. It pulled him back to that night over seventeen years ago.

Now, only a moment ago.

He was a college student with an identity crisis after learning he'd been adopted. She was a teenager put through hell by her alcoholic father. Rob had tried to ignore her—the most attractive girl in group therapy. But when he sat beside her to escape Tina's leer, Peg's sapphire eyes beguiled him.

The evening she finally came to him, it was February second—he remembered because the ground hog had predicted a long winter. An eternity, as it turned out.

She came into his room without a word. On his TV an old James Bond played, the one where the funeral guys mopped their brows with handkerchiefs and blew their horns in a slow march.

The movie was ignored as they moved in passion. When the screen faded to black, Rob was seeing colors he'd never known. Even the night light burned brighter, with a golden hue that branded her into his memory. He had found what he'd searched for: the artist who could paint him back to life, reveal his own colors.

The next day, he demanded Tina stop calling him her fiancé. He couldn't let her crazy rumors spread; he was in love. But as enchanted as that night had been, the artist disappeared as magically. Had Peg regretted their night together? He wanted to know that she was okay. Had her father taken her away? He couldn't locate her.

Eventually, his search for the color had taken him through rosy sunsets on cobalt oceans and golden dawns on emerald seas. The search had brought him young people with skins of ivory and taupe, eyes of coal and azure, all with hearts that beat with passion and a need for guidance. He had found satisfaction in taming their wild winds. But in the quiet moments, in the spaces between colors, the memory of *her*s came back to haunt him.

With effort, Grayson closed the door on the music and walked back to his desk. From the drawer, he pulled out that article. The one he could easily have missed last summer, if the dentist hadn't been running late. As he'd scanned that newspaper in the waiting room, a name caught his eye.

Worder. A name he'd encountered exactly once before. He read an incredible tale of attempted murder and history revised. It told of an identity hidden in 1812 when the name *Redrow* was concealed by reversing it. And it told how Margaret "Worder" Stowe had recently survived because of her teenaged son.

Grayson hoped the boy was a very young teen. Peg couldn't have found another love soon after *their* night together, could she? That special night, seventeen years ago last February. He liked to think that, though she'd disappeared, she had missed him desperately until she had finally, reluctantly, moved on to whomever the boy's father was.

Fielding had tracked down Peg Stowe's address. But she would not accept his offer of help to locate that missing treasure. Was she afraid to open a door to the past?

Robert Grayson Fielding, get yourself together. He had business to complete, trainees depending on him. They needed a leader, not some cow-eyed youth mooning over the past. He crumpled the news page.

He studied his keynote speech. The storm had necessitated some change: *Due to hurricane damage, we have arranged for additional aid for Haiti. The load will be distributed among ships heading for the Caribbean.*

Disasters had hit the island hard. Though much of the population had converted to Catholicism, many believed in angry spirits and, to appease them, resorted to the practice some folks called *voodoo.*

A ring tone interrupted his thoughts.

"The Lafitte room?" The home office was calling with updates about the workshops and lecture. "Okay, so everything's set? No, I haven't picked this year's flagship, I'll announce it later." Usually by now, he had some idea which ship he would join to work with trainees. Right now, he had no clue.

He opened the desk drawer to grab his itinerary. There was the *Gold Seekers Magazine* he had picked up in the bookstore. He'd almost forgotten it. He flipped the pages featuring a sunken ship at Pedro Banks, near Jamaica, before stuffing it into a canvas bag along with his lecture notes. He had no use for a briefcase.

7 OLD BATTLES

BATTLE OF NEW ORLEANS

"Jean Lafitte" scanned the letter. His band of pirates knew the bayou well and could be valuable allies to the British. "They offer land in exchange for our help," he announced, his black mustache bobbing against his cheek.

Corey, AKA *Lafitte,* had to scratch. He turned his head away from the other "pirates" and slid his finger under his mustache, a prop in the War of 1812 workshop. Corey liked analyzing facts and drawing conclusions; it kept his mind off other things. He patted down the mustache.

Think. Should he help the British or stick with the Americans? The British had disciplined soldiers who could overwhelm the ragtag Americans. Lafitte rested his foot on a stump and considered the British option. "But isn't that the kind of regimental behavior we rebel against?" He thought out loud, and his men respected Lafitte's need for silence. Except one.

"Why even consider an alliance?" Sharkbait asked in his annoying nasal voice. "This war is no concern of ours."

"Shhh!" Lafitte stroked his mustache. Wasn't he, Jean Lafitte, well versed in the art of deception? And didn't the Americans need time to prepare? He smiled. Yes, he had reason to offer the British his "help."

Corey took off the black hat and dropped to a tree stump. It was an eye-opener to realize that even pirates had to make tough decisions. He looked across the park at other crews involved in hands-on learning. When he'd heard there would be workshops, Corey had imagined whiteboards and Power Point screens. He laughed silently at his mistake.

He put on his hat and reviewed his options: 1. Stay out of the battle. 2. Ally with the British and be rewarded with land in the colonies. 3. Help the Americans and preserve the lifestyle he and his men valued.

The dilemma reminded Corey of Sam. What were his options? 1. Do nothing—and depend on fate. 2. Settle for Goldy—she *was* a hottie—and quit wasting time on a dream. 3. Run back to Sam and hope his demon had disappeared.

Lafitte's historical decision was a twisted fourth option: he pretended to accept the British offer, allowing the Americans time to prepare for battle; then he double crossed the British!

Corey thought of a similar idea: *Be with Goldy until you find a way—then go back to Sam.* No. He would never do that. Betrayal had worked for Jean Lafitte, but Corey was no pirate, and he couldn't stab Goldy in the back.

Even pirates had reason, though. By misleading the British, Lafitte preserved his lifestyle and enhanced relations with the Americans. Maybe pirates weren't so different from other people. *Everyone looks out for family and friends.*

Corey scribbled a summary of Lafitte's decision as Clarence, AKA Sharkbait, looked over his shoulder.

"That's good." The boy was a local landlubber participating for school credit. "Hard to believe the British were beaten by our frontiersmen, free blacks, farmers..."

"And pirates." Corey bumped fists with Clarence. After a bad first impression, he realized the boy's rudeness was just eager nervousness. Putting himself in Lafitte's shoes, too, had exposed Corey's assumptions. *What else have I assumed?*

The thought was interrupted by the boom of a cannon.

COMBAT & CANNONBALLS

Corey knelt at the embankment at Chalmette Battlefield and aimed his "rifle" beside Woody.

"This is as fun as paintball!" Woody picked off another British soldier. "Take that!" Woody might seem heartless to some, but Corey knew Olga was still a sore spot.

Having built a bulwark against the oncoming British regulars, Corey's team was now joined by "locals and Kentucky sharpshooters." The enemy advanced in bursts of gunfire and cannon. Several soldiers trying to scale the wall below them were "shot" as reported by flashing sensor pads on their red coats.

"I was wrong." Woody picked off another soldier and stretched his neck to be sure the guy stayed down. "This is *more* fun than paintball." But then he himself was targeted by one of the Brits, and his chest buzzer went off.

"Dang, I'm hit!" Woody staggered and pulled Corey close. "Tell my mama I won't be comin' home."

"Hey, let me go." Corey ducked and glanced over the wall as Woody fell to the ground.

"Tell my sweetheart..." he coughed pathetically, "Tell *Olga* I did it all for her." His leg gave a spasm, and he lay still.

After a barrage of cannon fire to the field below, a cluster of soldiers dropped to the ground. Corey glanced at the source of "fire." *So that's how the captain got her nickname.*

Cannonball Harper was barking orders. Her crew were all in a rhythm reenacting traditional firing procedures: pushing, angling guns; loading, tamping with cotton; lighting and standing back, fingers in ears. She wore a hard grin accented by a deadly gleam in the eye, and her aim was right on target.

THINKING OUTSIDE THE LOCKS

After the battle reenactments, the trainees spent several days learning to deal with weather conditions, pirate raids, and crew disputes; then they met in groups to prepare summaries to present in conference.

Now the *Golden Aye* had moved to the northern port, its sails neatened into harbor furls to show the ship at its best. Corey scrambled down the rigging. It had been a hot day, and the crews were sweating buckets. Corey wanted to get cleaned up before the conference in the Grand Hotel.

"Hear the news?" Woody called from the pin rail as he checked lines. "An extra half hour is slotted after the lecture and workshops—we get a personal meeting with Fielding."

"What—that's awesome!" Corey glanced around as he hurried past Woody. "Does Goldy know?" He still hadn't talked to her. "Wait 'til I tell her..."

Woody grabbed his arm from behind so Corey's feet almost flew out from under him. "You don't get it do you."

"What are you talking about?"

"Just watch out for that girl. She's not your friend."

"C'mon, she's all right." Corey pulled away. Woody was still holding a grudge against Goldy. Maybe she and Corey had a misunderstanding, but she was still his friend, wasn't she?

After they finished tripling up the mooring lines, Corey threw his sea bag over his shoulder and headed down the pier. That's when he saw Goldy filling water tanks with a hose. He waved, but she didn't seem to notice. He'd catch her inside. He had to hurry to the shuttle to get a shower at the hotel before his scheduled sessions.

Grayson Fielding was even more impressive than his pictures; from the podium, his penetrating gaze focused on each student, and the passion in his voice resonated throughout the amphitheater. The man's energy was catching as he gave his perspectives on sailing and life, and he welcomed feedback from even the newest sailors.

Corey clicked his pen as he listened but took no notes. His mind and body had become his recording system. Once he trusted Fielding's method and gave up on the rote system he'd always struggled with, his mind retained what he heard.

"Avoid 'crowd thinking,'" Fielding said. "Don't just accept what the experts say." After demonstrating several problems and solutions, Fielding posed questions. He referred to a seating chart and called on individuals by name.

For each question, students offered answers, and Fielding guided them to more fitting solutions. "In problem solving, we tend to add complications based on assumptions; if you remove them, you get a simple, direct solution."

Near the end of the session, Fielding was pacing the central aisle, one hand on the seating chart.

"We have just a few more minutes," he began. "Here's a riddle you've probably heard: Travel ten degrees south, ten degrees east, and ten degrees north, and you end up back where you started—where are you?"

Several voices called answers.

"Yes." he consulted his name chart. "Ms. Holloway." He grinned up at a blond in the third row. "Yes, the North Pole." He said, "Now, before I pose another problem, think about what you assumed when you first heard that puzzle." He paused while students called out "flat planes" and "triangles with straight lines."

"Now here's another," Fielding went on. "My ship is traveling in a constant direction for fifteen minutes, and yet I never change latitude or longitude." He scanned the curious eyes peering up at him. "Ask questions. Yes," he pointed to several teens, in turn.

"Are you still on earth?"

"Yes."

"Do you rely on known technology?"

"Yes."

"Is your 'ship' a submarine?"

"Nope!" he chuckled and called on others with questions Corey couldn't hear.

"Yes, I remain on the water's surface, and yes, all my movements are intentional."

It wasn't typical to move in the third dimension, but Corey's ship had done it. He waited. Surely someone else would answer, someone who'd traveled the Seaway or the Panama Canal.

Everyone was quiet.

Finally Corey spoke up from his seat near the back. "You're ship is in a lock, changing levels, like on the Seaway." Fielding zeroed in on Corey's position and referred to his chart.

Corey continued. "Your direction is up or down—only altitude changes." He watched Fielding's brow furrow as his gaze fixed on the name chart; then the man's eyes narrowed in on Corey. His smile disappeared.

Guess it wasn't the answer he wanted.

The hour bell rang, and Group B filed through the doors.

Corey's group had to move to the classroom next door for training on the distribution of aid. He was separated from

Woody until after the group had two more workshops and watched a video about how people were surviving in the rubble of Haiti.

ONE SICK SAILOR

"Redrow, that was pretty cool!" Woody told him as they hurried toward the fireside lounge, where they would meet Grayson Fielding.

"What?" Corey scowled. "Children starving in Haiti?" After being ravaged by a hurricane on top of an earthquake, they were lucky if they had a tent for shelter, and young girls had resorted to prostitution just to get scraps of food.

"Not that, I mean before—about the locks in the Seaway." He chuckled. "Why didn't I think of that?"

At least somebody appreciated his answer.

Corey had just noticed the directional sign pointing to the lounge when Goldy rushed up and shoved a piece of paper under his eyes. Woody groaned, but Cory's mood got an instant boost.

"Goldy!" he blurted with a grin. "I missed you."

"Corey." Goldy sounded secretive. "I heard the *Weather Aye* lost a couple of crew members—down with the flu. One's so bad their captain needs to replace him." She glanced around as Woody rolled his eyes and threw up his hands, moving toward the lounge. She turned back to Corey. "It's your chance to see your father. They're stopping in Key West!"

Corey could hardly believe it. "What? Where is the captain?" Corey turned his head to scan the lobby. If he changed ships, he would miss his new friends, especially

Goldy, but the ship would have enough crew without him; Clarence–AKA *Sharkbait*–had signed on.

"You'd better hurry up to room five-sixty-nine. That's where Captain Rathburn is meeting with his crew."

Corey looked down the corridor, where Steve huffed past Sherrie, his crush, who was holding hands with a sailor from the *Sharp Aye*. Even Morris, always late, was entering the lounge. They had to catch the shuttle to the pier right after that, so Corey would miss his chance to meet Fielding.

But he could be heading to Key West.

"Thanks, Goldy!" He spun around and ran for the elevator.

Twenty-five minutes later, Corey re-entered the lobby, where his shipmates gushed about Fielding. Corey felt like a punctured life raft. Not only had he missed Fielding; Captain Rathburn, who was actually in room *six-fifty*-nine, had already filled out his crew.

"Oh no, someone beat you to it?" Goldy forced her lips into a frown. "Oh, right..." She hit her forehead with her fist. "It was me!" Her laugh echoed throughout the lobby of the grand hotel.

A TURN OF FORTUNE

Goldy might as well have stabbed him in the back with a fish knife. It wasn't fair–Corey had misread her when they were in sleeping quarters. As he told Woody, she had taken him by surprise on his bunk, and he felt he had no control over his reaction.

"I knew that girl was bad news. She's the type to get revenge." Woody's voice was patronizing. "Don't you know that even a normal girl doesn't like to be called by another girl's name when you kiss her?"

The captain called for muster. They had cleared New Orleans and were nearing Mobile, Alabama, to take on relief supplies. This had not been the original plan, but after New Orleans, Corey didn't care. He had no plan of his own.

"The *Golden Aye* will be the key distributor for Haiti and Jamaica," Captain Harper said. "We will have to work as a team, no rest."

"Hey, buddy, quit moping." Woody nudged him. "You're better off without that girl around anyway." He pulled Corey's arm. "You're next to me in the fire line."

Wordlessly, Corey became a link in the brigade that formed from a pier in Mobile to the ship's hatchway to load crate after crate of aid packages.

One, two, three...

Corey swiveled left, right for each handoff.

Twenty-five, twenty-six...

As the crates blurred, he was barely aware of a tickle in his throat.

Ninety-eight...

Corey was a piece of machinery; the only hint that he was other than a robot was his cough every fourth swing.

One-hundred twenty-three...

Then every second swing.

They spent the night in Mobile. Corey tossed and rolled as he was poked and prodded: a blue-eyed demon dared him to abandon ship and hitchhike to Key West; Fielding's glowing face urged him to stay with the ship and deliver aid to the kids in Haiti.

As they headed southeast the next day, Corey lasted through the early watch then descended the companionway. He was exhausted, and he didn't want to watch as Florida glided past, just out of his reach.

Three-thousand-eight...
Nine-billion-forty-eleven...
Corey's semi-dream state was interrupted by a shout.

Corey forced his lids open. Had he slept through to dinner? Wait, that wasn't dinner...

"All hands muster, quarterdeck!"

Corey dragged himself topside.

"We're picking up a passenger." The captain winked. "You'll have a two-hour stopover."

Still groggy, Corey looked around and spotted land off the port bow. Had he slept all the way to Haiti?

"All hands for coming into port..." the mate called. "In Key West."

The crew buzzed about something, but Corey only heard Key West. Could this be real? Was he still asleep?

No, they were really here! *Calm down.* Rob might not even be home. But Corey's body summoned new energy, and he trembled with excitement.

"Stand by to come alongside."

Corey pinched himself.

He promised Captain Harper he'd be back on time. He hailed a cab and gave the address.

FIGHTING SPIRITS

"What a mess," the driver said, taking a hard right by a bus stop and cursing the street fair ahead. Blocked with orange cones, the route was a blur of colorful balloons and food stands, and the tones of an island steel drum band seeped through the taxi's windows. After two lefts and a right, the cab pulled up in front of a two-story stucco. It was topped by a widow's walk, a railed platform for observing the sea. Corey pulled the piece of paper from his pocket and checked the address one more time.

"You gonna get out or what?"

Corey counted out the steep fare, deciding to catch a bus on the way back.

Corey walked up the stone drive toward the front porch of the man who dominated his mind. He felt small as he studied the walkway and went over his words. He stared at the three steps that rose, like a mountain range, to the entrance. After two deep breaths, he scaled them and hiked across the wide, open veranda. Through the screen door, he could see shelves holding old anchors and ancient-looking carvings that could've been figureheads of old ships. Corey was sure the artifacts were stolen. But they were right in plain sight, where anyone could see them! The guy was shameless.

The force of gravity doubled as Corey hoisted his finger part way to punch the doorbell, but he let his hand drop.

He took a breath. *Why should I be scared?* Corey relocated the fire of anger in his belly. He was not some object that could be owned and controlled. No. *Rob is the one who should fear me!*

As he thrust his hand up, a movement caught his eye; he turned to the right to see a man on the other side of the veranda, sitting back in a porch swing. Corey edged toward him. The man had no beard, no cap, no cigarette. His off-white linen shirt exposed dark chest hairs that mingled with gray, and his lanky legs emerged from neatly pressed green shorts. The man's pale blue eyes were riveted on a bottle nestled between his large palms.

Corey was coming face-to-face with his father! He stopped breathing, and his lips twitched. He crept closer.

He cleared his throat.

The man jumped as his lids flew open. His blue eyes focused briefly then clouded over; he looked through Corey.

Corey hadn't come all this way to be ignored. "I'm your son. Look at me!"

But the man's lids lowered, and he said softly, "Andrew...Andrew."

The man couldn't remember his own child's name? Corey was irritated. *Wait.* He was actually facing his father... *Without freezing.* He checked his arms and legs and twisted his neck. Yes, he was past the first hurdle! Now it was time for shock and awe. Corey stood tall and raised his voice.

"Put that bottle down." Corey decided it was time to fix his problem, time to stop the demon ghost from haunting him. He towered over the man and demanded: "No more..."

"*Yes.*" It was little more than a whisper. The man stared at the bottle and seemed to summon all his energy. "No more!" His fingers sprang open, and the bottle bounced on the all-season carpet then fell over. The man's head dropped against his seat cushion.

Corey stared at the white face as he gave voice to the words he had rehearsed: "I may have your genes. But I'll never have your soul...and you can't have mine!"

Corey kept his eyes on the face, but the man's lids were closed. Corey poked his arm. No movement. Corey reached out and shook his shoulders. The chest rose and fell, but there was no other response.

Corey picked up the bottle, some kind of Scotch whiskey, surprised to find it unopened. The man had probably consumed a bottle or two and was about to start another.

He's passed out.

Corey backed away.

He stumbled down the stairs, a little unsteady. He had thought it would feel different, that's all.

No problem. He squared his shoulders as he trudged up the street. He had faced his father without freezing up! Even told him what he thought. But whatever else he'd expected, Corey hadn't planned on such an anticlimactic triumph. Something about the look in his father's eyes had made Corey ill at ease. He shook himself.

That was the old me. Corey deserved to celebrate his triumph. He had done what he came for, and his father's response was his own business.

Corey envisioned his father's demon rising from deep inside him and exiting through every pore. Corey's walk became lighter and faster as he persuaded himself: he was finally free!

Now he must be ready for the next step: facing Sam. Or at least calling her. He trembled as he pulled his phone out and punched her number. He couldn't wait to hear her voice!

Corey's arms and legs prickled as his body thawed out; he stooped over painfully to retrieve his phone from the sidewalk where it had fallen. It was only a few moments this time, but Corey couldn't deny it: he had frozen. Was it a delayed reaction to facing his father? The last thing he remembered was that masculine *Hello?* on Sam's phone.

He didn't know which was worse: turning into a statue again or knowing that some guy was answering Sam's phone.

His body was a lead weight that he dragged toward the bus station. He studied the cobblestones as he shuffled toward the sounds of the street fair.

In Harts Landing... MUSEUM SWITCH

"Hey, quit playing around and help me find the records." Sam scolded Auger from the door to the archives room at the Harts Landing Museum.

Auger said goodbye to his latest girlfriend and pocketed his cell phone. "If I'd known you were going to be a pain about it," he said with a teasing smile, "I would have picked a different partner for the debate."

"Yeah, well *partner* is the operative word here, and you need to do your share." Sam normally enjoyed research, but her concerns about Corey had distracted her. She had overheard his mother and knew he was okay. But was he *with* anyone?

She and Auger had settled into their chairs and were digesting a pile of documents when a ring tone broke their concentration.

"Now what?" She glared at Auger.

"Hey don't blame me. That's not *my* phone."

Puzzled, Sam pulled the phone from her own pocket and stared at the word *Corrections* on the caller ID. This wasn't her phone; she had laid hers down to sign in at the lobby. The guy at the front desk must have her phone.

She went to the sign-in counter and put the guy's phone down. "I got yours by accident."

The thick fingers tapping a page of *Metal Attractor* magazine now paused. Its owner glanced at the phone screen showing the call gone to voice mail.

"Oh yeah," he mumbled without looking up. "You got a call too." He tore his gaze from the article as he pushed her phone forward. "Just a wrong number." Then his eyes met Sam's and widened in recognition along with her own.

It was Charlie Stowe's nephew, that guy she'd seen at the pier in September. Must be working here part time.

"Hey, how's it going?" He grinned as his gaze wandered down her front. Sam stepped backwards in horror as she realized her blouse had gapped, showing a view to her abs. She grabbed her phone, punching buttons absentmindedly, and stuttered a "Thanks" as she backed away. But Derrick had turned around, phone to his ear, muttering, "Oscar?"

Auger smirked at her from across the lobby. "So now who's fooling around?" He ratcheted his voice up to mimic her: "Quit being a pain and get back to work!" She ignored him, red-faced, as they settled down at the table in the archives room.

But her chair faced the door to the display room, and the cutlass of Corey's ancestor was like a magnet. She tried to concentrate, but she could only think of the time she and Corey had found a clue on that old sword. Auger gave up and followed her gaze.

"Oh, I get it," he said. "Look, you've been stuck on that kid and his 'treasure' for weeks." He stared at his notebook and sighed. "If I'm going to pass this course, not to mention excel, you're going to have to snap out of it."

"I'm sorry, I just..."

"I know what you *just*. You're thinking about how to find that island and help the Worder kid—"

"Redrow kid, remember?" she said, mustering some attitude. "I mean *Hart*..." she wavered. Or—

"Whatever. Anyway, I don't know why you let him go. I hear it was just some kind of seizure he had."

"Right." She wished she could believe that. "More like a spell." The next words spilled out on their own: "A spell that Swedish girl put on him."

"What?" Auger's brows shot up. "You mean *Olga?*" His gray eyes warmed and drifted. "She was at the resort." His focus returned, sharp again. "But that girl was all about some guy from New York: 'Jerry' this and 'Jerry' that—said he was getting her an agent." Auger shook his head. "I tell you, if she wouldn't go for this..." He drew his right hand along his own body from head to waist. "I guarantee that Worder—*Redrow*—kid had no chance."

Sam hesitated then said, "You obviously haven't seen him lately."

Auger ignored her. "She liked him all right: 'Corey's so sweet' and 'Corey's a lamb.' He was like her kid brother."

Sam's mouth went slack. Could that be true? That squeeze the girl gave Corey...was it a sisterly goodbye? Maybe Sam had assumed too much. "Have I screwed everything up?" she whispered. "If only I could get in touch with him." She shook her head and slumped as she looked down. "It's hopeless."

Auger settled back in his chair, where he seemed to struggle with a decision. "Look." He suddenly leaned forward, "When I have a challenge, you know, a girl I'm not completely confident about..."

Sam narrowed her eyes. The great lover had a chink in his armor?

"I find something. Something to deflect the focus off me and onto the girl—something she needs."

"You mean like when you found that rare coin for Emily Grave's collection?"

"Exactly."

"But I thought you just stumbled across that." She leaned closer. "You acted like it was nothing!"

"It wasn't 'nothing.' I searched high and low for that stupid quarter."

Sam stared at him as he continued.

"The point is, you need something to help you *connect*."

"Yeah..." She let her eyes wander to the display room. "Like information about that treasure."

"No!" Auger was agitated. "I mean, there must be something he misses here. Maybe you get pictures of his dog that you happen to shoot while photographing scenery."

But she was sure it was the treasure that would get Corey's attention. "If we could prove his ancestor was right..."

Auger sank back in his chair and scowled. Finally, he sighed and closed his notebook. "I can see we're not going to get anywhere." He squirmed in his seat as he opened his mouth and closed it several times. He was the one acting weird now.

"What's up with you?" she said.

He looked at her sideways and said slowly, "I may have something." He looked toward the door and back. Then he leaned across the table. "I wasn't supposed to say anything..."

STREET FAIR FORTUNE

"Win a treasure!"

"Three rings for a dollar..."

"Your fortune in five minutes!"

Hawkers waved tokens and fliers in his face as Corey trudged toward the bus stop.

He didn't resist the palm reader who took his elbow and ushered him to a stone table. Not that he believed in that stuff, but he needed to sit down anyway. And she only wanted two dollars.

The cold granite beneath him helped him focus. He relaxed a little.

"Close your eyes," she said. She scolded him when they blinked themselves open. Then she held his hands and made a humming sound before articulating: "You will kiss a ghost."

Corey's lids separated. "Wha—?"

"Keep them closed."

What a waste. This girl couldn't tell him anything.

"You are troubled." She paused for a moment. "But you will see your father soon."

He couldn't help blurting, "You're supposed to see the future, right, not the past?" *She must've heard me talking about my father.*

She put a warm hand over his eyes. "Count to fifty before opening." Corey was surprised to find her touch calming. He counted.

When he opened an eye at the count of fifteen, the girl was gone. Along with the cash from his wallet.

He didn't have enough for the bus.

8 ZOMBIE TIMES

SURPRISE GUEST

The ship stood ready. The entire crew faced the pier as Corey coughed, panted, and staggered up the gangway. He fell to the deck and puddled ten street blocks worth of sweat.

He expected to hear shouts of "Walk the plank!" and "Twenty lashes!" But no one paid him any attention. They were still staring toward shore.

Corey was dizzy; his world reeled as he tried to make sense of the last couple of hours. Spending all this time so far from home had been a total waste. Facing his father had not kept him from freezing up. Plus some guy was answering Sam's phone. Then, at the street fair, he'd fallen for the oldest trick in the book. Now he just wanted to pass out.

No. He had to muster for the captain, even if he crewed as an able-bodied zombie. Corey caught his breath, heaved himself up, and stumbled past Woody for a drink.

"The mystery passenger is late," Woody murmured.

A rumble of excitement made Corey lift his head as water dribbled down his chin. Through bleary eyes he spotted a figure coming up the gangplank. The man's face was shaded by his cap as he hoisted a sea bag with a black monogram, *RGF*, set against tan canvas.

Captain Harper's voice, dominating the shouts, was a hollow echo in Corey's skull.

"I had a hard time keeping the secret—felt like a pregnant mare!" she chuckled. "But I'm pleased and honored that Mr. Fielding has chosen the *Golden Aye* as this season's flagship. Give him a *Golden Aye* welcome!"

The "*Aye Ayes*" buzzed in Corey's head. The man apologized for making them wait, something about blocked streets and having to stop by headquarters. The entire crew clustered to shake his hand.

The entire crew except for Corey, who slunk below. His head spun, and he felt the roll of the ocean in his stomach as he tossed his brass buckle under the bunk and collapsed.

In Harts Landing... UNDERCOVER MAP

Peg surveyed the icy shards fringing the bay below the window at Martin's Diner. There was more than one way to get treasure from that river.

She was on a lunch break from another fourteen-hour work day with Fred. The normal tourist season in the North Country was summertime, but the idea of a winter festival had generated enough interest to make the "Thousand Ice Lands" a reality. They had been working hard to ensure its success.

Charlie changed the subject to Corey.

"The last I heard, he was doing well," Peg said between bites. "You know, with Dr. Mason's exercises, and the sailing..." She quit chewing for a moment and let her gaze drift out the window of the diner to the iced-in harbor and the river beyond. "I just get the feeling everything's not quite as he expected." She flaked some salmon onto her fork and dragged it through ginger sauce.

But this—under the table, she pulled a paper from the purse on her lap—*might be just the thing.* Should she show it to Charlie?

Charlie took a gulp from his mug. On a cold day like this, most people went for hot chocolate. Not Charlie. When he was tense, he'd get an urge for a Genesee but order a non-alcoholic beer instead. She had a stab of guilt. He'd been on edge because, busy as she was, she still kept checking the blog.

"If I could just prove there was an Estar Island..."

Charlie sighed and sank back into his chair. "Look, Peg, we've been through this."

"But people say Patrice was unbalanced—" Peg knew she should keep her cool, but the bloggers were getting personal. "Think of what Corey went through to prove his ancestor was a hero."

"And he's stubborn, just like his mother."

"And he's stub—" she glared at him then continued. "That's why I let him go sailing. There's no stopping him when he's on a mission." She glanced at her food; she'd almost forgotten it was there. She took a bite. "Though I still don't quite get what his big mission is." Her words came out muffled.

"Anyway," she stabbed the air toward Charlie. "You'd do well to remember how he was stubborn enough to find me and bring me back to you! We owe him everything for that."

Charlie was shamed into an apology. "Touché. I can never give him enough credit." He took a bite of buttered roll, keeping his eyes on Peg. "So anyway, why do I have a feeling this has to do with Randy's daughter talking to you earlier?" He cut his meatloaf with the side of his fork. "I saw her with you by the car."

Peg took her time scooping croutons. "Samantha wants to help with the festival. She hopes it will bring business to the B&B." Peg could hardly keep her voice steady. "But that wasn't all she said."

Charlie raised an eyebrow.

"She seemed shy—" Peg rushed the words, and her hand darted to her lap. "I don't know why she didn't just contact Corey..."

"Not the shy type to me, a girl that gives 'save the planet' blurbs on the radio."

"She gave me this." Unable to wait any longer, Peg scooped the paper from her lap and slid it to the table top.

Charlie sat straighter.

Peg leaned closer. "Auger found it at the estate and gave Sam a copy." She sat back and smiled with trembling lips as she tapped the paper with her index finger. "The map of Estar Island."

Charlie's eyes widened. "You're kidding."

"No, I'm not." She turned the unlabeled map so he could see it better. Her smile partially dissolved as she admitted, "You still can't tell which island that is."

"But all you have to do is match the shape to an island on the river map, right? What is this, about a mile of coast?"

"Well, there's no key."

"So this could be a half-mile stretch out of a hundred miles or a five-mile stretch of an island that's ten miles around." Charlie pursed his lips and squeezed his eyes into well-worn creases. "Look, Peg, I hate to have you get your hopes up, but—hey, what's wrong?"

Peg's mouth hung open as she stared out the window. "She said *she*, not *he*. Samantha said *she* was holding back so as not to get our hopes up..."

"What do you mean?"

Peg's gaze followed the drift of a black cloud as it threatened the sun. The darkness came out in her voice.

"Sam meant Auger's grandmother was holding back." A wave of prickly cold rippled her flesh.

Mackenzie Hart had never intended to share this information.

It didn't matter how much Charlie protested that the woman was in jail, was monitored, could no longer do a thing to Peg.

Nothing could save Peg from a bout of the shakes.

OUT OF THE DEEP

Corey's stomach was a cannon ball plunging through the sea. A mermaid's red hairs were hot prongs on his chest, her mouth the opening of a bottle. Her lips sucked him inside.

A rope hung down from the bottle opening. As he hauled on the never-ending line from below, it coiled around him, piling higher and higher, reaching his throat, squeezing tighter and tighter...

After what seemed an eternity of fitful visions, Corey sank into a deep slumber. At last he was on a tall ship, sailing home. Someone sat next to him.

"You've been ill..." The soft voice wavered in and out. What a relief to come out of that nightmare, in his own bed with his mom taking care of him. He must've been really sick.

"But your fever has broken now." The feminine hand blotted his forehead with a damp cloth.

He uttered a weak, "Thanks, Mom." Then he heard a strange chuckle.

"It's Chazy, hon."

Corey's eyes flew open.

"You've had a nasty time, but we're all rootin' for you!"

He was in a bunk. On a rolling ship.

"You okay, buddy?" Woody's voice broke in. "We could use some help with those crates!" Corey caught his wink to Chazy, who scowled back.

It was December, and they were approaching Haiti.

FIELDING PROBES

Corey's reflection told him he hadn't changed, other than being a little pale, maybe thinner, but he felt different. He was there but not all there.

His mates, however, were charged with energy. Fielding had filled in to do Corey's chores and everyone was happy to work at his side. All were comfortable with "Grayce."

One day as Corey moved a sanding block over the ship's hull, someone fell into a rhythm beside him.

Corey rubbed hard on a spot that wouldn't come out.

"I think that's part of the wood," Grayson Fielding said softly. Corey quit sanding as the man continued. "Some marks are in the grain—they give it character."

Corey looked at the spot then moved on.

"I liked your thinking at the conference," the man said as he worked.

Corey turned to stare at his own reflection in Grayson Fielding's shaded glasses.

"The...conference." It was another world, and ages ago. Corey turned back to the hull. He hadn't done anything special. "We all came through the locks."

Fielding stopped sanding. "But *you* were the one that made the connection." He continued moving with the grain of the wood and hummed along with the steel drum band on the radio. Then he stopped and cleared his throat.

"I, ah, noticed your name. I think I've heard it before." Corey smelled mineral spirits and saw the edges of a rag flutter as the man wiped down the hull. "Lot of Redrows where you live, are there?" Fielding redoubled the rag and moved along the hull.

"I don't know." Corey didn't care to explain about his name. He hadn't cared about anything since the day he'd left Key West.

Near Harts Landing... BROKEN PROMISE

It's hot in here. Auger pulled at his collar. *Is this how they punish prisoners?* He shifted in his chair, avoiding Gran's eyes staring at him from behind the partition. "If you'd seen Sam..." Auger puckered his lips. "I didn't have a choice."

"Choice about what, Augie?"

"I know you wanted me to wait—" he blurted. "But I had to show her the map!"

Gran was more alert than last time. She laughed and said, "That's not a problem, Augie."

He wiped his brow, relieved. "Sam has been so distracted trying to figure out where that island is, she's making me crazy." He chuckled. "I mean, I know even if Estar Island is real, no one will probably ever find treasure there, but..."

"So it's called Estar?" Gran's wrinkles adjusted to remap her face. "They found a name? How wonderful!" Her eyes softened with the warmth she reserved for Auger, and he found his voice.

"Oh, yeah." Being in jail, she probably hadn't heard what everyone else knew. "The name *Estar* was on a loose page that fell out in their attic before you took the jour—" His smile froze. They both knew Gran had tricked Mrs. Stowe out of the old diary, but Auger would rather eat dirt than bring *that* up.

His grandmother gave a sigh. "It's all right, dear." She leaned forward. "I've come to terms with my actions." She looked at her hands and pursed her lips before leveling her gaze at him. "That is why I'm so keen to do what I can to make amends. Go ahead," she nodded. "Tell me more."

"That's really all I know." Auger studied his fingers. "The name."

"Well surely, if we have a name," Gran said with a twinkle in her eye, "it can be found. What's the problem?"

Auger raised his hands then dropped them. "They've looked high and low."

"And there's no record of that name?"

"Right. But, see with that map, they might have a chance."

"Do me a favor, Augie." Gran's eyes gleamed.

He stared.

"Get me a copy of that page." She leaned toward him. "My mind may not be quite what it used to be, but I'm getting better." She sat back. "You know, if I put my mind to it, I might be able to give some assistance!"

Auger knew that if there was anything to this treasure stuff, no one would have a better chance at solving the mystery than his brilliant grandmother.

HAITI

Dice spoke up first.

"Voodoo is where they stick pins in dolls of people they don't like."

"Actually, it's called *Vodoun*, from West Africa," Fielding corrected him. "And many of the stories you hear about sorcery and zombies are misconceptions."

The voices drifted by, mostly as noise to Corey, who gazed over the azure waves lapping Haitian beaches. He was carving the lid for a jewelry case. Mom might like it.

Captain Harper had mustered crew and trainees for a meeting about Haiti; Fielding was explaining how its history could affect relief efforts. His voice floated past Corey again.

"Vodoun has more to do with dance and spirits. Some Haitians continue the Vodoun tradition even though they are also Catholics. They offer gifts to the 'loa,' the spirits, to protect their families."

"Those are the ones that possess people, and they go wild, shimmying, shaking all over—I saw it on TV." That was Dice again.

"There are many loa who are believed to have power over different aspects of life. For example, *Ghede* is the loa of death and healing but is also a protector of children."

Everyone was quiet while Grayce continued.

"Some believers say the damage from the earthquake and hurricane could have been avoided, had they been more faithful to their Vodoun practices."

"But if they are so needy, how can they afford to give gifts to spirits?" Chazy asked.

"Good point. Some are giving even the little they have, in hopes of reaping rewards from their loas. We have a campaign to persuade people to come to distribution points for aid packages." Grayce sighed. "It's a lesson in diplomacy: how to give help without offending beliefs."

"But—these spirits don't really exist?" That was Hanna's soft voice.

A rougher voice asked: "How do you know they don't?" Morris's voice.

"You're kidding, right?" Darian said. "How can anyone believe such, such—"

"Some of us believe a man walked on water," the captain said. "Do you know how that sounds to some folks?"

Hesitation. "Well..."

"I went to this séance once where, I swear, the host was talking to a dead person..." Steve's voice.

"People say all kinds of things," Hannah said. "I never know what I'm supposed to believe."

Everyone pondered in silence. It was soon broken.

"There is no *supposed to*." The words were clear but sounded unfamiliar, even to the speaker.

Everyone looked at Corey, who spoke so rarely his voice was a shock. But he just stared at the deck and shook his head. He couldn't think of a single thing to believe in.

AN EXORCISM

Aloof as he was, Corey couldn't help being affected by the devastation around Port-au-Prince, and by children homeless among the rubble. Many people were in tent villages with limited access to drinking water and sanitary facilities. An awareness dawned on him and with it, a sense of shame. He had always had food, clothes, shelter, the freedom to go places, learn things. He'd taken so much for granted.

The ship had berthed near the outskirts of the capital, and crew members unloaded crates onto wagons that were pulled to distribution stations. Hunger was a good motivator, and many people had come for help. Uniformed police threatened anyone who dared think of jumping line.

Woody and Corey unloaded crate after crate from the wagons. On the fringes of the crowd, they noticed several children and older folks peeking from behind tents or piles of rubble; only their eyes and tops of their heads could be seen. Many of them were waiting for friends or relatives in line who would bring a supply package to share; from time to time they called hopefully to someone in line.

Except the small girl with the large brown eyes and dark, shaggy hair.

"I don't think she has anybody." Corey wasn't sure why he even noticed her. She blended in so well it seemed the wall itself was peering at them.

Break time came, and the boys were relieved by shipmates. Corey and Woody took several packs and crept around past the partial foundations then swung back to the pile of rubble. Corey could see the girl bracing herself against a broken pillar with one wiry arm, cradling a ragdoll with the other.

Not until they were several yards away did she notice them. When Woody stepped on gravel, the girl's head jerked and she jumped away from the wall, black and blue marks visible on her arms and legs.

"Don't be afraid," Woody called. "We just want to—hey!"

She had taken off like a jack rabbit.

"She must have springs in those skinny legs. C'mon!"

But Corey had already dug his toes into the dirt and pushed himself in her direction.

They darted through an alley, past bushes, and had nearly caught up to her near a tent among the trees. Suddenly, a man, short and slightly heavyset, stepped from behind a tree and grabbed the girl's arm. Her expression was a mix of anger and fear as she yanked the doll behind her.

The man growled something in French. Woody picked out the words: "*Gaby—thief—stole my bread!*" In the man's other hand was a thick, knobby branch that he was swinging, taking aim at Gaby's back side, when Corey and Woody surprised him. As his grip loosened, she pulled away and kept running. The man hesitated, probably not liking his chances against two muscular teens. He didn't follow.

Gaby was fast, given her condition, and she seemed to know the path. She skimmed over every root that tripped the boys, ducked every branch that slapped them. But when she stopped, they nearly stumbled over her. They were near the edge of a clearing, and ahead of them were about fifteen or twenty Haitians.

Corey and Woody regained their balance quietly as the slim girl hesitated. She seemed unsure whether to run into the clearing or stay with the boys. As she cradled the doll, Woody gently touched her shoulder and whispered some words in French. Corey took in the scene before them.

Some of the people had closed their eyes, and many were singing. At the center of the clearing were several tree stumps supporting bottles of liquid, jars of jam, wood carvings, clothing, cigarettes, herbs, and fresh flowers.

Corey couldn't take his eyes off the scene as the rhythm of drums and voices throbbed in his ears. The group swayed as a body and called for Ghede in a pulse that merged with Corey's own heartbeat. He felt something move within him, drawing him forward.

"Pssst! What are you doing?" someone hissed behind him, but the sound became lost among the rhythmic hum and the wind in the trees.

Corey felt as though he were moving through a tunnel. He seemed to be outside the confines of time and space, yet he was deep inside himself, where a dark cave was opening outward, and a healing pulse coaxed an infant to life. In this timeless space, it wailed in grief, it grew, and it gained a voice that resonated beyond the crumbling of the rock walls.

They were heading back the way they came. Corey felt amazingly light, and curiously energized as he followed Woody, who suddenly turned his head and tossed harsh words.

"What did you think you were doing?" Woody grasped the girl's hand firmly. "You might have gotten us into a lot of trouble!"

The comment surprised Corey. "Don't be so hard on the poor girl."

"The girl?!" Woody faced Corey directly. "I'm talking to you, Mr. Zombie. You know, the one who just walked right out in front of those people like he belonged there? Grabbing that black hat and pulling it over your head, strutting around laughing, dancing?"

Corey stared. "I have no idea what you're—"

"And then pulling whiskers, lighting cigarettes... chanting something like—what was it? 'I was dead, now I've come to life! Ho ho ho!' over and over."

Corey was speechless. Why would Woody make that up? All Corey remembered was stumbling onto a gathering in the woods and then...

There seemed to be a blank in his memory.

"It's like you were possessed," Woody said.

Corey shook his head. He didn't even believe in that stuff.

"I'm serious, dude. While they were singing and beating drums, you were shaking and gyrating all over—even drained one of those bottles."

Wide-eyed, the girl watched Corey closely, no longer attempting to run away.

"Then you put the hat back on the tree and collapsed, flat out."

Corey furrowed his brows. Something very strange had happened. Something on the inside.

Woody turned back, letting Gaby lead them through the trail, but he was still ranting. Corey ignored him and listened for the inner voice, the demon whisper—*You'll never have control*—that had plagued him since Key West.

But the voice was gone.

Chazy wanted to fill her empty nest, and her motherly instincts drew her to Gaby. It took a few days, but with Corey's help, Chazy finally found out that the girl's parents and brother had died in the hurricane. The only living relative was the man who allowed her a small mattress and beat her for eating too much.

Chazy consulted an attorney about adoption and decided to remain in Haiti until Gaby's fate was resolved.

9 NEW LIFE, SECOND WIND

JAY'S FAX

"It's coming through!"

"What's taking it so long?"

"That's a sonograph?" Steve screwed up his face.

"*Sonogram*, ducky! It's a picture of his baby." Sherrie tousled Steve's hair, which seemed to please him. It didn't hurt that she'd broken up with the guy from the *Sharp Aye.*

Finally, Jay grabbed the fax and tore out of the chart room. He halted in a patch of direct sunlight by the starboard rail. He narrowed his eyes and dropped his head as he held the fax under his nose.

"What's it look like?" Clarence—still *Sharkbait* to some—joined the others crowding around Jay.

"Is it a boy or girl?" somebody else said.

"There!" Jay stabbed the paper with an index finger and looked around in triumph. "I knew it would be smart—look at the size of that head!"

"That thing is a head?"

"No, that's the butt—"

"Well, it's got yours for sure—" Woody said.

Raucous laughter arose from the main deck, and each comment created more eruptions.

"Can't see the whites of his eyes yet!" Morris said.

"Can you tell the eye color?" Hannah said.

"No, not really," Morris patted her shoulder. "And even after they're open they all look blue for a while."

Woody raised his cream soda. "To the blue-eyed parents." He slapped Jay on the back. "Here's hoping for your sake, that baby's eyes stay blue!"

Everyone laughed and cheered, and Jay punched Woody with a right-left-right to the shoulder. It was obvious he was over-the-top happy and couldn't wait to get back to LouAnn.

Then the beginning divers were called to scuba class, and the group broke up.

Corey felt happy for Jay and told him so. "But don't screw it up. You're lucky to have her."

Woody sidled up to Corey. "Do I detect jealousy?"

Corey stared at him and realized something. "No. Not even a little."

"Good. You'll be the center of attention soon enough." He tried to hide a smirk as he turned away.

BIRTHDAY MAKEUP

It was mid-December, weeks after Corey's birthday, when Marty carried the flaming cake into the main salon where the early watches had gathered for dinner.

"Happy Birthday, Corey!" everyone shouted.

"Don't worry, it'll be good," someone said. "It's from the bakery." But mostly Corey heard singing along with Dice's guitar strums and felt the warmth of friendship. It had been a while since his "zombie" session in the woods, and though he had lived and worked aboard for months, he now felt more at home with his shipmates than ever. They were family.

"We missed your real day back in November." No cigarette dangled from Morris's mouth, and his shirt was clean.

"Yeah, with what's-her-name setting the place on fire," Woody added, to a chorus of laughter.

"The girl was a fireball, couldn't help it." Morris accepted a big slice of chocolate coconut.

"Plus we had a few other things on our minds back then," Stix said, tapping a rhythm on her deck shoe.

November seemed like years ago. Corey was sorry for Goldy's hurt feelings, but if she was unable to move on, that was her problem, not his.

He took a bite of cake. Since his Vodoun "exorcism," everything tasted better, and the dessert was delicious. He cut a piece for Gaby, who had come aboard with Chazy for the afternoon.

"Merci." The girl's face glowed as she took the slice and snugged herself closer to Chazy. Corey was glad the authorities had okayed her visit.

HEART TO HART IN WOOD

It was late in the day when Corey started carving the face inspired by the ship's figurehead. He could just imagine someone special arising from the lid of the box intended as a gift for that same someone. He smiled to himself. He'd never really intended it for Mom.

"Mind if I join you?" It was Grayson Fielding. "The thing about wood is..." He took out a piece of carved mahogany and oiled a rag. "Even old scarred wood has a soul inside that you can bring out by treating it right."

Corey relaxed as they worked side by side. Corey shaved thin layers to release the feminine face trapped in walnut while Grayce used his rag to rub a plaque on which a schooner had already emerged. Then the man pulled out a sheet of sandpaper along with a small chunk of oak that resembled a treasure chest. He started smoothing its edges. *Cool.*

"Did your dad teach you?" Corey asked.

"I had a good shop teacher." Grayce blew sawdust off the chest. He hesitated before adding, "My adoptive father was only good at drinking. Never met my biological parents."

Wow. Grayce grew up without his dad too. Corey continued to shape the walnut wood as he checked the photo of Sam next to him. Before he knew it, he was talking about his own father.

"When I found him, I wanted to knock him out, but the whiskey beat me to it."

"Ah," Grayce nodded his head. "Alcohol can mask the real person. My house sitter, Andrew, is fine—if you hide the Scotch." He muttered, "Just before I joined the ship, he'd made a breakthrough, but apparently it took a lot out of him."

Grayce held up the treasure chest and eyed it from an angle. "What you need to remember, Corey, is that who *you* are is not determined by whose blood runs in your veins." He lowered the chest and gave Corey a quick smile. "You are your own man." He started sanding some dark flecks in the grain then stopped. "But the imperfections can give you character. It's your responses to them that mold you into the person you are."

Grayce seemed able to look right inside him, and Corey felt a warm connection. As his nostrils filled with the rich smell of wood, he couldn't remember ever being so relaxed. When he had started carving, he'd struggled with every slice. Now his hands worked quickly and automatically, shaving a bump here, whittling an indent there. Words, too, came more easily.

"How did you know you wanted to sail, Grayce?" Corey asked, never taking his eyes from the carving.

Grayce turned his own work in the fading light. "I was studying to be a counselor." He paused and looked westward, at the diminishing blaze of orange sun. "But I needed to get away, be out in the open." He turned back with a grin. "I jumped on a sailing ship, like you, and I discovered I was a good teacher. I wanted to help kids who needed a focus." He ran his hand slowly over the rounded top of the treasure chest as they both adjusted their weight to a gentle roll of the ship.

Corey stroked the wooden face that conjured the softness of the real girl in his memory. "Do you...did you have a girlfriend?"

"Oh I've had a few." Grayce looked thoughtful. "But my partner is the sea. How about you?"

Corey lifted his head and looked out to starboard toward the distant coast of Cuba. Beyond that was the U.S. mainland, and much farther north...

"Only one that I really, you know." Corey stared at the carving.

"Oh." Grayce eyed the small wooden figure. "I wondered who your inspiration was."

"But I haven't had much luck." Corey grabbed some rags and began to wrap the carving for the night. "I messed up with her. I got played by the next girl, and I got robbed by the last one."

"Bad luck."

"Yeah, especially considering that last one was a fortune teller."

They looked at each other and burst out laughing.

"I had a few girlfriends—in my teens," Grayce said. "I was in my twenties when I found love..." He looked past the sails, toward the sea. "But if it doesn't work out, you substitute." Corey saw a gleam in his eye. "You find another passion and grab what treasures you can." He had opened an arm to the sea, now becoming a mass of darkness. A mist seemed to come over the man's eyes, and Corey waited to hear more about the treasures that were so enticing.

But the man started packing up his work. "The stars are coming out. By the way, happy birthday. I heard about your celebration."

"Oh yeah, there's an extra piece of cake in the galley." Corey didn't bother explaining why the celebration was delayed by so many weeks.

"Hmmm." Grayce looked down at the deck. He looked up and scanned the December sky then quickly raised his arm and pointed. "There it is. Your archer, Sagittarius."

Corey had stowed his sculpture in a canvas bag and started to place the carving tools in their case. He glanced up, still holding a chisel. Why the sudden interest in a constellation?

"Epsilon Sagitarii is a binary star, three-hundred seventy-five times more luminous than our sun. It's at the base of the bow. And see how the archer's arrow is aimed? It points toward Scorpio, a neighboring constellation."

"Hey that's—" Scorpio was Corey's horoscope sign, but he didn't want Grayce to think he believed in that stuff. Instead he lowered his carving tool and said, "Interesting."

Before disappearing into his cabin, Grayce turned back. "You may think you're unlucky, Corey, but don't give up." He shifted his gaze to Corey's bag—or was he looking at his chest? "Remember, what appears old and damaged can be made new with a little buffing."

Corey recalled how rough the wood had once been, before he had used the keen edge to transform the lump into art. He eyed the sharp blade in his hand and thought of the pain and struggles of his recent weeks. Had they smoothed his rough edges? Maybe. *But I could use some buffing.*

CHARLIE PICKS UP

"What's wrong with Mom?!" It was a new year, and the ship was just off the southern coast of Jamaica. It had been a couple of weeks since Corey had talked to his mother.

He couldn't help raising his voice to Charlie. Finding out there was a map was a surprise, but he no longer had anything to prove. And since that Vodoun experience, Corey had a sense of balance that smoothed his ups and downs.

Except where his mother was concerned.

Charlie was hiding something, Corey was sure of it. He asked again: "What's going on? Why are you answering Mom's phone?"

"Take it easy, son. She went for a walk and forgot to take her phone." He sighed. "Her PTSD is making her a little sensitive to...things."

"Things? What things?" It wasn't like her to forget her phone. "I thought Dr. Mason and the pills took care of that post-dramatic stress." Or whatever it was.

"She just gets a little anxious when people..." his voice trailed off, "make stupid comments."

Those bloggers! "She knows about them?" he shouted. "She shouldn't let those idiots get to her."

"That's what I've been telling her. But with all she's been through, you can't blame her for letting it bother her."

Charlie was right. Corey had over-reacted too, at first. He had wanted to punch "TruHart," "Lander," and the others who posted derisive comments. Then he realized Sam was right: the internet was full of dorks with nothing to do but take cheap shots. No one who mattered would pay any attention. Mom had to believe that.

"Listen, I'll worry about your mom," Charlie said. "Now, tell me about your adventures. You know," his voice softened, "you and I never got a chance to talk."

"Huh? Oh." Charlie had never questioned Corey's reason for sailing south, but he was no dummy. Charlie got around to the inevitable question.

"Did you stop in Key West?"

"Yeah, I did."

"Well?"

"I met him, Charlie. Three sheets to the wind—more interested in his bottle than in me."

"A drinker?" Charlie seemed surprised. "I wouldn't have thought that."

PORT ROYAL

The white sails of fifteen tall ships rippled in the tropical breeze as cannons boomed their salutes from Fort Charles. Crowds of tourists milled about the grounds of the fort and other historic buildings. The Fielding Foundation was partnering with a local coalition to raise funds for explorations of the old town.

Port Royal was the entrance to a natural Jamaica harbor. Old Fort Charles had protected the English military and its citizens and privateers in the seventeenth century. Now cannons held only empty threats, and the nearby military storehouse sat at a ridiculous angle to the horizon, as it had since a 1907 earthquake.

Corey could see fishing boats, piers jutting out from the palm lined coast, island greenery interrupted by sand and gravel roads, stucco and wood buildings, and stacked stone edging the island properties.

"So where are the saloons—you know, where they chased the wenches?" Steve said from his position near the helm.

"Dude, you've seen too many pirate movies." Dice swiveled back to the starboard rail.

"Those buildings are probably underwater," Brian said, capping a can of varnish. "And more to the north."

"Huh?" Hannah looked confused. "What are you all talking about?"

Darian sighed and looked aft from her perch on a deck box. "Don't you guys know? The old town sank in 1692."

"'Old Port Royal is an archeological site,'" Brian read over Darian's shoulder. "'Much of it sank upright, and it's well preserved, protected by the lower oxygen levels underwater.'"

"I'll bet it's a diver's dream, that and all the sunken treasure ships around here," Woody said.

"Awesome!" Dice said. "Let's go diving while we're here."

"You can't go," Jay said. "You're not certified."

Dice scowled and muttered, "I can snorkel at least."

The certified divers buzzed with excitement as they prepared for mooring.

Woody chewed with his eyes closed at the outdoor cafe. "There's something about this stuff." He lifted his gaze and sighed. "I mean we have pulled pork in Dayton, but this..."

"They sure know how to do it here!" Jay finished for him as he tore into his third piece.

"You know who would have loved this?" Darian said. "Chazy." But she was still in Haiti, awaiting the authorities' decision about Gaby's adoption.

Corey was sipping his cola and surveying their surroundings when Morris came by the cafe. What was different about him lately? He walked taller, seemed more alive. And no "cigarette" had dangled from his lips for days. *Must be the climate.*

"Let's see about touring that sunken city," Woody said as they finished.

"'There's a dive shop a block over." Corey wiped his mouth and pointed to his left without looking. His finger poked something solid. He turned to see what had blocked him and slowly raised his eyes to meet the captain's. He gave a silent thanks that he hadn't poked two inches higher.

Captain Harper took his hand out of her ribs and placed it on the table as she addressed everyone.

"I hate to break it to you, but they don't let just anyone dive here—even if you are certified. You have to have a permit." She smiled sympathetically, borrowed the spice shaker, and left to join the older crew at the bar.

Disappointed, the young people filed out to the street.

Woody broke the silence. "The captain only needs a skeleton crew after we deliver the aid packages tomorrow." They were down one crew member since leaving Chazy behind, so they would all have to work a little harder as they transferred supplies to the Relief Society trucks.

"At least we don't have to deal with distribution—the local group is taking care of it," Woody said. "Anyway, I hear there's a great self-guided tour around the island. I'll spring for car rental."

Nobody objected; by now they all knew about Woody's generous aunt.

TOUR JAMAICA

In Kingston, they went to the Institute of Jamaica, where the displayed chest of three thousand silver coins reminded them of sunken treasures they wished to explore. But as they rested by an open market, the reggae music and lulling sun cheered and relaxed them.

"Time to get a move on." Woody broke the spell, and they headed west.

Montego Bay had been a sugar harbor in the 18th century. Plantation slaves, torn from their homelands, had turned to Christianity, and an abundance of churches still salted the landscape.

They saw the museum honoring Bob Marley, the reggae performer.

They took a pontoon ride down the Black River, where fluffy orange-crested birds hovered, their long beaks bright red against the rain forest. Swampland alligators lay in wait in the channels as their boat passed.

"Protected by law." The guide nodded at one of the predators.

"What about us," Brian whispered. "Is there a law that protects us from them?"

Lily pads and green and reddish grasses dotted the waterscape, and several fishermen's huts were visible through the vegetation. Corey spied a man focusing on a fish below the water's surface as he aimed a harpoon.

"Doesn't he see that alligator looking at him?" he whispered.

"Oh, he and gator are old friends," the guide said. "Have a business agreement." Then he cracked a smile. "Man has much skill. Gator is no dummy."

They descended on a coastal market where fat fishes were selected and weighed. They saw white sand beaches lining the vivid green sea. Along the coastal waters were fishing boats, jet skis, and paddleboats. Farther along, divers soared from the cliff into the sea.

They took a bamboo raft, slicing through intense greenery as the barefoot guide steered with a long stick while overhanging branches protected them from the sun. Back in the car, they headed past Columbus Park, where Christopher Columbus had landed on his fourth journey to the New World. They walked the underground pathways of the native Arawak, where the stalactites and stalagmites, formed by dripping mineral deposits, reminded Corey of monster teeth ready to take a bite. *Must be because I'm hungry again.*

Bananas, mangoes, pineapples, coconut and unfamiliar vegetables imbued the air of the market place with fresh aromas. Corey tried a piece of raw sugarcane, chewed to extract the sweet juice, and spit out the fibrous wads. African coconut palms, citrus, melon, and papaya surrounded them, and the fragrance of vanilla pods filled their nostrils.

Island life was pretty close to paradise. *Only one thing missing.*

10 PIRATE LAIR

RELICS OF AN AGE

"It was an earthquake—about seven-point-five."

"We have them in California, but they don't demolish whole towns..."

"The buildings weren't built to code back in the sixteen hundreds."

"Plus Port Royal was hit by huge sea waves—"

"And the ground was like quicksand. The water table was only a couple of feet below the surface."

Corey watched the animated faces and felt the energy of his shipmates discussing what had happened to old Port Royal. He was proud of them; even Hannah had gained the confidence to express an opinion.

Underwater, archeologists had excavated part of a major street of the seventeenth-century town. Eating utensils, dishes, jewelry, and furnishings were on display in the nearby museum, and Corey's group used them to analyze and debate the actions of the residents. In Port Royal, even upstanding citizens had owned lavish items looted from Spanish galleons.

"Back then, people thought the earthquake was punishment for the debauchery."

"Because the city was a pirates' haven."

"Can you believe this stuff?" Steve said, ogling a strand of priceless jewels. "These were found in the home of a judge." He shook his head.

"Probably wanted it for his wife." Even William, usually quiet, voiced his opinion. "Bought it cheap off a privateer."

Corey's muscles tensed. "*Pirate*, not privateer," he said, narrowing his eyes at William. "There's a difference." Corey's own ancestors were privateers, authorized by the U.S.

government to engage enemy ships in the War of 1812, and he was proud of their contribution to the new nation.

"Actually," the guide cut in, "many privateers did cross the line into piracy. Both pirates and privateers brought in merchandise from all over the world, raising the general wealth of Port Royal. 'Decent' people went to church wearing the latest fashions and jewelry that people had been killed for."

Darian's voice was harsh. "Were these people aware they were contributing to bloodthirsty piracy?"

Dice challenged her. "Why shouldn't they take stuff from the enemy? To them, the Spanish were the bad guys."

"C'mon," Hannah said, her face flushing, "That was just an excuse!"

"No way!" Dice's voice filled the display room. "They were being patriotic—they were proud to display the spoils of their country's victory!"

What started as a lively debate threatened to turn into something darker. Was this how wars started? Corey was glad to see Grayce approach. He'd get things under control. The others clustered around the man.

"Nobody can come to an agreement," Steve said sourly.

"It's totally frustrating," Hannah added.

Grayce smiled. "That means I've done my job."

Corey's jaw dropped. "Huh?"

"I want to make you uncomfortable. We have to poke and prod, that's what makes us think about things and get to know how they work." He poked Steve good naturedly in the ribs and got a smile in return. "Especially the things that lurk beneath our skin." He grinned. "By the way, you might want to listen more and talk less, because your next assignment will be to argue against your own opinion."

Grayce was off his nut. Lafitte's betrayal of the British was understandable, but Corey couldn't justify stealing for your own gain, any more than he could justify a man traumatizing his son.

At sunrise, Corey and Woody were leaning on their elbows over the port rail as they looked west before a day of general ship maintenance. Then the *Golden Aye* would sponsor several days of three-hour sailaways for local youth.

"Would have been a perfect day for diving," Corey murmured. He imagined swimming between underwater buildings, snaking around corners of houses that stood upright just as they did in 1692. *What would it be like to find things no one has seen in two-hundred years?* Wait. He meant one-hundred. He must have been thinking about Patrice's treasure. But that wasn't what he was interested in now; it was history, knowledge. He forced himself back to the here and now.

"To think it's right out there, a few feet below us." Woody swept an arm outward. "Tempting us. And we can only dangle above it like—" He turned back toward the pier, shading his eyes. Something was clump-clumping along it.

Corey turned and saw Grayson Fielding wheeling a crate full of things dark and rubbery.

"Time to suit up." Grayce navigated his load up the gangplank and began tossing the contents of the cart in their direction. "Let's see what that underwater city has to show us."

Corey caught a flying wetsuit before it went over the rail. *Doesn't he know the rules?* Corey's eyes darted to Woody's as he cleared his throat. "Uh, well, they have restrictions..."

"Permits? I arranged for them weeks ago." Grayce winked. "I've been here before."

The students had buddied up and were all talking at once when Cracker called for quiet before turning them over to Grayce. They were eager to board and launch the small boat, but they knew this excursion was serious business, and they'd better listen to the details—like *don't take any souvenirs.* They stood near the hatch and listened as Grayce gave instructions.

Finally, he wrapped things up, saying, "Take care...the town is preserved just as it was on June 7, 1692, at 11:43 A.M."

They stared at him.

"Eleven forty-three?" Woody shifted his weight.

"C'mon," Dice whispered. "How could they know what minute it happened?"

"Good question," Grayce smiled at Dice, who avoided the man's eyes. Dice had come a long way; he probably didn't want to be thought disrespectful.

"See that buoy over there?" Grayce pointed. "It's over a church where one of the most interesting discoveries was made in the underwater town."

"A last-minute diary entry?" Hannah said.

"A clock?" Corey said.

"Close. A watch whose hands had stopped at eleven forty-three."

Near Harts Landing... YOU ARE GETTING SLEEPY

The minutes ticked by slowly as Auger listened to his grandmother.

"I've been thinking about that island. And that name, *Estar.*" She cocked her head. "I've had dreams...or were they memories?" Her eyes gravitated to Auger. "My granddad used to tell stories he'd heard about people and places before his time. I'm sure he mentioned an Estar. I assumed it was only a woman but—it was odd, the way he spoke. Looking back, I think he was talking about something else." Her eyes probed Auger's. "Did you know I can make people remember things?"

Auger scanned the floor. "Uh, Gran, did you get your meds today?" He leaned toward her and lowered his voice. "You know your grandfather is *dead*, right?"

"Oh Augie." Her eyes were bright. "Do you forget who made the cover of *Regression Today* three times?

Auger forced a smile. "Well, you, Gran, but..."

She glanced at her hands, and her voice was tinged with regret. "I've misused my skills." She glanced back at Auger. "But I want to make amends." She leaned forward. "I'm not just skilled at hypnotizing other people. I can do *self-hypnosis.*"

He stared at her.

"I mean, to help me recall the legends I heard from Granddad." She licked her lips. "But I'd have a better chance with the help of a trusted second party." She gave a shy smile. "Will you help me, Augie?"

Auger let out a breath. She *was* in her right mind. He scanned the script she propped up for him. She had really thought about this.

He began: "You are relaxing more deeply with every breath..."

BANKS ROBBER?

Corey drew oxygen from the respirator. He glided through blue-green water as flashes of color darted here and there. The fish were unlike those of the St. Lawrence.

He heard nothing but his own breathing as he caught an occasional glimpse of swirling sediment where other divers flicked fins or turned too quickly. Corey was careful to follow Grayce's movements, disturbing no sediment.

Grayce was pointing out buildings nearby as he held up fingers to show the number of each one as listed on the map they had studied. Corey gently altered his trajectory toward the buildings, aware that few people were allowed here, and even fewer got a personal tour by Grayson Fielding.

They were near the intersection of old Lime and Queen Streets, and below them was Building Three, a simple wooden structure. Next to it was One, a large brick building, which apparently housed a tavern as well as several shops. Building Two, on its other side, was made of wood and had suffered some deterioration. Numbers Four and Five were a complex of housing and shops. Coming around the back side of Five, Corey was able to make out first a cistern, and then the remains of several hearths as he passed to get a look at the street side of Building Four. This structure still had brick interior walls in place, but a section of floor and walls had been warped. When he backed away and got an overview, it was obvious why that structure had suffered a breach. From above the scene, the remains of another structure took on a familiar shape. It was as long as the building it overlapped, and lay at an angle to it. Corey recognized it because it was in the same form as his home of the last six months. A sailing ship had severed Building Four! The earthquake must have caused a wave that launched the ship over the street and through the building the day the town sank.

Corey had almost forgotten to keep track of Grayce, his diving buddy. He swam carefully toward the front of Building Five, where Grayce was examining something under a window. Then whatever the man held caught a ray of sun and seemed to reflect a flash of gold. Corey thought he saw Grayce slip the thing into a pocket of his diving suit. But then swirling sediment, sunlight, and water pressure could play tricks on your vision.

His shipmates were in a good mood at the cafe.

The setting sun cast a shimmering column of orange into the water beneath it. The sailors slurped frosted glasses of root beer as the sun sank into the sea, and the red-tinged ball of fire was soon swallowed by black hills of the main island.

"Too bad Grayce couldn't be here." Woody raised his glass of soda. "I'd give him a proper toasting."

"Where'd he go after we got out, anyway?" Brian said. "I thought he'd have us discuss and analyze all afternoon."

"Had to go check on other Fielding ships," Morris yelled over the noise of rowdy tourists at the next table, "from what I heard." He reached over, poked Corey in the ribs, and teased, "You fellows can't monopolize him all the time. He has other children to supervise." Before the "children" could protest, another voice cut in.

"Oh, Morris, you're the biggest child Grayce has ever seen."

Everyone looked up to see a striking woman, with brushed back sandy hair, wearing a sleeveless blouse and a flowered skirt; the toes of her sandaled feet were adorned with hot pink polish.

Morris choked on his punch before croaking, "You clean up very nice, Captain."

Corey sank into his bunk after a perfect day. "Grayce is all right, isn't he?"

Woody was surfing his laptop online. "Not everyone thinks so. Listen to this: *"R. G. Fielding: philanthropist or pirate? Perhaps it was his evil twin spotted near Pedro Banks today. Some say the thirst for treasure dies hard..."*

Corey sat up. "That's a lie!" Somehow he avoided hitting the wood beam, but his heart was racing like when he'd worried about Mom. "You heard Morris...he's with his other ships."

"Hey, I'm just reading a blog."

A blog. Corey lay back down. Nobody who knew Grayce would give it a second thought.

11 NEW DIRECTIONS

THE GREAT SACRIFICE

"What you love, you set free." Corey had heard that before, but now he began to understand. Grayce had loved a woman who chose another path, but he let her go and channeled his passion into helping kids.

The man had set his other love free, and Corey could too. Instead of moping, he could accomplish things. He gazed toward Haiti and remembered Grayce's words: "Take it one day at a time. Give your energy to those who need you."

When his controlling inner voice had vanished, along with it went Corey's impulsiveness. If and when the time came that Sam needed him, he would be there for her. Meanwhile Corey would help others. His inner turmoil was replaced by quiet confidence.

Corey set his sculpture of Sam on the hatch cover where he could see it. He caught the rhythm of a steel drum band on the radio as he repaired gear. Corey's body and mind were united in smooth movements—until the flow was interrupted by a fast talking news guy.

"...unauthorized activity at the Banks, one diver taken into custody, another may have gotten away with..."

That's harsh. Corey didn't need to hear what was wrong in the world. He went to change the station.

Corey twisted the dial through several blasts of static until he found another steel drum band that suited him. He turned back to midships just as the captain came toward him with an apologetic smile, holding out a sheet of paper.

"It was faxed in when you were down with the flu." Her eyes darted aft as she lifted her upper lip. "I've gotten distracted...must be the climate." She turned away. "Makes you feel like a young filly." Corey could almost hear a neigh in her voice.

He looked at the paper in his hand. *The map of Estar Island!* It had no key; it could be any island. Sure, he'd be happy if this map could put Mom's worries to rest. But what good would those squiggly lines do him in the Caribbean?

Near Harts Landing... THE BIGGEST CATCH

The four wheeler made tracks over the snow-covered ice, wavering slightly in the stiff breeze that channeled down the river valley and caused fishermen to pull scarves and earflaps to their heads. Samantha snugged her own padded hood and squeezed the sides of the vehicle as Auger sped them onward.

They passed fishing contestants boring holes with blue and red ice augers, fastening tip-ups with fish line to set over holes, and others relaxing in folding chairs, tipping back steaming thermoses. As the four wheeler raced downriver, they saw another fisherman struggling with a line, probably working a large pike and hoping to win the $1500 prize.

Sam had been avoiding Auger, though she was grateful to get that map. She was embarrassed that she hadn't sent it to Corey directly. Plus, Auger probably did it to get on her good side—though he swore he had no interest in her. Now she was forced to work with him as a festival assistant. They would help with the hockey tournament, the fishing derby, and the ice sculpture contest.

They had passed the eastern end of Rocky Island and were within sight of their target. The vibrations that had shaken Sam's derriere numb were now rattling her teeth. When Auger slowed down, the vibrations ceased. Both Sam and Auger jumped off and hurried, crunch-crunching over snow-covered ice, to the couple huddled next to a hole.

"Thank goodness," the pink-cheeked woman stammered.

"What a d-dummy I am!" The man had his arms folded, each hand inside the opposite sleeve. "So s-sorry to make you come all the way out," the man said. He had lost his gloves to his ice hole.

"Hey, we were passing by anyway," Auger said.

"Just glad we could help." Sam broke up a hand warmer pack and gave it to him, along with a large pair of mittens. "Sure you want to keep going?"

"You bet!"

"Who knows?" His wife chuckled as she waved goodbye and checked the tip-up. "Maybe we'll pull out the winning black-gloved pike!"

Auger and Sam headed farther downriver to check on some other fishing parties. As the four wheeler hummed along, Sam reflected on the past few weeks. She had been busy studying for exams and helping Randy with the books for the B&B. The mid-winter business had increased, thanks to the festival. But would it be enough? Randy had set up an interview down south at a pecan company to coincide with spring break. Sam was looking forward to seeing her grandparents, but she didn't want to live in Georgia.

As the four wheeler droned on, she allowed thoughts of Corey to surface. If he was running away from the online rumors and skeptics, he was taking it to great lengths. Was he still denying his feelings? Didn't he really want to come back, find Estar Island, and validate his ancestor's claim?

Most people couldn't relate to that obsession with heritage that the people of Harts Landing had. Here, the false Hart legacy had ruled for generations, and Corey's family had been burned by it. But Sam needed to reassure him that everyone who mattered believed he had uncovered the truth. And if it was proof he needed in order to give up his obsession with exotic places (and girls?), Sam wished more than anything that she could help him find the treasure.

Auger slowed the four wheeler a few hundred yards past the Sisters Island Lighthouse. Sam scanned the area but saw no derby participants. As Auger cut the engine, he stared past Sisters.

"What are you doing?"

He pulled off his fur hat, which attracted stray blond hairs, and he smoothed them down as he smiled back at Sam.

"I know where it is."

She rolled her eyes. "Where what is?"

He took out a thermos and offered her some hot cocoa. She shook her head in disbelief. He poured some steaming liquid into a cup and carefully took a sip.

"So..." Sam lifted her arms, palms up. "Are we here for the scenic view?"

Auger swung his right leg up and over the front of the four wheeler and sat sideways.

Is he really going to hit on me here? He needed to work on his approach.

Auger took a breath. "My grandmother remembered."

Sam was at a loss. "What?" She tried to be patient.

"Okay, I'm not a hundred percent convinced, but she said her great-grandfather talked about an island near Sisters." He nodded northwards toward the large island beyond the lighthouse.

"Early 1800s, some smuggler was in love with this woman, and he used the island to hide stuff for her. 'He'd smuggle the island itself for that woman.' That's what people said." Auger looked at Sam. "Can you guess her name?"

Sam's eyes widened. "Estar?"

Auger grinned and nodded. "So that's what they called the island: Estar Island." He took another sip then swept his gloved hand outward with a flourish. "Today we know it as Grenadier."

Sam looked to the north, snapping her mouth shut against the cold that finally penetrated her teeth, and surveyed the southeast coast of the Canadian island that dwarfed Sisters.

Within seconds, hot cocoa splashed all over the ice when Sam threw her arms around Auger, bulky jacket and all.

In Harts Landing... THE SECRET in the WASTE BASKET

Peg stared at a piece of paper as she wandered out of Corey's bedroom. Since he'd left, she had been in his room several times to dust and vacuum. She had even checked his trash. But she had never noticed the tiny paper stuck on a piece of gum at the bottom of his waste basket. Not until now.

From the kitchen, Charlie repeated a warning that hardly registered. "It's ten o'clock!" he called again. "Aren't you supposed to be one of the ice judges?"

As she entered the kitchen, the sight of Charlie reading the newspaper agitated her. "How on earth did Corey get this?" She shoved the torn scrap under his nose.

Charlie's head snapped up and the sports page fell to the floor. "He, ah..."

"Did you give it to him?"

"Now, don't get excited, of course I didn't *give* it to him." Charlie took off his glasses, shaking his head and muttering, "I knew I'd pay for this." He cleared his throat. "Look, he found the envelope in the trash and guessed the truth."

Peg dropped her hand and stared at the wall. "Was *that* why he went south?" She refocused on Charlie. "He knows who his father is?" Now Corey knew she had lied. She felt oddly exposed. Peg wasn't sure whether to feel angry or relieved. At least she didn't need to worry about him finding out any more.

"Are you going to tell him you know?" Charlie asked.

She hesitated. "I wouldn't want to complicate things for him right now." Maybe finding his father would help him get over the thing with Derrick. Peg knew what it was like to have an inner demon. She loved Charlie dearly, but now and then a memory of her own brought feelings she'd rather keep private.

She had been young. So in love! She was crushed to learn of Tina, Rob's fiancée. What could Peg do but get out of the way? It had hurt, and she had gone through a tough time. But otherwise, she would never have found Charlie.

His touch brought her back to the present, and she gave him a hopeful smile as he said, "Don't worry, hon, things will be okay."

MONEY IN THE BANKS

"Like this, Cheryl." Corey shaded his eyes from the blazing sun. "Pull up, roll back—keep doing it so the sail is even." Corey felt the swing of the footropes under him and adjusted his weight against the rolling of the ship. "And hang on tight. Never depend on footropes alone."

Among the broad stretches of canvas that hollowed to the breeze, the young Jamaican girl worked with determination.

Beads of sweat dotted her face and neck, yet she kept up with Corey while balancing on the foot rope.

Corey enjoyed working with kids. This would be the last sailaway before the *Golden Aye* headed north. Sure, there would be other towns on the way home, and other teens wanting to learn, but Corey would miss the bright smiles and contagious energy of the youth he'd met here in the Caribbean.

Cheryl was eager and quick. She kept her cool even through the rolling of the ship that made other first-timers green with seasickness.

Now the helmsman was avoiding an obstruction.

"I've heard the reefs can be dangerous," Corey said. "Aren't there a bunch of sunken ships around here?"

"Here? No, you're thinking of Pedro Banks—that way." Cheryl pointed southwest. "The Spanish *Genovesa* sank in the 1700s with gold, silver, and gems." She copied Corey as he secured the sail with a gasket.

"There's probably more than a billion dollars' worth at the Banks. Lot of people would like to get some of that." She smiled. "I'm one!"

"So why don't they? Can't they find it?"

"Oh they know where it is. The government is afraid hunters will damage the marine habitat and steal treasure that belongs to Jamaica. Treasure hunting is banned."

Corey leaned over the yardarm and looked to the south. "So you're telling me," he stroked the warm canvas with his fingers, "there's over a billion dollars in treasure out there, and nobody dives for it?"

"I didn't say that." Cheryl mirrored Corey's position and fought the swing of the mast to balance herself on the yard. "I said they aren't supposed to."

In Harts Landing... PEG SCHEMES

Peg had mixed feelings. It was just before the final judging of the Thousand Ice-Lands sculpture contest, and she stole a few moments in the warm-up shack. Charlie was there, recovering from the wind's bite after measuring fishing derby entries.

Peg stamped off the snow and rubbed invisible mud from her boots as she confided what she'd just learned. "That woman is up to something!"

"Here we go..." Charlie groaned, handing her a mug of hot tea. "Isn't it possible Mackenzie's turned a leaf?"

Peg nearly choked on the tea. "Right. She sees that journal page and suddenly, even though nobody else has ever heard of it, she can say which one is Estar Island?"

"Look, it's possible she did hear of it as a child. And she wasn't herself when, you know." He didn't mention last June. "She had that condition, and I'm sure she regrets it." He opened the shack door, and his breath hung in the air. "Everyone deserves a second chance." He hesitated before saying, "Where would you be if my sister hadn't given *you* one?"

Peg said nothing as she picked lint from her wool coat and walked with him to the marina lot. Instead of boats, it was now populated with frozen cartoon characters, animals, and even heavenly bodies, all competing for prizes.

"Apparently, Corey showed that journal page about Estar to Sam, who showed it to Auger, who showed it to his grandmother." Peg paused in front of a bust of Einstein. "And I thought Auger was a good kid."

"He is a good kid—" Charlie interrupted himself. "Hey look at that hair!" He gently touched twisted strands on the head of the frozen genius. "How'd they get those icicles to do that?"

Peg knew he was trying to distract her, but she was perfectly capable of handling this job and discussing Mackenzie "Hart."

"Okay, so maybe Auger was innocent, wanting to help Sam get information for Corey." She carefully set her tea mug down on a brown spot on Einstein's "desk" before grabbing a notepad from her pocket. Charlie scowled as he lifted the cup and handed it back to her, pointing out the circular impression and muttering that an ink well was not part of the sculpture. She ignored him and proceeded to the miniature solar system.

"I don't know what made Auger think his grandmother would be any help. I'll never trust her." Peg sipped her tea then absently set the mug on an ice model of Earth.

Charlie picked up the mug again. "Do you want to start a global warming incident?" He was trying to make her laugh.

She glared at him. "Work with me. The woman tried to kill me!"

Charlie tried to say more, but she kept going. "And I don't care how much she's medicated, she'd find a way to game the system."

If Mackenzie Hart had an opportunity for gain, she wouldn't hesitate to cross Peg and Corey. But what was the woman trying to do? Did she just want to see Peg and Corey chase treasure that wasn't there? No, that wasn't like her. She would have to get something out of it. Somehow, she had more information than she was letting on.

Charlie had left, and Peg was writing an evaluation of Sculpture Number Six when she heard crunching snow. A soft voice buzzed in her ear: "I, um, don't think Mrs. Hart meant for Auger to share that information. So, you know, maybe you could keep it..."

Peg's words came out automatically even as her mind rushed to new conclusions: "Oh, don't worry Samantha. We wouldn't want her to think I know anything."

Now there could be no doubt. Mackenzie *was* trying to hide information! Grenadier was so big it would take forever to explore all the areas that conformed to the shape on the map, but Mackenzie planned somehow to cheat Peg out of finding that treasure. Even from jail. Well, Peg could not let herself be intimidated by this woman any more.

Peg slipped her notepad into her pocket as she took a last look at the larger-than-life Pinocchi-Ice. She touched her own nose and ran her finger over its altered contour; she remembered the shocking impact of rocks once again, but this time, she didn't freak out. This time she had a focus.

We'll see who's grown the longer nose.

Mackenzie Hart had tried to rob Peg of her memory and her heritage, and even if she had to break her own rules, Peg would not let that woman beat her again.

She never thought she'd use it, but she had a trick up her own sleeve.

Near Harts Landing... MACK PLANS

"You'll need help," Mackenzie said to Oscar.

"No problem, I found somebody on a treasure-hunter site. The guy is definitely motivated."

"Good." She smiled. Oscar was well trained.

She wrote something on a notepad. "This is my man on the Commission up north. He must make the *rules* clear about permits."

Once she understood him, dear Augie had become quite reliable. Of course she had heard the rumors, like everybody else, about an "Estar Island" having treasure, but its location had been a mystery even to Mackenzie. By bringing that extra journal page and "helping her remember," her grandson had given Mackenzie a chance to make things right.

There was work to be done. Though coastal waters were now imprisoned in ice, preparations could be made. She was a well-connected woman. Oscar would make arrangements and get the original maps of "Estar." With those and the journal map Auger found—which she had memorized before hiding—she was sure to zero in on the specific site.

And there were other resources to tap.

12 MOTIVATIONS

COVERT PARTNERSHIP

Standing in the chart room, Grayson Fielding tapped his foot until the fax machine emitted a screech. He had just returned to the *Golden Aye* to find only a skeleton crew. The others had been given leave to go snorkeling.

He snatched the warm paper and scanned it. The outline of the island meant nothing to him...yet. She had come to the right guy. Grayson had experience and resources. He took a deep breath. Just another job.

Who was he fooling? He was excited to think fortune had put this opportunity in his grasp. He allowed himself a smile as he slipped into his cabin to change before going ashore.

MAP MISPLACED

Corey knocked on Grayce's cabin door. Wasn't he back on board by now? Well, back or not, Corey had to get the book Cracker wanted. Some of the trainees needed to prepare for their Able Bodied Seaman's certification test and needed the study guide. Corey waited at the door. Nothing.

Hadn't Grayce told Corey to "Take life by the helm"? Corey nudged the door open and entered. He looked around. Desk with notebooks and a few sailing magazines, calendar and charts on the wall over the desk, small bed stand by the tidy narrow bunk... Something on the top of a bookcase caught his eye. A magazine cover portrayed brilliant gold pieces spilling from a treasure chest under the caption, "Money Still in the Banks." Smaller print declared the article was about a sunken ship at Pedro Banks, near Jamaica. But what distracted Corey was the loose paper sticking out from under the magazine. A sheet with blobby lines forming an irregular closed shape. *The map of Estar Island!*

Corey didn't remember leaving his map here. He must've been distracted that day he'd come in to borrow a book on sailing history. Corey needed to hang on to this. He put the map in his pocket.

He hastily grabbed the study guide from a bookcase shelf. An envelope fell to the floor, and as he crammed it back into place, the words *Robert G. Fielding* disappeared behind a book.

CALLING NAMES

The ship had left Jamaica behind, as well as January.

Corey flipped open his phone. Service had been unreliable until they approached the coast. Finally, they were nearing the mainland and Mom got through to *him*.

"I need to talk to you." No "hello," no "sweetie."

Then her tone changed. "By the way, the festival was a success—we drew two thousand visitors!" Now she was rambling, avoiding something. *What is she afraid to tell me?*

"...and Charlie saw Randy selling off their stuff—so sad about the B&B—I'm sure he hated to ask his folks for help." What was she talking about?

"Speaking of which, Randy and Sam were flying south to visit—took one of those small connecting planes..."

He heard her take a breath. "Look, Corey I have something to tell you. I just didn't know how—"

He waited.

Nothing.

"Mom? What is it?" Did something happen to Sam's plane?"

Still nothing. "Is Sam Okay?" he shouted into the phone.

He'd lost the connection. He was seized by images of a small plane buffeted by the March winds over the Adirondack Mountains.

"Hey, what's with you?" Woody stopped as he headed down the pier. They had moored near Jacksonville, Florida, to get supplies and pick up a crew member from another Fielding ship. They were shorthanded because Jay had flown back to Montreal.

Corey grimaced again and pocketed his phone. It was his third try. He dropped to a bench.

"Still no answer."

"Sorry, bud....but I gotta run." Woody had to meet the new crew member.

"What I do is close my eyes." Another voice cut in. It was Grayce. "Look at the world as if from space, and see all the oceans." Grayce was standing next to Corey's bench, arms opened broadly.

He gazed at Corey, his eyes catching the late afternoon rays. "Anything you want to talk about, son?" He sat down.

Corey breathed the words out: "It's Samantha."

"Your figurehead."

Corey explained the phone call. "Now my stomach hurts and I can't think of anything else."

"I hear you," he said softly. They both sat looking at the water curl over itself as an outgoing motorboat cut a pathway to the east. Then Grayce turned to him.

"Corey, you have an awesome power that lies inside you." He was pointing at Corey's chest. Corey wasn't sure what he meant, but he trusted the soothing voice. "And you can access your own sea of tranquility whenever you're willing."

Grayce was a smart man. Corey closed his eyes and listened. The voice was soft and rich.

"Travel the rivers in your mind, pass the troubles like islands."

Corey felt his muscles relax.

"Go deep."

Corey felt as though he was swirling down a big drain.

"Find your core, the stable center where nothing can touch you.

When Corey opened his eyes, he had not solved anything, but he felt better. He had some time; he didn't have to be anywhere. He chatted with Grayce about nothing in particular, and he watched the activity on the ship as if through a hazy lens: Morris laughing with the captain by the companionway; Woody carrying a sea bag aboard behind the new crewmember, who wore a hoody; Darian and Hannah coiling line, looking up at them in surprise.

Corey realized it was pointless to worry about things he had no control over. He was in his sea of calm.

Until he heard a familiar voice shouting an old nickname.

"*Worder Deserter!*"

It was the new crew member. Goldy.

She was greeting old friends between complaints about life on the *Weather Aye.*

"...and I haven't even seen my favorite hair pin since I left the *Golden Aye*– Hey, keep up with me, *mate.*"

Woody didn't say a word as she harassed him all along the main deck. He must've found his own sea of tranquility.

A feeling of agitation was spreading through Corey's muscles, but he thought now he could calm himself. Maybe seeing Goldy was a test. He was glad to have Grayce beside him as he again heard that voice holler *"Worder!"*

Corey turned back to his mentor for reassurance. But instead of warm support, the man was giving Corey an icy glare through slits of amber. Fielding got up and left abruptly when the captain called him.

What had Corey done to deserve that look?

SAVANNAH

Corey still hadn't heard back from Mom, but he tried not to think about it.

At least he had ship maintenance to keep him busy. As he prepared the hull for new paint, he kept his calm as best he could. Whenever he heard Goldy's voice, he avoided her. She was on a different watch, and she had been preoccupied with updates from Woody.

Corey was opening a can of paint amidships when Grayce approached. He hadn't spoken with Corey since they'd shared a bench in Jacksonville.

"Been meaning to ask you." He seemed hesitant as he settled near the hatchway. "The new girl—Goldy is it? Does she know you pretty well?"

Corey stared at him. Where was this going? He scowled and returned his eyes to the paint as he mumbled, "Doesn't like me much." He dipped his brush in the can. "It's a long story."

"She called you *Worder*...I've heard that name. You're from the St. Lawrence, right?"

Corey's hand froze before reaching the can. He had only used the name *Redrow* since coming aboard. He stuck the brush in the can and looked at Grayce, wondering where he could have heard the name before Goldy blurted it.

The man was staring at his own hands, clasped around his knee. "I must have seen it in that article. You know, about the revised history at Har—er, some Landing."

"The article?" Oh yeah. The story had been published in some big newspapers.

Grayce continued. "I think it mentioned a woman, originally a Worder—"

"She's Peg Stowe now," Corey said.

Grayce looked up to meet Corey's eyes. The man stopped breathing, and there was a look Corey had never seen. It almost reminded him of himself when he froze up. Then Grayce put on a look of indifference. "You...probably don't know her well."

"She's my mom."

Was it the clouds covering the sun that made the man's face go gray? His eyes grew wide before he got up and paced. He stammered. "Y-you just turned...seventeen?" Then he mumbled something like, "That means mid-March."

The man suddenly took off toward his quarters, muttering something like, "Guess she got over me pretty fast."

Corey stared after him as his brush dripped to form a sticky pool on the deck.

A GHOSTLY YOUNG LADY

"C'mon, it'll take your mind off things," Woody said after Corey tried his mother again. He led Corey, Hannah, and Dice to a street corner where they boarded a bus. "It's just a few minutes away." When it stopped, they were at a Savannah cemetery, and some hokey actors were trying to convince the tourists they were witnessing something otherworldly.

Corey looked at Woody in mock disgust. "A ghost tour?" He shook his head and chuckled.

"Yeah, well, Goldy thought it was pretty good." His face turned pink. Since when did Woody care what Goldy thought?

It turned out that Savannah was full of secrets.

They visited an estate that had changed hands many times because the household ghost was picky about owners; an old house where people claimed to see a ghostly sea captain; and a place where the breakfast table was mysteriously set each morning. Finally, they entered an old plantation house with dark shutters.

The petite young guide, Gena, had long dark hair and a serious face. "In the early 1800s, the lady of the house found her husband with the maid in the servants' quarters. She went upstairs and threw herself off the balcony to her death."

The guide led the tourists up the white staircase to the second floor, where they viewed the balcony. Corey and his friends stayed at the rear of the group.

"Okay, so it's weird," Dice whispered. "That doesn't mean there's a ghost."

After touring the upstairs, they had descended the stairs and headed down a hallway when Corey heard a showering of particles near a side door. A dusting of plaster had settled on the floor near the sitting room.

The guide apologized. "That's happened a couple of times..."

"Wait for it," Corey whispered. "She'll tell us it's from a ghost walking around on the upper level!"

"The second tour must've started upstairs." She looked at the ceiling. "For now, let's just avoid walking there." When an employee came with a broom and started sweeping, Corey was almost disappointed.

They followed the guide to the servants' quarters, where they peered through a wood frame doorway into a small room with an old dresser and narrow bed.

"The confrontation took place here between the wife, husband, and maid," Gena said. "Since then, people have seen and heard odd things."

"I've heard plenty of odd things," Corey snickered to Woody. "Where's the proof it's a ghost?"

As if to answer, the guide said, "What about evidence? Well, it happens that Authentic Haunts International has done an investigation."

"Hey, those guys are supposed to be legit," Woody said. "Scientists, systematic methods, sensitive equipment..."

Gena continued: "One of the things that AHI did was to secure the area and set up a recording system."

"Bet it's just the wind," Corey said. "She'll say it's a ghost."

"Shh, she's gonna play the recording."

At first they heard nothing but static, and Corey gave a "told-you-so" look. Then the silence was broken by shrieks and vocalizations. They were clearly human sounds.

Hannah was shaken. "How could that be?"

Dice tried to laugh it off but sounded unsure.

"That's the real deal," Woody said, his eyes popping. He was buying into it.

"Come on, somebody messed around with the recording." Corey was still pretty sure the whole thing was silly.

The guide had moved on to a story about a lady named Sheila who lost her lover. "Most ghost stories involve people haunting the place where they died. But Sheila died in Jamaica before her ghost came north looking for the man she loved, who had fought here in the Civil War."

If a ghost came north to get here, could one travel south? Corey felt his face flush. Now he was thinking of Sam as a ghost? Ridiculous! But what if she *had* become a ghost? Would she come looking for him?

He followed the group back through the house to exit the front door. Before they got there, Corey gasped.

Near the sitting room, a young woman appeared, the color of ash. A sun bonnet framed a sad face.

A face just like Sam's.

He blinked at the vision. Was he that obsessed—to see her *here*? Corey ignored the group as he gave in to the specter and felt his skin prickle. It drew him like a magnet. Could it be true? Could people return as ghosts? Had Sam gone to the "other side"? As he drew near, he felt his knees buckle under, and he struggled to walk upright. He couldn't deny it: before him was the face of the girl he loved! Conflicting emotions swirled through his body: desire, anger, sadness. He had wanted her so and gone through so much, and now she had finally come to him...as a *ghost?!*

As he looked at her face, his emotions funneled into a new wave of shock. Her mouth had dropped open and her eyes grew large. Could ghosts be surprised?

"Corey?" She blinked and wiped a cheek with one hand as she shook white dust from her hair, and the ghostly young lady transformed into the living Sam. Suddenly Corey was feeling real arms squeezing him in a tight hug.

He sank into her embrace, his own eyes swimming in liquid relief. They hung onto each other for several moments before they drew back, each staring in wonder at the other. Their words tripped over each other.

"How did—?"

"What are you—?"

They both laughed. They made their way outside and found a moonlit bench in the sultry evening, where they sorted out the events that had brought them together.

Sam was killing time while Randy finished a meeting at the Blue Falcon Restaurant down the street. Then they would drive back to her grandparents', where they would stay two more nights. She told Corey about her hopes for a scholarship, her projects, and the winter festival. And how she couldn't stop thinking about him.

"But," she added shyly, "I thought you were with that Swedish girl."

"I—I thought you were with Auger..."

Each stared at the other until shock turned to laughter, and again their words collided.

"So sorry—"

"Should've known—"

They grinned silently at each other until her eyes drifted to his arms.

"You know, you look really...*fit*." She stroked his bicep and added, "A little scary."

"I haven't changed." He shifted closer to her, reached out, and brushed a fleck of white dust from her cheek.

Her eyelids were closing, and her head was drifting closer to his. Was he about to kiss a "ghost"?

He leaned in. He closed his eyes. His lips softened.

"Corey, honey!" The voice jarred him. He opened his eyes and turned to see the last person he wanted near Samantha.

Goldy walked over to Corey and sat right on his lap, wrapping her arm around his neck.

"I've been trying to tell you—I found my tortoise hair pin!" She lowered her voice to a whisper loud enough for Sam to hear: "I left it in your bunk, sweetie." She winked at Corey. "You know that space by the wall, where things slip through the cracks?" Then she added. "Just beyond your reach!"

Goldy got up, gave Sam a sweet smile, and turned back to Corey saying, "See you later, darlin'!" She sauntered with a sassy wiggle toward the corner, where Woody seemed to be hypnotized by her approach.

Corey felt sicker than the first time he'd climbed the mast. He hardly dared breathe. He glanced sideways at a stunned Samantha.

"Was that girl...really in your bunk?" She furrowed her brow and narrowed her eyes. "With you?"

Corey stuttered, "No...I mean yes—well, it didn't mean anything."

Sam's lips were stiff. "You were together...with her—" she choked, "and it didn't mean anything?" She stood up. Then she turned to him and punctuated her words with stiff fingers: "That's how you treat women?" Sam stared at him for a moment before running toward the Blue Falcon. Long after she disappeared, her look of disgust was still etched in Corey's mind.

PATIENCE

Was he back to square one? Would Corey ever see Sam again? Finding his calm spot only helped so much. He needed advice, but he wasn't sure Grayce would want to help him. Not after that last time on deck, when he'd weirded out on Corey.

But Grayce seemed to have forgotten about that, and he encouraged Corey to spill the latest episode of his love life.

"It's a roller coaster." Corey spread his arms and dropped them. "I was almost ready to give up on Sam, but now that I've been with her..."

Corey had screwed up by misreading Goldy, but hadn't he paid the price? How much more would he have to endure?

"Sam was really upset," he said out loud.

"Look, Corey, if it's in your stars, you'll work it out."

Corey was irritated. He would never dream of disrespecting Grayson Fielding, but—well, Sam was *real* now. He'd felt her silky skin against his. How could he wait for the stars to bring her back to him?

THE MAKE UP

At lunch the next day, Corey shoveled potatoes, corn, and roast beef into his mouth; he was surprised by his own appetite, not to mention the improvement in Marty's cooking. Somehow, a dream of binary stars convinced him that his problem would work itself out.

Other crew members in the salon were teasing each other about last night.

"Was that you I saw in the scuppers with a redhead, William?" Brian said.

"Wasn't me, I was on watch!"

Even Morris contributed to the gossip: "I'm sure I saw our little red-haired girl in a dark corner."

"Yeah, but I never thought I'd see her with *that* guy," someone said.

"I'm glad she's back!" Morris exaggerated his voice on the way out as Goldy herself appeared. He extracted a "cigarette" from his pocket and held it near her head. "I needed my lighter!" The crew around the table erupted with laughter.

Goldy smiled sweetly then directed a piercing gaze at Corey. "I have a surprise for you."

Not again. "Thanks, but I'm full up on surprises. Closed for business." He studied his food as he continued to eat.

The table had become quiet as the others found excuses to leave.

"Oh, don't carry a grudge, sweetie," Goldy smiled. "I figured, since you couldn't have the real love of your life—*moi*—I'd give you a consolation."

"I don't want anything you have." The girl Corey had considered his best friend was now just annoying.

"I said to myself..." She put one hand on her hip and twirled her hair with the other. "I said, look Goldy, if the guy would to go to such lengths for this girl, enough to sacrifice *me*—" Her voice filled with drama. "Well, he must be insane, in which case I wouldn't risk having his children. Or, you and this girl..." She dropped her arms, along with the attitude, and her voice softened. "It's the real thing."

What was she trying to pull?

She stood aside. When Corey saw Samantha smiling shyly from behind Goldy, he jumped up and hit his head on the cupboard.

"I told her that you were too lame for me, and would she please get you out of my hair?" She moved to let Sam pass through the door.

"Anyway," Goldy said, looking down. "I guess I assumed things. Someone had to hit me over the head." A voice barked orders from topside, and Goldy turned to go out, saying with a grin, "A bossy dude, but one I can count on."

Corey barely heard Goldy as Sam took his hands in hers.

WEAR MY BRASS

Corey felt like a human decoy as he directed a "Quaaack!" across the table at Sam.

Sam quacked back at him before pulling the orange plastic away from her own mouth. She grinned and spoke in human: "I must say, that bill looks natural on you."

They had taken a tour on an amphibious vehicle, where they had received their very own "duck bills." Then they'd checked out the Maritime Museum's history of sailing display, and finally found this outdoor cafe for a late lunch. Sam kept looking at something in her lap.

What is she doing—texting? Corey felt neglected until Sam looked up and said, "Dot-dot-dash, dot-dash-dot, dash-dot-dash-dot, dot-dot-dash, dash, dot."

Oh, *duh!* He pulled out his own Morse code guide as she repeated the message. He grinned, happy that she thought he was cute. "Ditto," he said.

A date on the town had been a good idea. Six months had changed them both, and they needed time to get used to each other. She admired his deep voice, his bulging biceps, and his confident walk. He noticed how mature she looked with her shorter haircut, and how her eyes became consuming flames when she launched into one of her "causes." He didn't want to miss a thing: how she laughed at the duck bills, how she cocked her head to hear the waitress, even how she walked the cobblestones with her slow-motion hopscotch, her flowered skirt swishing against her legs.

The twilight sky turned inky and the water below flashed with sea life as they stood at the ship's rail. Sam's hair glowed in the moonlight, and Corey couldn't resist stroking it. Then he had a sudden urge.

"Ouch!" Sam drew back. "What was that for?"

"Sorry." Corey rubbed her arm. "Didn't mean to pinch that hard." Was the girl of his dreams really on his ship? On his deck?

Sam looked up at the moon for a moment before turning back. "Corey I've wanted to be with you since last summer."

Corey's smile widened to rival the ship's beam.

"I'm glad your captain let you switch watches," she said. "The 'Cannonball' must be a real romantic!" She laughed then let her eyes go soft and tilted her head close to Corey's.

This was the moment. He wouldn't wait any longer to taste the lips that had teased his memory since August. He was aware of all he had endured—the torture of wanting something, failing, and then surrendering to fate—as he leaned toward Samantha.

Corey drank in her aroma, and he felt his lips touch hers. As he immersed himself in Samantha, he knew that everything had been worth it. Her kiss melted away everything else; it was an eternity within a moment.

Corey had never felt this way about anyone, and he wanted to mark the occasion. The jewelry box wasn't finished; besides, he would rather give her something she could wear.

"I wish I had a ring," he murmured.

Samantha gave him a teasing smile. "I'll take a rain check if you'll do that again."

He lifted her chin and kissed her, this time pulling her into him as their lips mashed together.

"Ouch."

He leaned back as she put her hand on his chest to feel the metal hidden under his shirt. He pulled the lanyard over his head and smiled.

He looked up at her as he bent down on his knee and held out the brass. "Would you wear...my buckle?"

She suppressed a giggle as she took it and looped the cord over her head, "Oh, Corey! I will keep it with me always." She gazed at the object before swinging it over her shoulder and diving into his open arms. Corey devoured her lips and was exploring further delights.

This is too good for public viewing. He began to move her toward the bow when her cell phone went off. She brought the buckle back to rest under her neck as she answered. It was Randy.

Corey frowned and paced the deck with a selfish wish: *Maybe he didn't get the job.* Corey had finally committed himself to the ship until it returned to the St. Lawrence, and he did not want to disappoint the captain. But would Sam still be there when he returned home?

When she turned back to face Corey, her eyes were watery. "I have to move down by August." She pulled a tissue from her purse. "I was hoping the winter festival would have made a difference."

Corey's mind swirled. He should have expected this. It was just one more of the obstacles life had been throwing his way. He willed himself into his calm spot as he listened to Sam.

"Randy can't keep up with the costs. Grandpa can help cover us until summer, but Randy says we have to be practical." She dabbed her eyes as Corey stroked the back of her neck.

There goes our senior year together.

"If we just could have gotten over this hump, I know the B&B could have made it." Sam shook her head.

Corey thought of something. It was a long shot, but hadn't he learned to keep an open mind?

"Look, I've got that map of Estar Island. When I come north, we could look for the treasure, you and me."

She smiled weakly. "I'd love to search with you, but it's a big island—your mom told you, right? Plus I'll be busy right up to when we leave. I'll be working on Dark Island as a tour guide."

Her sentences were running into each other, but Corey caught that last thing and raised his brows.

"I start in mid-May," she added.

"So, you're working at Singer Castle," Corey said aloud. He knew she would have been honest with her employers, and he wondered: Why would they hire someone who might be leaving mid-season?

13 THE RACE IS ON!

ESTAR REVEALED?

"Hey, did you grow another foot?" Randy gave Corey a hearty backslap when he came aboard with Sam before flying north. The man was tall, but Corey could now meet his dark gaze without straining his neck. Randy asked about classes and seemed surprised to hear that Corey was getting grades in the nineties in all subjects.

"And without Sam's help?!"

Corey was warmed by Randy's enthusiasm, but he was glad when Captain Harper dragged the man off for a show-and-tell about sailing. Corey wanted to pick up with Sam where they'd left off.

It seemed like only a moment later that Randy was tugging Sam's arm, and then she was gone.

Corey wanted to feel sorry for himself, but there was a problem to solve, and he needed to use his head. He had a map, and maybe that treasure could help save the B&B. What was it Sam had said—something about a big island? And Mom?

Mom! He felt a stab of guilt. After finding Sam, he'd completely forgotten Mom's phone call.

He tried her cell number, and this time he got through. Charlie answered.

"I was just writing an ad for early summer help," he said. "I'll only have Derrick on weekends since he got a management job. Anyway, your mom has her hands in the batter—first chance she's had to cook since fall," he laughed.

"She was trying to tell me something, and I—"

"Ah, I think what your mother wanted to say," Charlie lowered his voice, "was that we found out where Estar is."

"What?" Corey's mind started churning. Hadn't Sam mentioned something about Mom and the island? Maybe things were falling into place. "That's fantastic!"

"The Hart woman remembered something her granddad had said. Turns out it's Grenadier Island."

Grenadier! That made sense with what the journal said. "I can use the map to do a search," Corey rushed on. "And when I get back—"

"Uh, about that..." Charlie hesitated.

"What?"

"That's not all your mom needed to tell you." He cleared his throat. "What you should know is..." He sighed. "She told him, too."

"Told who what?"

"Your father, Rob, about the map."

It took a moment to register. *No!* The phone almost cracked in Corey's grip.

Charlie sounded defeated. "I was against her emailing him after you said he was drinking. But she's so paranoid, thinking the Hart woman wants to cheat her. Plus, she didn't know anyone else with experience."

Corey felt sick. "He'll just steal it for himself." Sure, Corey's father had looked harmless when he was passed out on his porch in Key West, but if he had the chance for treasure... "You can't let her tell him where it is."

"She already faxed him the map."

Corey's heart sank. "If he finds the treasure, he'll take it and run."

Charlie was quiet before saying, "Your mother's still fragile." His voice cracked. "I'm afraid if Rob double crosses her, she'll get worse."

Corey bit his lip. "We've got to find the treasure first! When does...Rob get there?" He stuck out his tongue at the distasteful name.

"It takes time to get the Canadian permits, but he plans to start by June."

The *Golden Aye* was not to return to the Thousand Islands until June. Corey had to find a way to get there before his father. He could ditch the *Golden Aye* and fly home... But he didn't really know how to get started on a treasure hunt. How would he get permits? What equipment would he need?

What Corey did know was that he had a fire burning in his chest—but it wasn't for gold. It was to keep Rob from stealing Mom's peace of mind.

Now Corey knew the truth: Key West was child's play—a no-risk face-off with a temporarily weakened man. The *treasure hunt* was what Corey had been training for. This was where he had to confront his father at full strength. The stakes were high, and Corey would have to use all his resources.

TREASURE ALLIANCE

The captain announced that several port cities had requested that the *Golden Aye* join their battle re-enactments. Her lip twitched into a smile. "Seems they need a crack gunner." She had responded in the affirmative, and it would be weeks before the *Golden Aye* would head across the Gulf of St. Lawrence.

It was mid-April, and Sam had left days ago with a promise to meet Corey in Harts Landing when he returned in early June. But he had to get to Grenadier Island early enough to find the treasure before Rob made off with it. How could

Corey beat him? He had to be calm and think it through, like Grayce would.

If only Corey knew someone really smart and experienced in treasure hunting.

When the answer hit him, Corey laughed out loud.

Duh.

Corey explained the situation, and Grayce's brows met in a scowl. Would he even consider helping Corey?

A smile crinkled around softening lips. "Yes, I remember something in that article, something about British treasure hidden by your ancestors." Grayce's eyes shifted from Corey to the horizon and back.

Corey let out a sigh of relief. "The thing is, we know what island it is. The problem is, Mom thinks the old lady is out to steal it, so she's desperate." He paused to make sure Grayce was keeping up. "So anyway, I found out she told *him* too."

"Your...father?" Grayce's smile vanished. "Isn't this the guy you met recently, the one who traumatized you as a kid?"

"She's in denial—she doesn't understand what he's really like," Corey said. "I saw what he was before he passed out on his porch."

Grayce furrowed his brow. He said nothing for several minutes as he stared over the starboard rail toward the east. Finally he turned to Corey.

"You're really committed," Grayce turned and squinted back at the horizon. "I have the feeling nothing will stop you once you're fired up." He scratched his head. "I think I know where you're going with this." He grinned at Corey. "The answer is yes."

"Yes?"

"As you may know, I have some skills." He put his arm around Corey's shoulder. "Okay, Corey. Let's you and me beat your dad to that treasure!"

Corey was so elated he whooped. He couldn't wait to get his hands on the gold, look into his father's cold blue eyes, and tell him he was too late! Corey's smile faded. *Revenge is hollow.* And it usually got people in trouble. What really mattered was finding the proof for Mom—the proof, for once and for all, that their ancestor was telling the truth. That should keep her on the path to healing.

Maybe it could even save Sam and Randy's Bed & Breakfast.

"See this inlet here? And the way the coast juts out right...there?" Corey squinted and used a sharp pencil point to trace a small segment of Grenadier's coast.

Grayce nodded. "That makes seven possibilities so far."

Corey wasn't sure whether to be glad or frustrated. If they found too many matches it would take forever to search them all.

"If we only had a clue about the scale of the original," Grayce said.

"Then we'd find the right place in about fifteen minutes," Corey finished.

Certain areas of the Grenadier coastline looked promising; they would check those first. If none of those panned out, they would go on to the next best matches. But there was so much of Grenadier.

Another problem was that some of the promising spots were under wetlands protection. Grayce would take care of that end of things. Because of the historical importance of the treasure chest, he thought he could get permission. It was questionable whether Corey's family would get to keep much or any of the treasure they found. It wouldn't help Sam, but if they found the treasure, they would keep Rob from stealing it and prove Pat Redrow's journal was not just fiction.

Grayce noted the potential treasure sites in a log book. "So she told your dad the location, huh?"

Corey furrowed his brows; hadn't they already been over that?

"How could she trust a guy like that?" Grayce was saying.

"Maybe she still had feelings. Maybe love does make you blind." Corey thought of how wacky it had made Goldy. *Oh yeah. And me.*

A revised schedule was in the works. Corey found out when Woody came out of the chart room staring at something in his hands. Corey could just make out the shape of the illustration as he climbed down the ratlines. *That's the map from the journal!* Corey hurried over to Woody.

"Hey, where did you get that?"

Woody jumped, and put the map behind him. He looked around then whispered. "Okay, but don't say anything. I overheard the captain and Grayce talk about a secret team-building event. It sounds like a blast!"

"So..."

"We're going on a treasure hunt! I ran their map through the copier when they weren't looking. This must be the island."

"That's uh..." Corey's map. Grayce must have copied it, probably even mentioned doing it, when Corey was distracted.

"It has an *X* on it, see." Woody squinted and pointed. "Right there."

SECRET UNLOCKED

Grayce had streamlined the schedule, but the parades and celebrations seemed to take forever. The captain only got to do two battles. Again, she hid her disappointment.

Finally, they left Maine behind them and headed across the Gulf of St. Lawrence. In Quebec, they picked up a few supplies, and in Montreal they met Jay, who showed pictures of his early-born baby and swore he would rejoin the ship—once his son got old enough to sail with him.

It was torture waiting to pass through the locks; there were always a couple of commercial ships in front of the *Golden Aye*. Otherwise, Corey's spirits were high, along with everyone else's. The whole crew knew they were on a special mission; they just didn't know the details.

Goldy sensed that Corey was hiding something. "I figured it has to do with your ancestry," she said. "Is it the treasure you told me about before? You know when we were...closer?"

He avoided her eyes as he looped a line on the deck. "I promised Grayce I wouldn't give the locations."

"Locations? How many treasure troves are we talking about?"

"Only one." Corey looked around guiltily. "We had to run a program to find matches between two maps. Anyway, there are a bunch of possibilities." He hoped Goldy wasn't going to think he didn't trust her, but for now he had to keep this to himself. "I just can't tell you which island."

She narrowed her eyes at him and puffed up like when she was about to lose her temper. "Sometimes you just suck... it up and take one for the team." She smiled. "Don't tell me any more. Just let me know what I can do to help."

Corey relaxed. Since getting with Woody, Goldy had learned how to chill.

AN ACKNOWLEDGEMENT

So far, they had held each other at arm's length, communicating only through fax and email. *Grayson* Fielding was all business. Now, at the sound of Peg's voice on the phone, adrenaline coursed through *Rob* Fielding like wild winds. He was young again. Feelings that had been buried welled up and cycled in waves. The ecstasies of new love, the bitterness of love lost, the uncertainties, the frustrations gone stale. His feelings confused him. He'd been an accomplished master of his fate for thirteen years, and suddenly he was a school boy. He managed to conceal his emotions as he outlined his plans for searching Grenadier. Peg voiced her approval. Then she hesitated before changing the subject.

"So you met Corey at Key West...?"

"He's a fine boy—" Rob's throat tightened at the reference to her child, fathered by another man. Corey obviously didn't know she had also asked Rob himself for help, so he hadn't mentioned it to him either.

"Look, I..." She seemed to have trouble getting the words out. "I know I left, back then, without telling—"

"You had your reasons." He was abrupt. He did not need to hear how Corey's father had swept her off her feet. He cleared his throat. "And now you've told his father about the treasure..."

She paused then with a strange chuckle said, "Of course—he's the best!"

Rob felt a stab of resentment. Corey was right, she still thought a lot of the guy! Did she forget that *Rob* himself was an expert?

He let out the air that was fouling his lungs. "Look, Peg, I'm glad to help find what belongs to you and Corey. I'll do what I can too, to save your treasure—and your name."

The call had taken a lot out of him, and the search at Grenadier would require all his strength. He needed time alone to re-charge. Unfortunately, Grayson Fielding was needed on deck.

FULL SPEED

It was Mom's news that made Corey tense. They had just gotten through the locks when Corey had a chance to call and tell her his position.

"What a coincidence. I just heard from your father." She sounded excited. "His ship has arrived in the area too."

Corey's heart sank. *He came by ship?*

"Maybe with the two of you searching, we'll have a chance."

Corey had hoped the guy would have trouble getting the permits. *Wait a minute.* Would such a pirate even bother with permits? And if he was going to search in secret, why would he tell her he'd arrived? Wouldn't he just take anything he found and disappear?

When Corey told Grayce that his father was closing in, he ordered, "Throttles to 1600!" To Corey, he added, "Keep your eyes out for other ships."

Near Harts Landing... A SINGER TOUR

Sam led a group of fifteen tourists into the "drawing" room. "If you feel you are being spied upon, you may be right!"

Some of the tourists were interested in the furnishings, some in the construction, but all were caught up in the romance of the old English style castle and its secrets.

"Direct your attention to the gilded frame on the south wall, and notice the portrait of King Charles the First." This castle was modeled after the one in Sir Walter Scott's novel, *Woodstock*. Sam still found Singer Castle fascinating even after giving five tours a day.

"A hidden mezzanine—an upper hallway—surrounds the room." Samantha swept her hand to indicate the expanse of upper walls. "Someone standing in the mezzanine could look through the eyes of the portrait to spy on people in this room." In the early 1900s, the likely spies were just servants checking to see if guests needed anything.

Sam pointed out other features of the drawing room: the window alcoves with their plush Pullman seats, the fireplace of pink marble, the antlered heads on the walls—a testament to Frederick Bourne's hunting skills—and the entrance to the office, which was located in the turret at the castle's southwest corner. She smiled, remembering the fun she'd had decorating the turret space in the floor directly above the office. Back in October, that level of the turret had been repurposed as a "dungeon" for Halloween, complete with a skeleton attached to ball and chain. Someone had suggested they reuse the props for Memorial Day. Sam had worried it might be too macabre, but the tourists got a kick out of it.

Sam loved the entire estate, from the clock tower, which pealed out rich tones every quarter hour, to the massive pillars in the great hall, the wood paneled library with its antique books, and the former chapel into which the group now proceeded. Gothic window panes lined three walls. Here, the north windows overlooked Canadian waters.

It had been a sunny day, but as the group lingered, Sam noticed a mist gathering outside. Still, it did not obscure the back yard which, as she pointed out, had served as a grass tennis court. "Frederick Bourne had two thousand loads of topsoil imported to create a level lawn over the rocky island surface."

The crowd scanned the manicured yard.

"What's that building over there?" A young boy pointed to the structure that rose from a level below the lawn on the northern edge of the island.

The building had been off limits since Sam had arrived, and lately she had noticed the manager visiting it frequently, busy as he was. Derrick hustled to complete his job here during the week and sped to the Landing on the weekends to help his uncle, Charlie Stowe.

Today, she'd heard sounds of machinery coming from inside the building.

"It was once used as a squash court—squash is a game like tennis—but it's being renovated." When the boy asked what it was going to be, she gave a wink. "There was talk about making it a haunted house." The boy's eyes grew larger. "But they decided to make it a rainy weather reception hall..." She referred to the numerous couples who chose to exchange vows on the island. "To keep the castle safe from rowdy wedding guests." The adults chuckled as she led them back to the main stairs.

Where did the time go? Sam was always amazed when quitting time came. She went to look for her purse, and then she remembered leaving it in the manager's office this morning when she'd gone to ask Derrick about scheduling. At the time, she had been distracted by something she had read in the castle archives. Now as she stood before the office right off the great hall, she realized the door was locked. Fortunately, she had seen Derrick replace the key in the hinged helmet of a nearby suit of armor.

ABANDON SHIP

The *Golden Aye* had left Ogdensburg behind them and passed through the Brockville Narrows. The weather had deteriorated from sunny and warm to cooler with patches of mist. The ship was passing Butternut Bay and, with his binoculars, Corey could make out the lighthouse at Crossover Island. On the way to Grenadier, they would be passing Dark Island, where Sam would be finishing her day's work. He hoped she would be outside waiting for the shuttle to Harts Landing. He could wave to her!

The *Golden Aye* crept toward Dark Island, still invisible, and Corey was sure they had never moved so slowly.

They were just below Crossover Island when his phone chirped. The caller ID was Sam's, and he answered eagerly—he hadn't heard from her since she'd told him she won her scholarship.

He was hearing nothing on the other end of the phone. "Sam? Hello?"

"Corey," she finally said in a low voice. "Where are you?"

He couldn't help grinning as he checked to see that his wristwatch registered nearly seventeen hundred. Five o'clock for her. He didn't expect to see her in person for a day or two, but he was excited just to hear her and know she was near; he would soon pass right in front of the castle. Maybe she was out front. "We're getting close." He held up his binoculars and gazed southeast as they crossed the border. Following the shipping channel, the *Golden Aye* was shifting from Canadian to American waters. Wasn't that Dark Island just appearing in the distance, sliding out from behind Crossover Island? "I think I can just make out the castle from here."

"Corey." She spoke in a low voice. "Something weird is going on. I found a copy of your journal page in the office—"

From the background, a voice butted in, a voice that gave Corey the chills.

"Hey, what are you doing—give me that!"

"No!"

Was it Corey's imagination or did Sam sound frightened?

"Sam? Sam!"

Nothing.

Was Sam in trouble? He had a bad feeling.

He went to Grayce and explained what had happened. "I think we need to stop at Dark Island!"

Grayce looked tired. He grasped Corey's shoulder and said, "You care about her." Even his voice sounded tired. "It's natural to be concerned, but I'm sure there's nothing to worry about."

Corey tried to set aside his fears. He remembered how he'd misinterpreted Mom's phone call. Maybe Charlie had given Derrick a copy of the map and asked him to keep an eye out. He probably passed Grenadier every day on the way to Singer. And Derrick would protect Sam. *We need all the help we can get if we're going to beat Rob!* Corey calmed down.

Grayce was saying, "You'll see her right after we complete our mission." He put things in perspective, as usual.

Then the man lumbered off to his cabin, calling to Woody, "You're in charge...mate."

Woody's face lit up. "Yes, Sir!"

Corey climbed the ratlines; as he rose above the cloud bank, he remembered the time he'd missed a potential collision because he was so distracted. He'd learned his lesson; it would not happen again.

No ship in sight. He swiveled his head. No other masts were showing, but he'd never seen such an eerie sight. They had barely passed Dark Island, and he could see the castle rising above the fog like a fairy fortress, the turrets and spires illuminated with a golden hue. Sam was probably boarding the island shuttle right now to head for Hart's Landing, without a care. *Grayce is right: I was imagining things.*

Corey was just turning his head back to the southwest when something flashed in his peripheral vision. His head snapped to the northeast again. There it was! A flash. No, not a flash, several short flashes. Then longer ones. Three short, three long, three short. Someone was sending an SOS from the castle turret!

It had to be Sam.

Think. Don't panic.

Corey climbed into the life boat and made sure it was equipped with a ditch kit before securing himself. Goldy was the one who had suggested he abandon ship. But she drew the line at enlisting Woody's help.

"He'd never make first mate or even get to be a deckhand again!" She didn't have to mention the sacrifice she herself was making. Neither of them would likely be allowed to sail again after this. But Corey didn't care if he got kicked out of the fleet. Saving Sam was more important.

"Are you in?"

"Almost...Okay—"

"No, wait!" Goldy removed something from her hair and tossed it carefully. Corey caught it and recognized the tortoise shell hair pin.

"For luck," she whispered. "It finally worked for me."

He gave her a smile, remembering that Sam had his brass buckle. He grasped the tortoise shell object close to his chest as Goldy said, "Ready to cast off the falls."

With pulleys unhooked, the life boat lowered to the river. As it hit the water with a jolt, Corey felt the jab of Goldy's hair pin, still in his hand. He cursed and sucked blood, his palm throbbing, as he slid the pin into his pocket. Still, he was able to start the motor to power safely downstream, away from the *Golden Aye.*

He slowed and turned to stare back at the tall ship heading upriver without him. He felt divided, like part of him was still on the ship. He hated to abandon the search for the treasure, but he could trust Grayce to follow through. Corey had to follow his own course. Wouldn't Grayce understand that? Corey had to focus on finding Sam. He turned back and throttled up. The motor hiccupped. *Now what?* Corey adjusted the choke, but the motor sputtered and died. It would not restart. He would have to use the oars. Could he get to Sam in time?

Corey scrambled to position himself and get leverage. He grabbed the oars and pulled hard to get headed north, toward the western end of Dark Island.

He had to calm his mind, focus his strength.

Corey envisioned Grayce coaxing him onward, his amber eyes warm with encouragement. For some reason, the underwater scene at Port Royal flashed in Corey's mind: Grayce gazing at a piece of gold. Then the magazine showing Pedro Banks popped into his mind, along with the news of an attempted theft. Grayce a thief? *Ludicrous.*

Out of the corner of his eye, Corey noticed a navigation light downriver, a light that glimmered in the foggy channel. It was heading right for him, and though it looked far away, it was probably doing fifteen knots. Way faster than Corey! He hauled on the oars with a burst of adrenaline. When he glanced again at the upbound ship, it seemed larger. He had heard that freighters sometimes used desensitized radar so they were not distracted by every piece of flotsam on the river. Would they even notice Corey? He stared into the lights of the freighter that bore down on him.

He yanked at the oars. He had to get well beyond the channel or he'd be swamped by the wake of the Seaway monster! He ignored the pain in his punctured hand as he pulled. *Sea chanteys help you concentrate.* That's what Grayce had said. If Corey ever needed a chantey, now was the time. His mind churned with random tidbits.

Grayson Fielding, (Row, Row)
He could do the job, (Row, Row)
He'd find the treasure, (Row, Row)
And keep it from Rob! (Row, Row)

The chantey was working. Corey had gotten into a rhythm, powering the small boat through the chop. He kept his eye on the western point of the island and rowed hard. He was slowly cutting the distance as the freighter neared. *Keep it up.* He sang anything that came to mind. He thought about Jay and his new baby. What was it Woody had said about his eyes? Corey turned that into a song too.

> *If Mom and Dad have eyes of blue*
> *Baby's eyes will have that hue*
> *Peg and Rob have eyes of blue*
> *So Corey's eyes should be that too—*

Corey skipped a beat with the oar. His eyes were brown. But there could be exceptions, right? He dipped the oar.

> *Fielding hunts, but not like Rob*
> *Helping kids is Grayce's job*
> *Grayson is his middle name*
> *Key West, the port from where he came*

Corey's rowing slowed along with his chant as scenes flashed through his mind:

Key West porch swing; Scotch whiskey; a man repeating the name *Andrew.*

Grayce describing his house sitter, Andrew, drinking Scotch.

An envelope in Grayce's cabin addressed to Robert G. Fielding.

Rob Fielding?

Corey stopped moving the oars. He remembered Grayce's questions about Mom, his weird stares, the maps in his possession.

And then it hit him: Grayce had amber eyes. Eyes like Corey's.

Corey was barely aware of the monster wake sweeping toward him as his grip remained frozen on the oars.

Near Harts Landing... MACKENZIE'S CONCERN

"You've got to find that cache tonight." Mackenzie used her no-nonsense voice. "While the boy has his head in the sand." Or at least in the coves of Grenadier.

Oscar furrowed his brow. "I wondered why you didn't find a way to keep him from coming back."

"I know this boy," she sighed. "If he wanted an answer, he would never stop until he figured it out." Auger could use some of Corey Worder's mettle. "I supplied an answer."

Oscar grinned. "To keep him busy."

"He got his smarts from his mother." Mackenzie thought she had beaten Margaret Worder Stowe before, and the woman had bounced back. But now she was vulnerable—enough to be managed. The blog posts were putting her on edge; though she'd seen the map, her head wouldn't be clear enough to figure things out.

No one else even knew that the map existed until Mackenzie's grandson ambushed her. But things were turning out fine now that she had learned how to use him, like others, by manipulation.

Leaking the map to the Worders was fine, but it was too bad it had to go through that clever girl. Now she was too close for comfort. Who knew what she might conclude if

Auger gave details about pulling that "memory" out of his grandmother?

Oscar was apologetic. "I told Derrick he was supposed to run the new hires by me—"

"Just don't let her interfere," she told Oscar.

TAKEN IN

The swell grabbed the small lifeboat and tossed it like a toy. It was all Cory could do to hang on while its contents, including the ditch kit, were pitched into the river. When the craft finally settled down, he was nearer the island, but it took the rest of Corey's strength to raise the broken outboard and maneuver between rugged granite rocks. Finally, the bottom slid over gritty sand.

Had he really partnered up with the man who was trying to beat him? Had Corey let his father sail off to Estar Island on the *Golden Aye* without him? What a fool Corey had been, looking up to Fielding as an ally.

With his pants dripping wet and water squishing in his shoes, Corey dragged the lifeboat onto the island. He stubbed his foot on a boulder, lost his balance, and collapsed on the damp ground. His head spun with thoughts of Grayce. Was he really... Could he be Corey's own father?

Corey's mind was a kaleidoscope of scenes reinterpreted. The porch guy with blue eyes as Grayce's house sitter. The Pedro Banks treasure thief as Robert Grayson Fielding, who had put on a good act as a role model.

Corey had secretly wished the man was his father. Now the impossible had come true, and Corey wanted to reverse it. Despite everything, his own father was beating him to the treasure, and Corey himself had invited the man!

Corey stared up at the dwindling light. He squeezed blades of grass from the ground beneath him and flung it away. Patches of mist floated above him. Wasn't he supposed to be doing something?

Sam!

Corey scrambled to his feet and sprang forward, ignoring the chill of his wet pants and shirt sticking to his skin. He had to find the castle turret.

An old "Indian path" wound from the west end of the six-acre island to the clearing near the castle. Sam said old arrowheads had been found here. People had found spoons from 1812, too. They had found an old grinding stone. Corey tried to think of anything but Grayce as he wound through evergreen groves, trotting and hopping over occasional branches. The shadows and light played tricks, making him jump and dodge what looked like creatures moving in the shadowy forest. Despite attempts at distraction, his thoughts formed a cadence to his running: *Pedro Banks, Port Royal.*

Robert Grayson Fielding had probably realized who Corey was even when they first met. But he didn't care any more about Corey than his house sitter did. No wonder Fielding had asked about Mom. He wanted her treasure.

Corey came to a clearing in the pines. Ahead of him was the main entrance to the castle, bathed in the moonlight. To the right of the entrance, at the southwestern corner of the castle, a turret rose through several stories to a conical red roof. The lowest level of the turret was one floor above the main entrance, and he could see two sizable windows. The one visible window of the turret's second-story was a mere slit. That's where the SOS must have come from. Corey was amazed that he had seen the signal at all. Fortunately, the narrow band of illumination had intersected Corey's position on the *Golden Aye.*

Before him was a treeless expanse of maybe seventy-five feet; all he had to do was cross the opening, make his way up the walkway, and open the massive red door. Then he was sure he could get to the turret. He was about to dash out in the moonlight when he noticed a curtain flutter in the upper window. He halted in the shadows as a man's face appeared in the glass.

Corey froze—voluntarily this time. Which brought up something Corey hadn't thought of before: If Grayson Fielding was his father, why didn't Corey freeze up around him? Was it because Corey believed he had already confronted his father?

Corey's thoughts drifted to the ship and his mates. *Woody didn't know about Fielding!* Corey had to warn him. He squeezed his hand into his pants pocket and forced the phone out, but it was waterlogged. Woody would have to wait.

The curtain fell back over the window, and the man disappeared. Corey dashed to the entrance. He gently pulled the handle of the door, and it creaked with weight. Corey felt just as heavy himself at the thought of Grayce taking the gold at Grenadier. But if the gold was at Grenadier, why was Grayce taking the crew with him? Corey was sure the man would not want any witnesses when he stole the gold.

Corey slipped inside and closed the door

On Grenadier... ROB'S EYE OPENER

"Two...three...four." That should keep them busy for a while. Grayson Fielding had assembled equipment for four pairs of crew members; each pair would don scuba gear and carry metal detectors and communication devices. The first set of targeted areas were at the farthest reaches of the island.

It had taken longer than he'd wanted to get through the channel past Sisters Island in the fog. Once they turned northwest from the channel, the mist had dissipated, and they glided past the country club, its neat line of evergreens glowing like torches leading the way to the western end. They had picked their way carefully among the shoals.

"Too bad the best spots weren't closer," Woody said. "Are you sure the permits allow us to be here now?"

"Of course I'm sure," Grayce snapped. "Sorry, I'm a little anxious." He had been surprised himself to receive clearance so easily—with the stipulation that the search begin no sooner than today.

By now, all divers were certified and experienced in night diving. They had gone over safety procedures and were versed in the use of dive lights and signaling. They would drop in pairs at site A. If that area didn't pan out, they would move along the north side to B.

It wasn't until they arrived at the first site that Grayson learned he was missing a crew member.

"He's *where?*" Woody, too, appeared shocked as Goldy explained the situation.

"But it's okay," she added, "I found Sam's number in Corey's things and heard her voice message. They've had some electrical problems disrupting business today, and she has to work late."

Grayson tightened his lips and scanned the deck. He tried to remain calm. Leaving without permission was serious business—and while the ship was underway! Maybe he should have paid more attention when Corey came to him. The boy must have been very worried to abandon the search he'd been so eager for. But the flashes he saw had to be from some kind of power surge.

"I know Sagittarius is supposed to be the explorer," he muttered, shaking his head. "But to abandon ship..."

"Sagittarius?" Woody's brows were furrowed as he spoke robotically: "Corey's sign is Scorpio—he was born November first."

Grayson blinked several times. He counted the months from February to November, and the blood drained from his face. His legs buckled and he choked, "He was not?!"

14 DUNGEON DAMSEL

SHH! THE LIBRARY

Corey entered a large space with stone arches and high ceilings. It was the room Sam called the "Great Hall." He turned right; he knew the turret base was in that direction. But there was no door, no stairs. How could he find a way in? He moved quietly near the wall, watching his step in the room lit only by wall sconces. He lifted his gaze when he met a pair of legs and gasped to find himself face to face with an armed guard. Then he let out his breath to see that it was only a suit of armor. Corey crossed the room, heading for the main stairs; then he saw that they were boarded over. He tried to stay calm as visions of Sam loomed in his head. Was she okay? Had someone hurt her? He had to find her!

Corey scanned the wall clockwise and spotted several closed doors. The man he'd seen earlier could be behind any of them. Corey had to remain unseen if he was to have any chance of helping Sam. He stood like a statue in the shadows as his eyes adjusted to the darkness. After glancing back at the large door he had entered, his gaze shifted to a set of stairs opposite the base of the turret. They led up to a raised entryway. Corey tiptoed up to the door, barely breathing, and peeked inside. *Looks like a library.* The light was on. He crept into the room. He glanced past a fireplace, chairs, and bookshelves. Toward the rear, an outside door was ajar.

The bookshelf opposite the fireplace held information about the property. *There must be a floor plan.* He glanced through a book describing Dark Island. It had been known by other names: Bluff Island, Lonestar Island... No blueprints. He moved to a book case beside the fireplace. He was tilting a book at the end of a shelf—a book that seemed to be stuck—

when he heard footsteps near the outside door. Someone was coming in!

Corey jammed the book back into place. He hesitated. Should he spring out the front door or duck behind a chair? Before he could move, the paneling next to the fireplace swung back.

Whaa—? He must have activated a switch. He stumbled inside the wall and shut the paneling behind him as he heard the slam of the back door.

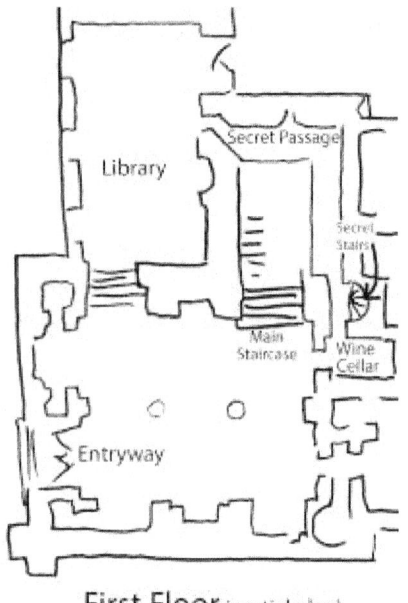

First Floor (partial plan)

He didn't dare move as a voice seeped through the wall: "Did you take care of her? She better be out of our way."

What is he talking about?

The other man said something Corey couldn't hear.

Were they talking about Sam? What did that mean, *Take care of her?* No, he couldn't mean... Corey almost burst through the door. He forced himself to stay still.

The first man spoke again, saying, "The search will be hard enough without Miss Nosey interfering." Pause. "Remember, we have to go through Canada." Then both men laughed, sending prickles up Corey's spine.

They must be in cahoots with Grayce! Was Dark Island their headquarters for planning the search on Grenadier? That's why Grayce didn't want Corey stopping at this island—he didn't want Corey running into his partners.

It sounded like one of them was moving toward the Great Hall. The other was walking toward the fireplace. Corey backed up. He turned around to find himself in...a hidden hallway?

Corey tiptoed quickly around a corner just as the secret panel door again sprang open behind him. Ahead was a room with wine bottles in the wall. On his left were stone stairs that spiraled upward. Which way to Sam? He darted up the steps just as footsteps approached the corner behind him.

He arrived at the second story level and was breathing a sigh of relief to hear no footsteps from below—the guy must've gone for a bottle of wine—when the sound of padding feet descended from above. His eyes darted between two narrow doors opposite one another. Corey pushed one open a crack then stepped out into a large room, closing the door quietly.

ROOMS FOR THE LIVING?

He edged to his right into an elegant living room with animal heads on the walls. *Must be the "drawing room" Sam talks about.* Across the room, the windows by the booth-like seats gave a darkening view of the river. He looked up past the chandelier and saw a large gold-framed portrait of a mustached man. That should be the south wall. Sam's turret would be to the right and up a level. But how to get there? He squinted past the third window on the opposite wall. That should be the first turret level. He crept across the Oriental carpet and past an ornate table. To his right, past the third south window, was an alcove. Between two large corner recesses was a narrow door opening.

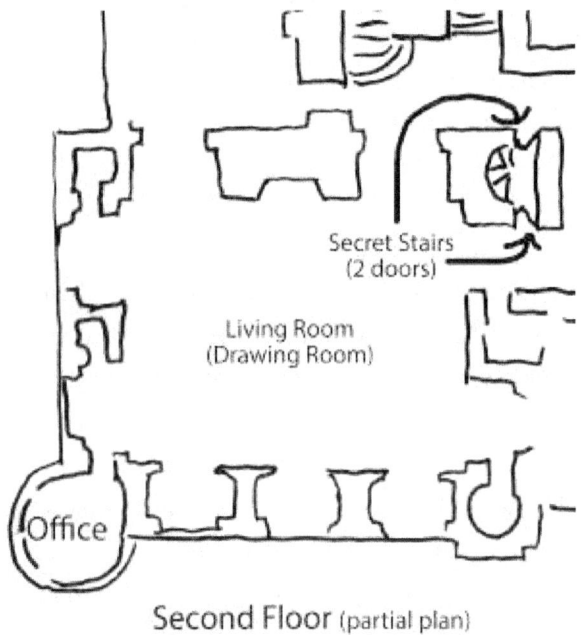

Secret Stairs
(2 doors)

Living Room
(Drawing Room)

Office

Second Floor (partial plan)

Enclosed in the rounded stone walls were a desk, file cabinets, and a monstrous safe inscribed with the name *F.G. Bourne.* Corey pivoted between windows. Three in all. From the middle one was a view upriver to where Corey's ship would have been when he saw the SOS. He had to get to the level above this, but he could see no staircase or even a trap door allowing passage upwards.

Time was wasting! He scurried across the room, back to the secret staircase, and came to a halt. The door he had exited was now invisible. He was still staring, his mind racing, when a soft creak interrupted his thoughts and the door started to open. Someone was coming out! Corey crept around the wall.

He came to the opposite side of the enclosure. But that door, the panel door he had seen from inside the stone staircase, was also hidden. He used both hands to feel all around the wall. Now, whoever had opened the other door was circling around to his side—and he could hear two people whispering. As he slid his hands randomly over the wall, he jarred a small portrait hanging by the panel. The stair door sprang open in time to swallow him from sight.

Corey raced up the winding stairs, his heart thumping, keeping track of which way the turret would be. He had only taken a few steps when he saw another door. *I can't be at the next floor already.* He wasn't. This one opened onto a hallway—the mezzanine Sam had told him about—that ran behind the animal heads in the drawing room.

The turret would be on the opposite corner of the mezzanine, above the office. He crept south along the narrow passageway then right-angled at the corner of the upper hall to make his way along the south side. He would be just above the booths by the drawing room windows. Midway along the south hallway was a circular hinged panel to his right. It was the back side of the portrait of the mustached man.

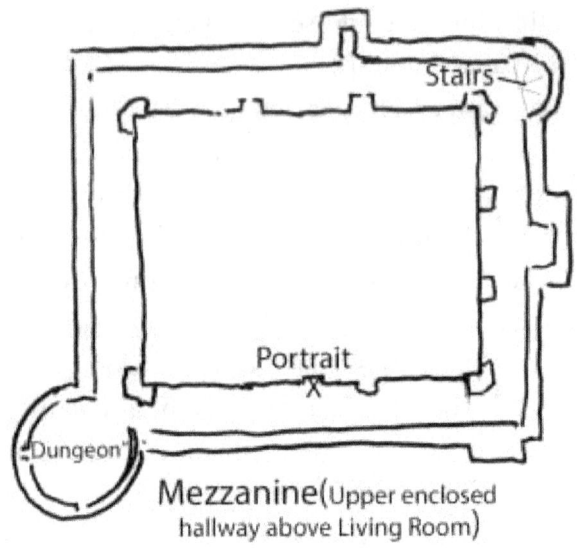

He hadn't heard footsteps lately. Was someone still in the drawing room? Or had that someone followed Corey? He thought he heard music. The back of the portrait had tacked-on canvas patches where the eyes would be seen from the other side. He carefully rotated them to the side and looked through the two holes. Was the moonlight playing tricks on him? He stepped back and rubbed his eyes then peered again through the picture. The vision of a couple swaying, circling the table to a three-beat rhythm caused him to jerk backwards, hitting a loose rod that fell to the floor with a twang.

Corey held his breath as he looked again through the holes. The waltzing couple looked real, but they gazed only at each other. Still, someone else might have heard the rod fall. Corey listened for footsteps. Nothing.

He hurried along the mezzanine, hearing a muffled sound. There at the corner, the light of a small ceiling bulb illuminated an entrance...to a round structure. The turret!

Corey pressed himself against an iron grating. Inside, a narrow window admitted a sliver of dusk. Corey could just make out a form that made his skin crawl—a human skeleton. *Don't be ridiculous.* It was only fake, probably somebody's idea of a joke.

His eyes adjusted slowly before they recognized the silhouette of a girl lying nearby, beneath the window.

"Samantha!" His voice was a harsh growl. Was she alive?

He heard another muffled groan. *Thank god she's conscious!* But why did she turn away from him?

The last rays of daylight from the window were no match for the ceiling light behind him; all she would see was a silhouette. She probably thought Corey was that other guy.

"Sam, it's me, Corey!" he whispered.

Now she squirmed and whimpered with energy, but her arms were behind her, and her mouth was bound. Her ankle was clamped by a cuff chained to the wall.

Corey had to find a way through! He trembled as he checked the hallways before shaking the metal door. It was rigid. As he watched Sam struggle to her feet, he noticed a familiar shape that hung away from her work blazer. That brass buckle. He should have kept it—it sure hadn't brought her luck. And if he had it now, he could use its small rod to probe the iron lock. He had to get Sam out of here before someone discovered him rescuing her.

Corey leaned against the wall beside the iron grating. *Think.* He had inherited his mom's lock-picking skills, but they did no good without a pick. He racked his brain as he glanced around, wrenching his hands together.

"Ow!" The pain from his hand pricked his memory, and he pulled out Goldy's pin. He had the cell unlocked in seconds.

"I'd almost given up!" Sam cried as he removed her gag.

Whoever tied her hands was no sailor, and Corey quickly loosened it. "Let's not make this a habit," he said, remembering how he had untied her in a cave last June. Then he turned her carefully for a gentle embrace, but she surprised him with a crushing squeeze.

"It was a long shot you'd even get my signal," she said, teary eyed.

"Yeah, how did you—?" She couldn't have used her hands.

"It wasn't easy." She described how hard it was to position herself at the window so the polished buckle reflected the sinking sun. "Turns out the thing was good luck."

"Not luck," Corey said, impressed. "'Applying your mind.'" He scowled to realize he was quoting Fielding again.

"There's a contractor working out back," Sam said as Corey worked at the clamp on her leg. "Derrick goes out to 'check' on him. Says the owner wants him to keep an eye on Oscar."

"I guess Derrick didn't do his job then, or this Oscar would never have tied you—"

"Corey, it wasn't Oscar who did this. It was Derrick."

Charlie's nephew? Corey had never actually met the guy, but he had thought of Derrick as an ally. He frowned again as he remembered another quote: "Never assume."

"He made me change my cell message to say I was working late because of some power glitch earlier. He even called my dad so he wouldn't come looking for me.

"Anyway, I had started to suspect Derrick and Oscar were in on something after I found your map. Plus I heard

Derrick say to someone on the phone, 'Don't worry, we'll find it before the Worder kid.'"

She paused as Corey absorbed the information.

"When he realized I was onto them, Derrick locked me in the turret."

Corey just stared at her, wondering. Were the two men getting ready to meet Fielding at Grenadier?

LONELY ESTAR

They needed to call someone to stop Fielding and his search partners. The life boat would do them no good with its dead engine. Corey and Sam needed to get to a phone.

"We can't risk the manager's office, even if you pick the lock. Derrick pops in and out. But his bedroom has—" Corey thought he saw her face go red, even in the dim light. "I mean, I think it has a land line," she mumbled. "We have to get to the chart room at the top of the castle."

As they passed the portrait on the way to the spiral stairs, Corey told Sam about the couple dancing in the room below.

"Josh and Eliza!" she said. "I almost forgot. They're renting the honeymoon suite—I've walked their spaniel, Kappy, a couple of times. And they're ballroom dance addicts; they dance everywhere there's room. Anyway, they could help us!" At the sound of a motorboat roaring away, her face fell and she checked her watch. "But they were leaving for shore right about now."

Her only option was to lead Corey up the spiral staircase to a small room at the highest point in the castle.

"Wow." Corey glanced around at the windows offering views in all directions. On the chart room walls were maps of the surrounding river and islands. The room had a fireplace, a bed, and a desk, where Sam was tunneling through a messy pile of papers. "He must've moved the phone."

She dropped to the bed, receiving a jolt, and jumped up to rub her backside. "Did he stuff the mattress with rocks? It used to be softer..."

Corey went cold as he narrowed his eyes on hers, which had widened.

"You seem pretty familiar." He swallowed hard. "Were...were you on that," he nodded at the mattress, "with *him*?"

"Corey, it wasn't what you think."

She looked awfully guilty. It was exactly what he thought.

She stared at her hands. "It was only once—"

"Once is plenty!"

"What?!" Now she sounded angry. "You won't even listen, after I forgave *you*."

He folded his arms. There had been nothing to forgive him for. They stared at each other in absolute silence.

Until Corey heard it. A *creak* out on the main stairway.

Sam sprang to life, put her finger to her lips, and pulled Corey out of the room. They ducked back through another door that led to a huge room with windows cut into the gabled roof. The maids' dormitory.

The footsteps continued to the chart room as Corey and Sam moved to a large recess in the slanted ceiling, out of sight of the door.

They stood uneasily, angled away from each other, tense as they heard the manager moving back and forth through the hallway.

Corey couldn't stand it any longer. After what they'd been through, all the risks he'd taken for Sam—he had even given her his precious buckle!

"Why'd you do it?" he growled.

"What are you talking about?" she hissed.

"You know, getting together with him?"

He stared at the wall for an eternity before she spoke.

"With *him*? What are you, nuts?"

Corey felt Sam grab his shoulder and turn him to face her.

"I only ended up in his room because he tricked me. Said he wanted my opinion about whether his new bedding was 'earth friendly.'

That would get Sam to his room. Corey relaxed a little.

"Then the guy says his lips are *Sam friendly*."

Corey suppressed a cough.

"I pushed him away and told him in no uncertain terms that mine were not *Derrick friendly*."

Corey chuckled silently as he watched Sam's expressions. Then she smiled. They grinned at each other. They held hands as they heard Derrick move around in the chart room.

Corey frowned. "What if he already checked the turret...and is looking for you?" They both waited tensely and flashed worried looks whenever they caught each other's eye. If Derrick was looking for Sam, he would be running around in a flurry. But they just heard a chair scrape the floor, and then nothing. Derrick must have settled down at his desk.

They would have to wait until he left. But there was nowhere Corey would rather be than here with Sam. How could he have thought she would...?

Love can make you nuts. He gazed at her face reflecting the glow of the nearby exit sign: the soft brown eyes, the small straight nose in profile against the window. He shifted his focus past her to the darkening sky and noticed that several stars had emerged between bands of dispersing mist.

His stars had led him back to the Thousand Islands and Samantha. He lowered his lips to her ear to whisper, "Even if we're stuck here, at least we're together." Like binary stars, connected no matter how others shifted around them.

They stared into the night, heads touching, as the stars grew numerous. More numerous than the Thousand Islands. He glanced toward the islands, still visible, near the shore. Lonestar, the old name for this one, seemed appropriate. Dark Island was separate, unique. As he stared upward again, the spaces between stars seemed to grow and shrink. It made Corey think of the journal. Something about the spacing of the words that said what Corey's ancestors did with the treasure:

LEFT IT ALL ON ESTAR ISLAND

It still seemed strange that no search had turned up an Estar Island.

Was he making an assumption? *Is your premise flawed?* He hated himself for letting another Fielding quote pop into his mind. But it was interesting how the mind could see—or ignore—what it wanted to.

"Too bad we don't have the journal page. There's something about it..."

Sam fiddled with the lanyard around her neck. "But we do, or *I* do." She opened the buckle.

Corey grinned as she took out a lump of paper—a copy of his ancestor's paragraph about hiding the treasure—and unfolded it.

The letters seemed uneven, gathering here and separating there. Had Patrice written this in a rocking boat? Corey's head was close to Sam's as they squinted at the page.

"This is silly." She gave up and led him to the nearby exit sign and held the paper so he could see.

"Look, the letters are irregular." She pointed at the text. "And sometimes words run together."

Something had always bothered him about that first *L in ALL*. The foot seemed different; short, like it was an afterthought. "Isn't that curve at the bottom more of a curly tail than a horizontal line?" He looked closer.

"And isn't that a white splotch?" Sam pointed at the top right side of the first *L*.

"Like a tiny bird dropping." Corey stared at it. "It's covering a black cross mark."

LEFT IT ALL ON ESTAR ISLAND

"I think that first *L* in *ALL* is really a *T!*" she said.

"But *ATL* doesn't make any sense."

"No, I think that's supposed to be a space, the *L* goes with the next letters."

LON? Look beyond the obvious; free your mind from assumption. Corey looked at the next grouping.

"What if that *L* and the *ON* go with *ESTAR?*"

Corey could feel Sam's warm breath on his neck. They stared at each other.

His lips barely moved as he began the revised sentence: "We left it *AT*..."

"*LONESTAR* Island!" Sam finished. Her large eyes reflected Corey's own amazement. He was beyond amazed when she poured her passion into a kiss that swept him off the subject. Only the sound of a scraping chair and footsteps could break them apart.

Corey's insides were awhirl. He wanted to be with Sam where nothing could touch them. But they had discovered something. *Focus.* Something important...

The treasure island. They were standing right on top of Estar—*Lonestar*—Island!

The footsteps were fading down the staircase. Sam held her finger to her mouth as they crept out of the dormitory. She listened at the circular staircase until she was sure the footsteps had descended below mezzanine level.

As they continued the search for a phone in the chart room, something was still bothering Corey.

"If Fielding knew Dark Island was the treasure site, then why was he gung-ho to head for Grenadier? To take the crew there, take me there?"

Then he caught his breath. It was obvious, wasn't it? "He wanted us to pass by Dark Island because it *was* the treasure site—"

Sam, who had been searching the corners of the room, stood up straight. "He didn't want you interfering. He wanted you out of the way!"

"But why didn't he just come without me in the first place?"

"Corey, if he knew you at all, he'd know you were determined—"

"And he was smart enough to keep an eye on me while making me *think* I was finding the treasure." All that stuff about permits was just to throw Corey off. He only knew what Fielding had said, so there probably never were any permits!

Meanwhile Fielding's partners were busy preparing the real dig site. They must have made arrangements with the owner of Dark Island. And Fielding would come back here— to claim his share of the loot and then disappear.

"But when Fielding finds out I'm missing from the *Golden Aye*, we won't be able to hide for long."

Sam nodded. "That's why we've got to find a phone!" She was pulling clothing and furniture away from the wall to find a phone jack.

"Charlie's nephew is a slob," Corey said, dropping onto the bed to look for a jack under the headboard. "Not much like his uncle."

He, too, was surprised by the hard mattress. He lifted it and found a binder full of documents, and he opened it to see a familiar page.

"That's the treasure map." Attached to it was a copy of the other loose page from his ancestor's journal. Corey recognized the handwriting of his ancestor Patrice Redrow:

After ensuring no one was around to witness, we placed the chest within the rocky cave at the inlet at the north side of the island.

"But there's no rocky cave on Dark Island," Corey said.

Sam's brows rose and her eyes widened as she unfolded a pair of smaller pages that had fallen from the binder. "But there was!" She pointed at the top paper. "This is a copy of the original island map—hardly anyone knows about it." The north side showed an indentation and a label: *Rock Cave*. On the modern map beneath the original, that section was filled in, showing a smooth coastline.

"What do you mean? Which is the real map?"

"They're both real—before and after Bourne altered the island."

Corey just stared at her.

"Look, I know the official history of this place—as a guide, I have to. But in my research, I found out things never mentioned on the tours."

She moved her finger in a jagged line. "The rock cave was here." She let her finger rest near the north shore. "It was blasted and filled in. A guy was killed in a faulty detonation." She wiped bangs from her eyes, looking up. "Some have even claimed to see—"

"His ghost!" The one they had joked about on their picnic last summer. "The one seen on full moons?"

"Right. In fact, the owners were so spooked they banned employees from telling that part of the island's history."

"Wait." Corey needed information, not ghost stories. "So you're telling me that Bourne had the island reshaped?"

"Yes, like I said, this original map shows the island as your ancestors would have found it in 1813—long before Bourne came along and modified the north coast in the early twentieth century."

Corey shook his head. He knew that the guy who built Boldt Castle had changed his island into the shape of a valentine for the love of his life. Were all island castle owners total nut cases?

But Corey had to admit, if he were rich enough, he would change planet Earth for Sam.

She continued. "Bourne used the blasted rock, along with tons of landfill from another island, to fill the inlet and the north lawn." She gestured toward the back of the castle. They glanced out the window to the back yard.

Corey looked down at the map, comparing it to the map in his head. "Let's see, the *X* would be about..." Corey moved his finger on the map. "Here."

Sam looked north and formed a frame with her hands against the window. "Which would be right about there." She pointed at the roof of a building that appeared out of the darkness. "That," she caught her breath, "is the squash court."

Corey shook his head. How lucky could Fielding get? The treasure spot was hidden from view, where he could set his partners to work unseen.

It was hard to believe that after all their searching and all the dead ends, they were actually standing right above the treasure! But it might as well be at the North Pole for all the good it would do them.

"That's why the guys have been spending so much time in the squash court," Sam said. "They're digging right where Patrice and Warren left the British chest."

Corey thought of something and dropped to the bed. "But this is the U.S."

"What are you talking about?"

"It doesn't make sense." Corey wrapped his hands over his arms. "Why would those guys say it was in Canada?"

Sam's smile fell. She dropped the maps in her pocket and sat next to him. They were silent for several moments.

"Wait—" her eyes locked on his. "What did they say *exactly*?"

He thought for a moment and shrugged. "They had to 'go through Canada.' But I don't know why they were laughing about it."

"Hold on." Her eyes grew large and shifted back and forth.

"Oh." Sam's mouth dropped open. She shut it and gave him a smug look. "Guess what else I learned about the island?"

He was not in the mood for games, but he waited.

"The soil Bourne brought in to fill in the north lawn. It was from a Canadian island!"

Corey stared at her. "And these guys are digging through *that* dirt—"

"So they have to *go through Canada* to get to the buried treasure!"

So that explained it. Fielding had gone to Grenadier to dump Corey and the crew. He planned to maroon them looking for non-existent gold while he came back to the real treasure island.

That meant he would be back here soon.

"There's no way for us to look for the treasure now," Corey said gloomily. "Not with these guys zeroing in on it."

"You're right." Sam talked faster. "Corey, we have to notify someone before these creeps take off with the treasure."

Corey found the phone jack behind the bed, but though they searched everywhere, there was no phone.

"Probably removed it because he didn't need that and the cell phone," Sam said. "There's only one other place where we might get to a phone without getting caught. It's at the north boathouse."

Corey stared down, as an overshadowing cloud drifted away, to see the long boathouse roof that rose from the other side of the squash court. How could he and Sam walk unseen—over a back lawn lit by a full moon?

Near Harts Landing... MACK TRACKS

Mackenzie's mind was like a filing cabinet. With her eyes closed, she reviewed the contents of her mental "files" and cross-referenced them with new information. She was always making new connections that might prove useful. She was amending her list of staff members and their weaknesses for the purpose of future exploitation—*redhead in food services has eyes for night guard*—when her pocket hummed. It was the untraceable phone Oscar had smuggled in for her.

It was a status update, and things were going as planned. He mentioned the one small snag only as an afterthought. "It's not a problem," he claimed.

"The girl knows?" Oscar shouldn't have let Derrick bring her there. No doubt he'd hired her for her looks, but in this case, looks were matched by intelligence.

"Keep her contained," she told Oscar.

"Don't worry, she's locked up."

"And watch for the boy. She's like a magnet to him."

CANADIAN SOIL

Corey put his ear to the doorway of the spiral steps; from behind it came a scratching sound. Sam heard it too and put her finger to her lips. They darted toward the main staircase and crept downwards. By the time they reached the blocked portion, they could hear soft padding coming from above, but it was too late to turn back.

Corey's eyes darted wildly for an escape route; when Sam started pulling him sideways, he resisted—they would be sitting ducks! But Sam was dragging him into it a closet camouflaged by the wall paneling. She closed the door from inside, yanked on a coat hook, and once again Corey found himself stumbling down a circular stairway.

He should remember to trust Sam.

She led him, twisting and turning, to the lower levels of the castle. Back in the Great Hall, they took a door that led to the clock tower and to the basement from which they entered a tunnel.

"Ready to 'go through Canada'?" she asked.

They walked without speaking through the dank, musty air as a low rumbling noise penetrated the earthen walls. They were walking under the back lawn. Corey shivered; his damp clothing had sucked out a lot of body heat.

By the time the tunnel opened to the breezy night air, Corey was shaking. They looked carefully to the left, where the roof of the squash court rose near the north shore, before hurrying into the upper story of the boathouse. They descended a stairway to the middle floor.

"Some of the original workers slept here," Sam whispered as she nodded toward several doors off the landing. Then her face froze as they heard a shuffling sound near the lower stairs. Corey pulled Sam into an old bedroom. He looked around for another escape—maybe this closet had secret stairs. He opened its door just as Sam said, "It was only a mouse!" She let the door swing open, creating a draft.

When Corey turned back to shut the closet, the moonlight streaming through the bedroom window revealed a mass of whiteness billowing from the door.

"Aaagh!" he jumped back with alarm. He clutched at his chest and felt the thump-thumping under his scar. Then the old shirts settled down under their hangers as Sam closed the hallway door. His breathing slowed, and he looked at Sam, embarrassed.

"Surprised me, that's all." He composed himself and tried to sound casual. "What are those old shirts doing here anyway?" He could tell she was trying not to look amused.

"They belonged to the detonation specialist who was killed. He always wore white shirts—kind of his trademark. I remembered his name because it rhymes: *Donald Knight, dynamite.*" Anyway, he's the one who's supposed to be haunting the place. He's the one they blamed for the strange things."

"What strange things?"

"Legend says that if his belongings are disturbed, his ghost will seek revenge. In fact, when a hired hand was clearing Knight's drawer, a beam fell and nearly killed him. After that, Bourne insisted that all of Knight's things be left just as they were."

Corey gave a derisive laugh. He still sounded a little shaky, even to himself, and he was clammy from his damp shirt.

"Corey, you're shivering." Sam shook her head. "I should have found you some warm clothes in Derrick's room."

He peeled off his top and reached into the closet. *Ghosts?* Yeah, right. "It's okay, I'll use one of these." He pulled the musty shirt around him to make up for his earlier reaction. It was scratchy, but it sealed his body heat inside.

Sam's look was a mix of anxiety and admiration.

They made it downstairs to an office where there was an old land-line phone. Sam picked up the receiver. Frowning, she rattled the cradle. "No dial tone."

"Let's try this one." Corey grinned as he held up the receiver of the more modern phone sitting nearby.

"The treasure is where?" Charlie said.

Corey quickly explained that Estar was Lonestar. He would tell him later about Derrick tying Sam up.

"So you decided Grenadier is a sham?"

Corey was getting impatient. "Yes, but Fielding will be coming back any minute to steal it—"

"Rob Fielding, your father?" Far from the voice of concern he expected, Corey was surprised to hear Charlie burst out laughing.

"Thanks, kid," he said between chuckles. "I needed some comic relief. We've been working hard."

We? "Charlie where are you?"

"I'm here on Grenadier with Rob."

No! "But he's gonna steal the gold, with Derrick and—"

"I don't know what you and Sam got into over there in fantasy land, but Rob's okay. I admit I had my doubts after what you said. But I've been known to tip a bottle myself."

His voice became serious. "Derrick is the one who always wanted easy money... But I thought he had changed after the drugs—and threatening you as a child. Your mother was devastated to hear he had traumatized you."

Wait. What?

"I thought finding your dad would take your mind off what Derrick did to you."

"Derrick traumatized me?" No, it was Fielding, he was the one...

In a matter of seconds, Corey's world reversed itself.

15 ISLAND HAUNTS

CONFRONTATIONS

"We should have stayed where we were," Sam hissed.

Corey rubbed his chest as he parted pine branches and straddled a protruding root to spy on the squash court.

At first, it was unbelievable. The idea that Fielding could be a stand-up guy now swirled around in a ball of emotion that threatened to swallow Corey. He forced his mind in another direction.

So what about this Derrick? He had to get a glimpse of him. Corey had tried to make Sam stay at the boathouse, but she had insisted on following as he edged along the northern shore. Now he scrambled up the bank near the squash court.

"You can't stop them by yourself!" Sam followed him closely.

"I'm not stopping them, I just want to get a look." Corey had to see the real man who had traumatized him. It was the sight of Derrick that had made Corey freeze at the pier and at the Wedgewood, the voice of Derrick from Sam's phone that stopped him in Key West. What would happen if he saw Derrick now? He had to know.

Corey had wound his way through a clump of bushes to scan the squash court, now partially hidden under cloud shadows. Once again, the moon's light was obscured.

"Shhh." He took another careful step, spotting a wide plywood-covered door opening, and craned his neck.

From inside the building came a rumbling and the sounds of metal scraping dirt.

"I know you want to see the treasure for yourself, but it's dangerous! Those guys are just inside that wall."

Corey wasn't listening. He rubbed his chest again. Something in the shirt had been irritating his scar. He reached into the pocket and pulled out an envelope, yellowed with age. Its corner had scraped against Corey's flesh whenever he moved. He squinted to read the addressee, an Alice Knight. She must have been related to the man named on the return address.

"Donald Knight," Corey whispered.

Sam looked over his shoulder, grabbing his arm to keep her balance. "That's the guy who owned the shirt."

Feeling her warm breath brought Corey to his senses. What was he thinking? The man who had tied Sam up was only a few feet away! Who knew what these men would do if they found them there. Sam's safety was the reason Corey came to Dark Island in the first place. He could resolve his issue with Derrick later.

Corey threw the envelope down and spun around to lead Sam back to safety.

She blocked him. "Don't throw it away! I mean...you know how I feel about littering."

He suspected she was more afraid of Knight's retribution, but he retrieved the envelope. He jammed it into his back pants pocket, promising to return it and the shirt to the closet "soon as we get back to the boathouse—" He stopped talking as he noticed the stillness. When had the digging stopped?

Corey turned back toward the squash court, stepping on a dry branch just as the clouds drifted away from the moon. A figure had emerged from the squash court and headed toward the castle, but at the sound of the crack he turned back.

Derrick's face was illuminated. His eyes locked on Corey's.

Corey stared at the face that had nearly ruined his life, the face that took him back to the scratch of a beard, the smell of a cigarette, and the warning, "Move and you're dead!"

Corey stood like a statue. He was finally facing his real tormentor! Even at this distance, he could tell those were the same blue eyes that had pierced him, the same lips that uttered the death threat so long ago.

Stay calm. Thoughts drifted by Corey's awareness like clouds passing the moon. Corey would remain frozen. The treasure would slip through his fingers and the thieves would get away with it. *At least I'll draw Derrick's attention away from Sam.* As long as she escaped, Corey didn't care what they did to him.

Corey remained still as the moon strobe-lit his face through evergreen branches.

He stayed still as dark strands of his hair floated over his eyes.

He remained still as Donald Knight's white shirt billowed in the breeze.

"D-don't come near me!"

Corey blinked. Did Derrick say that?

Derrick had raised his hands, palms forward, as he slowly backed away. "We didn't take anything, honest... *Mr. Knight.*"

Corey slowly opened his own arms in a gesture of confusion as Sam whispered from behind, "He thinks you're a ghost!"

Very slowly, Corey's lips curled into a smile. He looked at each of his arms. He was not frozen!

And Derrick was afraid of *Corey.*

"P-please..." Derrick whined. "I—I never meant to disturb your...your domain!"

Elated, Corey realized he had the advantage. Why not make the most of it? He mustered a ghostly moan. "Leeeave this plaaace...and never return."

The guy was nodding, still walking backwards. He stumbled over a rock and scrambled to get up, hollering, "We have to leave—now!" Another figure had emerged from the squash court, and Corey could just make out the man's back side as he walked toward Derrick. That must be Oscar.

"Might as well leave," Oscar grunted. "All that work just to find a few rotten boards." He sounded disgusted as he held up a bundle of old wood fragments and rusted hardware. "There's your so-called 'treasure chest.'" He tossed the debris on the ground.

Corey had only a slight sinking feeling to hear there was no treasure. At least the broken remains of the chest might be enough to verify the journal. Enough to keep the bloggers at bay for Mom. And he had managed to keep Sam safe!

Yes, everything would be fine.

Or might have been, if it hadn't been for the mustiness of the old shirt. Or was it the chill? Corey surprised himself with a sneeze.

Derrick turned back. "Hold on." He growled, "Ghosts don't sneeze."

Oscar, too, looked toward Corey. "Ghost? What are you talking about?"

This time, Corey did freeze up. He noticed the hulking size of Oscar as the moon's light played on the man's bare shoulders, highlighting his bulging biceps and washboard abs.

"Hey, I know who that is," Derrick said, catching up to Oscar and approaching Corey with more confidence. "That's the guy in the picture at Uncle Charlie's." His expression turned to anger. "It's that Worder kid! He's the one your boss lady warned you about." He pushed Oscar forward. "C'mon, make sure the girl isn't with him."

They both ran toward Corey.

"Sam, run!" he whispered, forgetting to be a statue. Corey would take on both of them by himself. They were ten paces away. He braced himself for bad trouble. It would take a cannon load of luck to get out of this one.

The men were three steps away when they all heard it.

Ba-boom! The two men stopped in their tracks, eyes focused behind Corey. He turned in time to see the flash that accompanied another *Boom!* Over glinting waves of the St. Lawrence, the sails of a ghostly tall ship reflected golden beams of moonlight.

Cannonball Harper's timing was perfect.

Corey turned back toward the castle at the sound of running feet on the lawn, followed by thumps and groans. Law enforcement officers were clapping handcuffs on Oscar and Derrick. Charlie and Randy were close behind them. They must have moored at the south side pier.

As Corey sank to the ground in relief, he heard Charlie say to Derrick, "Consider yourself fired."

Corey was tackled by Howler, who had escaped Charlie's trawler. As they rolled on the grass, another dog, a spaniel, circled and yapped.

"Kappy, how did you get out!" Sam caught the dog and scratched his head. "You're the one we heard on the stairs, aren't you!" The dog must have escaped the honeymoon suite.

FATHER FIELDING

Woody and Goldy came ashore, and Sam led them into the castle as she walked with her arm around Randy. Kappy followed them through the back library door. Meanwhile, Grayson Fielding appeared, and he lingered behind with Corey.

"I just got a clue," he started softly, "a little while ago when I got a call from your mother—" his voice seemed to break, "asking how my son was doing." His chest heaved. "When you said you'd met your father, naturally I believed, as you did, that it was someone else."

For the first time, Corey noticed how much the man's eyes resembled the ones in his own mirror—except for the sheen over them now.

Corey stared at the ground, not quite ready to unravel his own ball of emotions. *Grayce never knew he was my father!* Some of the man's words came to mind: Never assume.

"So, when you went to Pedro Banks you were..."

Grayson seemed taken by surprise. "I was helping the authorities. Catching pirates requires secrecy."

"And diving at Port Royal," Corey said, not daring to look into those eyes, "you took something. Something gold."

"You do have a sharp eye, Corey." There was a smile in his voice. "You caught me in one of my greedier moments." He cleared his throat. "I found a missing piece of the recovered window, a gold shard. I just wanted to hold onto a memory before giving it to the museum." He murmured, "It reminded me of your mother."

Grayce laid a hand on Corey's shoulder. "I'm sorry we didn't have more time...son."

Corey tried to stay in his calm spot, but his insides were whirling.

"You really thought," he said, not knowing what else to say, "Mom's treasure was at Grenadier?" His voice started leaking emotion without permission.

"That's where I was told it was." Grayce's eyes were definitely cloudy with a chance of rain. "And I wasn't about to fail, for hell or high river!" He scratched his head, looking embarrassed. "At first I wanted to prove I was better than that guy she left me for—or that I thought she had." He licked his lips. "Then, I find out you're my..." He mouthed words robotically: "Well, I decided I'd have to make up for not being there." But his eyes said so much more. "For you. For my *son.*"

Corey threw his calm spot to the winds, and his body shook with emotion. Grayce grasped him by the back of the head and clasped him in an embrace. Corey let his father squeeze the laughter and tears right out of him.

Finally, he stepped back, tilted his face to the full moon, and howled.

KNIGHT MESSAGE

"Oscar was right about the treasure," Corey told Woody and Goldy, who had joined him and Sam in front of a roaring fire at the castle library. Woody had brought Corey a warm set of clothing from the ship, and Corey laid his damp pants and the white shirt on a chair to dry.

"It was nowhere to be found under the squash court."

"After all that planning and time, getting your hopes up...?"

"It was just a waste of time," Corey said.

Sam nudged his leg with hers. "So it was a waste of time to come find me?"

"Oh, you know what I mean..."

She gave him a mock scowl. "And finding your father? Would you even have known he was your father if you hadn't come to look for the treasure?"

No. Corey stared into the fire. He would have gone on thinking his father was that guy on Grayce's porch swing.

Sam brought him back to the present. "Anyway, you did find your dad. And you did save me...and you made a promise." She insisted that Corey take the shirt back.

He grinned. He got up, took the shirt off the back of the chair, and said, "You coming? No time like the present." He had finally gotten warm in front of the library fireplace, but after all the excitement, he wanted to be alone with Sam.

"Oh, I almost forgot—" Corey felt the back pocket of his jeans. "I better put that letter back in the shirt or Donald Knight will haunt me!" Warm as he was, he melted further at Sam's smile in the glow of firelight. *Who needs gold with a smile like hers?*

When he reached into the pants pocket and pulled at the envelope, the corner came off in his hand. The dampness of his jeans must have weakened it. He fished it out and held up the shredded envelope, exposing the original note. Sam sighed and shook her head.

"Well, it's too late to put it back the way it was," he said. "Let's see what the dead man had to say."

Heads touching, he and Sam sat on the library floor and read the letter.

My dear Sarah: The job is nearly finished, and when I return to you in a few days, I will bring a surprise beyond your dreams. *Work is difficult, but it paid off when I examined the cave to set up explosives. I found a fortune in an old chest! I've stowed the contents in pouches I hid underwater next to the island. Imagine if I hadn't—no one would ever have known it was there! Before I come home, I will pack them in my empty cases (I'm sure the "Explosives" label will discourage close inspection!). I can hand truck the treasure right under people's noses when I ship out for home.*

I'll post this letter tomorrow when we go for supplies and I launder my work shirts (yes, you'll be pleased to know that I always wear white ones, as you insist they make even a workman look like a gentleman).

To keep on schedule, we must finish blasting tonight— luckily for the surface workers, the moon will be full.

I must go now, my love, but be assured I will not rest until the treasure is retrieved from the "cat's ear" and gets into deserving hands!

> *Yours forever,*
> *Donald*

Corey and Sam sat, stunned, as the letter slid to the floor. They looked at each other.

"The treasure...may still be here?" Sam said.

Corey furrowed his brow into a continuous line. Another mystery. "Like trying to find Estar all over again." He rolled his eyes.

"But Corey, this letter helps prove there was treasure!"

She was right.

"I know as much history as the owners themselves, and I have to admit..." She shook her head. "I've never heard of a 'cat's ear.'" She sighed. "I'm sorry, Corey, this might be beyond us."

He had almost come to the same conclusion when he blurted, "Don't you still have that map?"

She looked at him blankly then pulled out the folded pages she had taken from Derrick's binder.

He spread the original and stared at it. He cocked his head, looking at it from another angle. "I know where it is!" He rotated the map so the northern coast would appear horizontal. "Look this way."

Then she recognized the feline shape. "The ear is the point near the west end!"

TAKING THE GOLD

Several concentrated deposits of iron set the detector off, causing false elation. But with his father's help, it didn't take Corey long to pinpoint the treasures. His guess that Knight would have dropped the pouches among granite pillars to protect them from the current proved accurate. Rob aimed the detector at the thickened muck around rock pillars just off the northwestern end of the island, and the device signaled again.

They dug together to discover the first of the gold pieces that had been covered with a hundred years' worth of silt deposited by the current. Though the pouches had disintegrated, it didn't take long to find the remains of the other four among scattered pieces of treasure, within inches of the first. Luckily, the surrounding rock formation had prevented the gold from being washed downstream, and it also enabled the buildup of silt that protected the whole cache.

Corey and Rob stripped off their gear before joining the celebration on the deck of the *Golden Aye*. The cheering, back-slapping, and laughter died down quickly as they all stared at the British treasure, once sent as payment for military contractors in the War of 1812.

"I'm glad we proved Patrice's journal, but I wouldn't want to have to do it again." Corey handed a gold piece to his mom. "Though exploring with Sam last year *was* fun."

"You couldn't have found anything so dull as this," Rob said, waving a gold piece, "when you were looking at the real treasure." He tipped his head in Sam's direction.

Sam grinned at Rob then said to Corey, "I can see where you get your charm, Mr. *Worder-Hart-Redrow-Fielding.*"

Though his lips quivered from all the recent grinning, Corey couldn't help smiling once again. The name Corey O. Fielding had a satisfying ring.

He and his friends were relaxing on deck chairs that Morris had set out for the treasure hunt, to which only Corey and Sam's families and the crew of the *Golden Aye* were invited. Morris, looking clean-cut in a Bahama shirt and Panama hat, was in an unusually upbeat mood.

"It's great you're so excited for us," Corey told him. "But you do understand, this treasure is not for *you*, right?"

Morris's face split into a grin. "Kid, why would I want your money, I got everything I need." His eyes drifted aft, from where a vision of loveliness approached in swirls of lilac and lace. Her bright smile was framed by a strong jaw.

"And that would be," Morris murmured, "my new bride."

Corey nearly choked watching Morris and the captain ogle each other, oblivious to the conversations around them. But he smiled yet again.

Rob and Randy chatted about sail training, tourism, lodging, and how to combine Randy's management skill with Rob's creative vision. The B&B as base of operations for a youth sailing camp could double as vacation center for the young sailors' parents.

"After all, now that I've found my son," Rob glanced at Corey, "Why would I want to leave?"

Corey was happy. He'd been afraid his dad would be disappointed to find Mom satisfied with Charlie, but Rob claimed his quest was not about rekindling romance. "It was all about connection, continuity. And after all these years, I've found my *family*." He squeezed Corey's shoulder and glanced at his mother, with whom he shared a warm smile.

Guess they've reached an understanding.

Corey didn't even mind that ownership of the treasure would be contested by the feds, the State of New York, the owners of Dark Island—and probably the British! The glow on his mom's face was reward enough. She had been vindicated.

"I really don't resent the Hart woman." His mom fondled a gold piece between her fingers. "In fact, I feel sorry for her."

Corey had heard the woman's trial was coming up; she was sure to be sentenced to a long incarceration.

For Mom, the last few weeks of therapy had been a breakthrough, and she seemed like her old self. Sam was the one who dropped a bombshell.

"You really have Auger's grandmother to thank, Corey."

He gawked at her. Was she crazy?

"Well, if she hadn't misdirected you and put Oscar up to finding the treasure, I wouldn't have sent that SOS and you wouldn't have come to Dark Island. We would never have found the treasure."

He pondered that for a moment before answering. "Remind me to send Mackenzie 'Hart' a thank you card," he said. "In care of maximum security."

16 HERITAGE REIGNS

"The B&B is turning around!" Sam said from the passenger seat as Corey drove east in his mom's car. "Thanks to Rob." She shifted to face Corey. "Plus, it's great finishing the season at the castle—it's been fun leading the ghost tour." Corey had seen the new tour Sam had designed, and he was proud of her. She had a real talent for combining education and entertainment, which she hoped to use in a new radio show for teens.

"The owners were grateful that we exposed the thieves," Sam was saying. "Did you know that Mrs. Hart had blackmailed them into hiring Oscar and Derrick?"

Corey had figured that much. He glanced over at Sam and smiled, still amazed to have her beside him. She turned out to be an eager student of sailing, and they spent time with Rob when he wasn't working with Randy. Mom was feeling great; Corey suspected her progress had to do with personal reconciliations. She and Rob had settled into a friendly and supportive relationship, and Charlie had even taken Rob fishing.

"Anyway," Sam continued, "no one has claimed to see the *real* castle ghost for weeks." She softened her voice. "By finding the gold, you released Donald Knight."

"*We* released him," Corey corrected her. Though he still didn't believe in ghosts.

Corey left Sam in the lobby of the correctional facility. He waited for an officer to usher him to the visitation area. He hesitated before entering.

Corey was about to face the madwoman responsible for Mom's problems, the one who had perpetrated a fraud against Corey's family. He had mixed feelings about meeting this woman face to face. At least he was glad he wasn't the one with her genes. *Poor Auger.*

"You got Augie's message." The voice sounded old but still strong. "I'm glad you consented to seeing me."

Her eyes were sharp. "The last time I saw you, I wanted you dead."

The cold voice gave Corey goose bumps, and his eyes shifted wildly. Was it possible in here—would she try to kill him?

But she was looking down, shaking her head. "What a mistake that would have been."

Corey stared in disbelief. What was she trying to pull?

He had to say what he thought. "Mrs...Hart. How can I believe you're sorry?" He crossed his arms over his chest and squeezed the words out: "After all you've done to me and my mom."

"Yes." She sighed. "I did put my faith in the wrong things. I regret it." Her eyes burned into him. "Everyone makes mistakes." She was quiet for a minute before saying, "I thought Augie was the one to carry on the family...mystique."

Is that the new word for fraud?

"But I was foolish to think we could build on a weak foundation."

Whatever. Corey sighed and rolled his eyes when she looked away.

"I knew my heir would be courageous." Her eyes searched his. "Augie does have courage. But you know, his heart wasn't in it."

What a waste of time. Corey looked at his watch. "Uh, well, my girlfriend is waiting, so..." He grabbed the chair's arms, ready to launch himself.

She ignored his comment. "Let me tell you a story."

Corey scowled and let his arms fall back on the rests. *Two minutes and I'm gone.*

"I was a foolish young woman. Of course I had to give up the baby."

She was rambling. Her eyes darted here and there.

"I worshipped Granddad, but he wouldn't tolerate a scandal." She leaned forward and whispered, "But I kept tabs on him."

On her grandfather? *Definitely nuts.* "Well, I..." Corey gripped the chair arms to get up.

"I've been able to track the movements of my secret son. It seems I have another grandchild. *He* had the heart to go for the treasure."

Corey's eyes widened and his arms went slack. *Derrick.* Charlie's nephew was Mackenzie's grandson?

"This grandson and I will be more powerful than I ever could be with Auger." She settled back with a satisfied smile.

Corey was dumbfounded. "Are...are you trying to scare me?"

She looked genuinely surprised. "Oh, no my dear."

"But Derrick..."

She looked thoughtful. "Derrick *was* more than willing." Her eyes were wide. "He's got that itch, the taste for gold. But he wants things the easy way."

She leaned in again, her eyes riveted on Corey's. "But what do I care about Derrick? *My* grandson is smart and courageous." Her smile broadened. "You see, dear, the son I gave up never married. Though I followed his successes, I never could have known—until *he* found out—that he had fathered a child." She sat rigidly, her eyes never wavering from Corey's. "Born eighteen years ago this November."

Corey's head whirled. What was she saying? She had given birth to Corey's dad? Robert Grayson Fielding was a Hart? Or more correctly, a *Poole?*

"Yes, Corey *Hart-Poole.*" She beamed at him. "You are the mingling of the best genes."

Corey's cheek twitched, and his mouth hung open.

"Your grandmother can help you." The woman leaned closer. "My incarceration is no obstacle. In fact, I can exert power undetected." Then she whispered, "The bloggers have stopped, haven't you noticed?"

He struggled to process what she was saying. Had she orchestrated the blogging thing to sabotage Mom? His head reeled and his stomach churned as the woman went on.

"We'll work up a positive spin, can't be disparaging your mother can we... And what would *you* like? To captain your own ship?" She winked. "Please your girl? College, jobs closer to home? I have influence you know...*contacts.*"

Corey hardly remembered walking to the lobby.

"What was she like?" Sam asked on the way to the car.

"Just crazy." Corey tossed his head as he unlocked the car. "Wanted a look at the guy that beat her." He spoke robotically and avoided Sam's eyes.

But as he drove, a gradual smile replaced his frown. His eyes widened as they passed the radio station that was considering Sam's show. As they passed the marina, his gaze lingered on the yachts.

Now and then, Sam brought him back to the present.

"You're going to miss our turn! And what is that goofy grin?"

He swerved onto the exit road. "Nothing." He glanced over at Sam. He could see her adoring look even through her scolding. He never wanted to lose that look. He wanted to keep Sam happy, always. And he could keep on pleasing her, with help from his...

Corey choked so hard he had to pull over. The thought of that woman's blood in his veins gave him a panic attack.

"Are you okay?" Sam asked.

No. Corey's heart pounded as he wiped cold sweat from his palms. What was he thinking! Was he like that woman? He had her genes. Was her seed taking root? He closed his eyes and breathed.

From somewhere deep inside it came: "Who *you* are is determined by your choices." Fielding's words. Rob had that woman's genes too, but he had chosen a life of hard work and generosity.

Corey's breathing slowed. He looked at Samantha and felt the warmth of her gaze. She loved him for who he had chosen to be.

Focus. He would always have to be vigilant. But he would make the right choices...for Sam.

He took another big breath. Then he leaned over and kissed her before pulling the car back onto the road.

He put the woman out of his mind and answered Sam's question. "With you beside me, I'm way beyond okay."

The two of them smiled all the way back to Harts Landing, a dot on the St. Lawrence River that held their loved ones, their hopes, and their dreams for the future.

****

Thank You

...for reading *Taking the Gold.* I wrote it for your entertainment, and I would like to hear what you think. Here's my email:

MANoble@rocketmail.com

ABOUT THE AUTHOR

Mag A. Noble lives with her husband, Bob, in St. Lawrence County between the Adirondack Mountains and New York's Canadian border along the St. Lawrence Seaway. She enjoys playing keyboard and drums and singing harmony, working and playing outdoors, and—if stuck inside—writing to inform and entertain. This, her second novel, is a follow-up to her first, *Taking Hart.*